SPIRITED LEGACY

A LOST LIBRARY NOVEL, BOOK 2

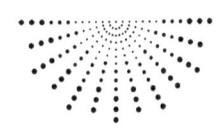

KATE BARAY

Copyright © 2014 Catherine G. Cobb
All rights reserved.

BONUS CONTENT

Sign up for my newsletter to receive release announcements, bonus materials, and a sampling of my different series. Sign up at http://eepurl.com/b91H5v

PROLOGUE

Lizzie felt a hard yank on her scalp. She wanted to cry out, but no sound emerged from her lips. Someone was dragging her down the garden path. Her muzzy, pain-filled brain tried to put the pieces together.

The painful pulling at her scalp was joined by a steady wrenching feeling in her shoulder. She must have passed out for a moment, because suddenly she was inside the house and being pulled across a floor. She could feel the wood floor and then the rug underneath her—but it was all distant and fuzzy, like she'd just woken from a dream but wasn't yet able to think clearly or move. She could feel even those sensations start to slip away as her thoughts became hazier. A sharp pain pierced through the darkness. Her body slamming into a wall? A doorway? Briefly she tried to grab at the doorjamb she was being yanked past, but her fingers wouldn't move to clench the frame.

She was so tired. Even the mounting terror couldn't keep her awake. She didn't want to die like this. She didn't want to die *at all*, she thought right before she lost consciousness.

She woke briefly as a guard pulled her body this way and

that, tying her feet. Her shoulder screamed with a tearing pain, and tears were running down her face. She could just barely make out Worth speaking in the background. He was giving instructions to one of his men for evacuation. As she struggled to hear anything that might hint at their destination, the guard had finished binding her feet and moved to her hands. He pulled her hands together, wrenching her damaged shoulder. She bit frantically down on the inside of her cheek as waves of pain tore through her. She didn't want Worth to hear her scream, she thought, a fraction of a second before her mouth filled with her own blood, and she lost consciousness.

CHAPTER ONE

Nine Days Earlier

Home for slightly more than twenty-four hours, Lizzie Smith was just starting to feel a little more like her old self again. She'd slept and slept. Apparently being kidnapped, rescued, rescuing others, and besting an evil genius made a girl tired. She smiled. After she'd slept—well, then she and John had *not* slept. A small blush bloomed at *those* thoughts. John Braxton, quite possibly the love of her life, Alpha of the Texas Lycan Pack, and completely gorgeous specimen of a man—she sighed. *Yum.* She snuggled closer to the solid warmth at her back. And then her stomach growled.

Her appetite had returned and then some. She hadn't realized how little she'd been eating over the last several days. She'd dropped around ten pounds during the "Lizzie Kidnapped" episode of her life. She'd warned John not to get too used to the svelte her, because she had every intention of eating like a normal person again. He'd just looked at her like she'd grown an extra head.

At the sound of her growling tummy, he hopped out of bed and slipped on a pair of jeans.

"Eggs and bacon good?" he asked as he headed to the kitchen.

"Sounds lovely," she'd replied to his retreating back. *Smart man.*

She was settling into a deep, warm pile of sheets and comforter when her phone rang. She sighed. She'd been avoiding most calls since she got home. Avoiding life in general—work, laundry, leaving the house. But eventually, she'd have to return to the reality of her boring, normal existence. And John needed to check in with the Pack. That was a depressing thought and quashed any desire to continue lounging in sheets he'd warmed just moments before. She slid out of bed, pulling on her robe, and debated whether to answer.

She could hear John letting the dogs out in the yard as she picked up her phone. He really was a keeper. He'd already picked Beau and Vegas up from boarding at her friend's mom's house. Weirdly, they'd been fine with him after lots of sniffing and curious looks. Given their initial, highly suspicious and vocal reaction to him, it was a pleasant surprise.

She glanced at the caller ID screen before she answered… Idaho? "Yes?" The single word came out short, clipped, and irritated.

Wow, she must still be tired. That was *not* her typical phone etiquette.

"Lizzie?" a male voice inquired.

"Who is this?" she asked pointedly. Would her manners ever recover from this adventure?

"Lizzie Braxton? It's Clark, Grant Clark. Calling to congratulate you on your union with Braxton." Since Clark was Alpha of the Idaho Pack and a co-conspirator from the first time she'd been kidnapped, he should be concerned about her reaction to a phone call out of the blue. He may have aided John's rescue, been respectful during her brief imprisonment, and seemed like a decent sort, but—he kidnapped her.

Clark waited until the silence was almost awkward, and when he continued his tone was cautious. "On behalf of Idaho, I'd like to extend official congratulations. It is our hope you'll accept a token of our good will and look to the future, not the past, in building a relationship with Idaho."

Then she realized she'd missed something. *What?*

The doorbell rang. She was already on her way to answer it, when her good manners kicked in and she replied, "Thank you, Mr. Clark. I'm afraid now isn't a good time, but I appreciate your call." Click. *Appreciate, my ass.* Her thoughts were sinking well into the depths of profanity when she answered the door to a UPS deliveryman and a florist delivery driver. "Lizzie Braxton?" the florist inquired, politely.

In the silence, the UPS man shifted from foot to foot, clearly in a rush, and asked, "I need a signature. Can you sign for Elizabeth Braxton?"

She shut the door on them both, and...

"JOHN!!!" She couldn't remember a time she'd yelled so loud. But if ever there was a time to start, it was now.

∽

Two Days Later

"ARE YOU SPEAKING TO ME YET?" John asked her.

Lizzie gave the question serious thought before she answered. She sat down at the kitchen table, and after about three seconds, she said, "Hmm. No."

John poured her a cup of strong tea and added a dash of milk, handing it to her before he sat down next to her at the head of the table. She couldn't keep this up. The man knew how she liked her tea. And cooked her breakfast. The smell of perfectly crisped bacon was softening her resolve even faster than the sight of him sitting at her kitchen table. With his bright blue eyes, his slightly scruffy chin, and his long, muscular legs stretched out in front of him. *Hmm.* Maybe John rated a little higher than bacon.

Sitting down at her kitchen table across from a man she was not speaking to, Lizzie's expressive face scrunched up in a frown as she remembered Zack Worth, the man who had orchestrated most of the grief she'd suffered over the last few weeks.

"Stop it," John said. "You'll ruin a beautiful day, and he's just not worth it." He paused a moment, then smiled wryly and said, "No pun intended."

She looked at him as he quietly drank a cup of coffee, his dark hair sticking up at odd angles. It was frustrating that he was so composed, so at home. As if their adventure several days earlier, and now their fight, didn't bother him at all.

His reference to Worth was right on the mark. She was dwelling on that horrible man, and thinking about him would ruin an otherwise beautiful day. The fact that John knew her so well after such a short time made him even more appealing. He was very nearly her perfect man. But two days ago—one day after she'd shared her growing feelings with him—she'd discovered a problem. She woke up after a mind-blowing evening of just-rescued-from-near-death sex to find that her last name had mysteriously changed—at least, within the magic-using community. And Lycan society recognized her as John's mate.

The plane ride home after the confrontation with Worth in Prague was a little hazy. She'd been tired—exhausted, actually—but she did remember the excitement she'd felt when John asked her to be his mate. How could she not?

After the flirting and tension, the growing feelings she'd held close to her chest, and the agonizing fear she'd experienced when Worth had begun to steal John's magic, she was thrilled to have their relationship out in the open and official.

Was she giddy from their victory over Worth? Tired from days of sleep deprivation? Or just so excited that she and John were finally together after so much had happened that she wasn't thinking straight? Whatever the reason, she had failed to ask about the odd wording that John had used. He'd asked her to be his mate. And she'd said yes. She was an idiot. Wait a minute.

"You even said it was like being your girlfriend. I remember that now. It wasn't just me being a complete idiot. You said that." Her tone was thoughtful. She'd been about as mad at herself over the last few days as she'd been at John. Maybe she'd been too hasty. Just maybe she'd been justified in her anger at John, and she wasn't as responsible for this mess as she'd been feeling.

"So you are speaking to me?" he asked.

She just ignored the question, waiting.

He scrubbed a hand over his face. "Yes. I don't remember the specifics, but I wouldn't be at all surprised if I used the word girlfriend."

Lizzie considered misleading her to think they were only dating, when she'd actually agreed to something much more serious, to be a large flaw in her nearly perfect boyfriend's character.

The magic-using community considered them married for all intents and purposes, but she'd never been properly asked and certainly hadn't gotten a ceremony. Or a party. Hell, not even a ring. She reminded herself that she wasn't upset that she had no ring. *Really.* She was upset at her ass of a boyfriend because he unilaterally decided on the next huge step in their relationship. And then announced it to the Lycan world.

Granted, he had his reasons. She glared at him over her tea. Her tasty, prepared-by-John tea. And just like that, some of her anger slipped away.

John must have caught the glare, because he said, "What? What did I do this time?"

Maybe two days of silence, and pouting, was enough. Lizzie was an honest person. She even tried to be honest with herself. So she admitted it. Juvenile as it was, she'd pouted. She sighed.

She mentally girded herself. Then she said, "Let's talk." She hadn't literally been silent for two days, just silent on the subject of Lycan mates, meeting the Pack, and her future with John. She thought she was justified in her anger. She was a grown woman, more than capable of making her own decisions, and he had yanked this momentous decision right out of her hands.

She wasn't sure what she wanted to do or how she felt, other than angry. But she wasn't so mad she was seeing red—literally. The first time he'd tried to explain his actions there had been red sparkles. And not the pretty kind—the scary, uncontrollable magic kind. Her magic did weird things when she experienced strong emotions, so she'd decided to give herself a little time to calm down. Because she wasn't so angry that she wanted anything or anyone to explode—or start bleeding. She thought of the house in Prague where Worth had held her, of seeing Worth moments before he'd fled the house. He'd bled from his nose, ears, and eyes. She shuddered, her insides suddenly feeling ten degrees colder. She'd done that.

She gave her head a tiny but emphatic shake. *Enough.* He'd deserved it. And it was over.

John had waited patiently to discuss the situation. As well

he should, since the whole thing was his fault. Well, mostly his fault, she conceded. More than half his fault, she finally decided. It was past time to have an adult conversation. Especially since the thought of discussing it wasn't triggering an unexpected magical light show. "Okay. Tell me when this mysterious ceremony took place. The one that seems to have resulted in us basically being married. Oh, and when I said yes." Lizzie's voice had a hard edge. "When *exactly* did I say yes?"

John winced. "How about I explain why first." He leaned forward in his chair, forearms on his thighs. His face was intent, and the movement shifted him closer to Lizzie.

Lizzie bit her lip and nodded. He was so incredibly appealing in this serious, earnest mood.

"We've never talked about what it means to be Lycan. Most of the time, I'm just a man. But sometimes it gets complicated." He huffed out a frustrated breath. "A lot like your magic when you're upset, the wolf in me doesn't always handle stressful situations as rationally as the human in me might like."

John never spoke about his magic. She'd thought it was too private, and he wasn't comfortable discussing something so intimate. So she was surprised that this was the beginning of their discussion.

Then Lizzie thought about what he'd said and frowned in confusion. "You talk about your wolf like he's another person. I thought that you were always John, the human, but sometimes you were furry?"

"Not exactly." He shifted in his chair, leaning back again. "I'm always the man. And there's not actually a wolf, more that my magic has the feel of a wolf. The man and the wolf aspect of my magic are like two aspects of my personality that live in harmony. Most of the time." John looked at Lizzie intently, his face tense and worried.

Suddenly, Lizzie realized that John—who never seemed to lack confidence—might be unsure. Worried about how she felt about him, how she felt about the differences between them. She waited.

"When you're in danger, I'm anxious. Unsettled. Even if I know rationally that there's nothing I can do, or that you can take care of yourself." He caught and held her gaze. "Those facts don't alter the way I or my wolf feels."

Lizzie was sure he was thinking about the magical confrontation she'd had with Worth. Lizzie had come out the victor—even if she wasn't entirely sure what had happened. Or how she'd done—whatever she did.

"Add my wolf's anxiety to the very real threat you were under as an unaffiliated Record Keeper. And the fact that you've been reluctant to commit and affiliate with a Lycan pack. It was stressful." John looked tense. His eyes narrowed, and Lizzie occasionally saw the twitch of a muscle in his jaw. Lizzie looked at the large, muscular, competent man sitting in front of her. He'd been worried. Okay, probably very worried. *Dangit.* Her heart warmed a little at that thought.

"You know why I was reluctant. I know almost nothing about Lycan, and what little I do know has left a mixed impression." Lizzie thought of her experiences with Clark, on the one hand, and John, on the other. "And making me your mate in the eyes of the Lycan community was the only way you knew to mark me as Pack right away?"

Pissed as she was, she could understand his argument—up to a point. As a pack member, she would be protected by the laws and customs governing Lycan packs. That much she did understand. If she'd been a member of the Texas Pack, Clark's pack wouldn't have grabbed her.

Lycan may consider her a Record Keeper, or a person with a particular talent for reading magical texts, but she'd learned she was actually a spell caster. So her talents were broader than just reading magical texts. If she could develop her skills—particularly offensive and defensive warding—she might not need a pack to protect her.

John spoke into the lengthening silence. "I acted rashly."

And that was the heart of the matter. He *had* acted rashly. Both in making her the Alpha Mate of the Texas Pack and in moving their relationship forward. Understanding why John acted as he had didn't change the facts. And she wasn't sure she was ready to take the next step in their relationship. They'd just discovered their feelings for one another. Taking a day or 600 to let those feelings slowly mature and deepen seemed like a good idea to Lizzie. Especially since she thought John was the One. She wanted this to work. Her heart cracked a little when she thought it might not.

The creamy filling to this sticky situation was the role of mate to the Texas Pack's Alpha. Texas was the largest pack in North America, and the position of Alpha was the most powerful single position in the pack structure. Lizzie wasn't even sure exactly what an Alpha Mate did, but it sounded a lot like being a politician's wife. She couldn't even *imagine* being involved in politics.

She needed time to figure out magic, to learn more about Lycan, to let her feelings for John settle. And John had taken that away.

"You were worried about me, and you thought making me your mate would keep me safe. I get it." He frowned in response to her words but waited for her to finish. "But you and I need time. You can't rush certain things. I'm not sure how I feel about taking on a completely new set of responsibilities…especially when I don't even know what a mate *does*. All while we're trying to give us—this, whatever it is between us—a chance."

John stood up and walked to the counter. It was as if he couldn't stand still and tension radiated from him. "I don't think you do understand. I wasn't worried; I was terrified. I've been in relationships before. I've even been in love." Her gaze lifted immediately, but he was staring out the window.

He hadn't told her he loved her. It was early days; she wasn't even sure she wanted to hear it. What would she say in return? *I think I'm falling in love with you—but give me a sec 'cause I'm not sure if I'm quite there yet?* Her feelings for him were complicated, a little confused, and very new. And what part did magic play in their relationship? Everything had happened so fast up to this point, she needed more time to assure herself that her feelings were real and based on something—attraction, passion, friendship, trust—not magic or wolfy pheromones.

John turned away from the window. His eyes briefly made contact with hers; then his gaze skittered away to a point a foot or so in front of her. Like he was shying away from too much intimacy. "Not only do I have feelings for you, but my magic, my wolf aspect, my wolf—however you think of it—is involved in my feelings. The need to protect you and to know where you are, those feelings are intense. It's disconcerting, and it certainly impacted my actions. And while I'm sorry that I've jeopardized our relationship, I can't be sorry that you're safer now."

Lizzie stood up, walked over to John, and wrapped her arms around him. She rested her cheek against his shoulder and just held on.

"Does this mean you're not mad?" Lizzie could hear a teasing note in his voice.

"You know it doesn't." She snuggled a little closer. "It means I care about you, and we'll try to sort it out." She took a step away from him, arms still draped over his shoulders, and said, "But I think I'm still allowed to be mad. We should have had this conversation before you even thought about announcing to the world that I'm your wolfy-wife."

He tried to suppress a grin and failed. "Is that what you are? My wolfy-wife?"

She decided he was irresistible, and she grinned right back. "Sure. If I can call you Fluffy."

He chuckled. "Don't you dare. Though there are some fond memories attached to that name."

After a quick kiss, she turned and sat back down at the kitchen table. After a few seconds, her forehead wrinkled. "Ugh. We haven't even begun to discuss the Pack's book, let alone the whole Record Keeper job. And I haven't had any time at all to study the book." She dropped her head on the table, forehead resting lightly against the surface. When she spoke again, frustration vibrated in her voice. "I only just learned how to use my spell caster talent. I can finally read that darn book, but there's no time. I haven't even caught up on my sleep yet." She lifted her head off the table and scrunched her nose up in annoyance. "This is what I'm talking about. Too much stuff, happening too fast. Who can keep up?"

"Sorry about the sleep part," John said sheepishly.

Her expression turned mischievous. "Hmm. You're so *not* sorry. And you'd be in serious trouble if you were." She sighed. "Are you going to tell me what exactly a mate does? What role I would have in the Pack?"

"Maybe tomorrow?" he asked hopefully.

Lizzie eyed the small piece of bacon and half slice of toast still left on her breakfast plate. "I think now would be best," she said with resignation.

He looked like he was debating his options. Lizzie tapped her fingers on the table and considered chunking her toast at him. But before she could pick it up off the plate, her cell rang. She dug it out of her back jeans pocket, and, once she saw the caller ID screen, she immediately answered it.

Scowling, she said, "Hello, Harrington. This is a surprise."

CHAPTER TWO

"Hello, Lizzie. I hope the trip home went well." Harrington sounded calm. But he always sounded calm and controlled to Lizzie, even in the midst of a major crisis.

Harrington was the Director of Investigations for the Inter-Pack Policing Cooperative, or IPPC. His call wasn't expected, and she couldn't guess why he'd need to speak with her so soon. She'd last seen Harrington four days ago in Prague when he'd taken possession of the Lost Library—after Worth had been injured during her rescue, fled, and then abandoned the Library.

Lizzie sighed wistfully. She couldn't help but remember the vast number of magical texts housed in the basement Library. It had been awe-inspiring to be in the same room with so much history and magic. And without the stress and fear caused by her captivity, the Library held even more appeal.

"I'm thankful to be home safe." Lizzie's reply was short. She was never sure how much to tell Harrington. Or how much he wanted to hear. All business, that was Harrington.

"What can I do for you?" she asked.

"I hope I can do something for *you*," Harrington replied unexpectedly. "I've hired one spell caster to staff the Library, and I'm actively searching for a second. Until I can find another caster, I'd like to offer you a job. And a mentor."

Lizzie's brain immediately started to work through all of the ramifications. Spend time with all of those gorgeous and fascinating books. Definitely good. Spend time away from John. Definitely very bad. Especially given the unresolved question of her role in the Pack and in John's life.

"How long will you need someone?" she asked.

"Not someone—you. I know you're in need of a mentor. I think it would be a mutually beneficial arrangement and worth the trouble of the temporary move. For both of us." Harrington paused and then finally answered her original question. "I'm estimating about a month."

Mentoring with a spell caster like Harrington was impossible locally. She didn't have any magical connections in the United States. And casters didn't exactly advertise. If the information she'd gotten from her European friends was correct, the spell caster community was much smaller in the States. She'd also heard Harrington was unique in the strength and breadth of his talent.

Certainly, this was an exciting opportunity for all of those reasons.

Lizzie bit at her lip. The thought of having ready access to someone who wanted to share magical knowledge was incredibly appealing, but her graphic design clients were already somewhat neglected after her recent kidnap adventure. "I'm not sure leaving my business for a month is a good idea."

"Did I mention this was a paid position? Technically, you'll be a consultant. Room, board, flight, and a small stipend for the stay are covered. Your free time is your own.

So you can keep in touch with clients during your off-hours, if you choose." Harrington had an answer for everything.

Just as Lizzie was about tell him that she'd need a day or two to think about it—and talk to John, but Harrington didn't need to know that—he added, "I know you'll need to get Braxton's permission before you can commit—"

"I'm sorry. What?" Lizzie interrupted.

"As the Texas Pack Alpha Mate, any travel across pack territory lines would be approved by the Alpha." There was a brief silence, and then Harrington said, "I assumed. Probably incorrectly."

Lizzie's eyes narrowed as she looked over at John and her pulse kicked up a notch. He'd been quietly sipping coffee and checking email on his cell throughout her phone conversation. "I'll get back to you." Then she hung up on Harrington.

She really needed to reevaluate her manners these days. Add a little stress and she became a stranger to herself, a rude person. One who cussed. *Dammit.* She barely recognized herself.

"What did I do?" John said.

"Your crazy-keen wolfy hearing didn't pick up the other end of that conversation?" She still wasn't sure exactly what he could and couldn't do. But she'd been in the same room; he should have been able to hear both sides of the conversation with his keen hearing.

"I wasn't paying any attention, and I have no idea what Harrington said to upset you." John's temper was slow to ignite, but Lizzie may have managed to prime the pump by avoiding "the talk" for two days. He sounded like he might be losing his patience. "I don't actually try to listen in. Sometimes you just make it impossible to avoid."

"According to Harrington, I need your permission to leave town. Is that true?" Her tone was grim. Fair or not, she was upset. No. She was more than upset. Frustrated? Angry?

Disappointed? She rolled her shoulders, trying to stretch out the tension gathering in her neck. All of those and more.

John shifted uncomfortably, avoiding direct eye contact.

"What exactly am I supposed to do? Run my travel plans by you for approval every time I decide to visit my parents or want to take a trip with friends?" Her nostrils flared and her face flushed. She knew her fair skin turned a brilliant shade of rosy pink when she was flustered or angry, and she was both right now.

"What the hell did Harrington say?" When she didn't immediately answer, he said, "Lizzie, take a breath. Calm down."

He avoided the question and told her to "calm down." *Calm down?* After she'd just been told her decisions were not her own, her life was not her own. That she needed permission to travel, from a man she'd known less than a month. That she was expected to live by rules she hadn't known existed a few weeks ago, rules she still didn't actually know. Lycan society, Lycan rules, were just as new to her as magic, as new as John was in her life. It was all too much.

Calm down? She didn't think so.

"I'm leaving for Prague. As soon as I can make arrangements with Harrington for a flight."

"What? Why? What's happened?" John said, his voice shaded by confusion.

"He's offered me a job." As John's face tightened at Lizzie's words, she revised her statement, reason compelling her to be more explicitly truthful. "A temporary job, just for a few weeks. I'm taking it."

His tone cold, John said, "You're leaving." It wasn't a question. He seemed certain. "You'll damage my reputation and harm your relationship with the Pack." Not just cold—icy.

Lizzie's breath caught in a small hiccup. She didn't want to leave *him*; that hadn't been the point. *Damn.* She was going to cry. She forced a slow, even breath as the sting of unshed tears prickled her eyes. She wanted to make her own decisions. No, she needed to. She couldn't lose herself in this new world, in her newly acquired magic. Not even in John.

As much as his chilly anger hurt, she knew that going to Prague was a good, if rash, decision. And John was the Alpha of his pack. Even if he didn't influence every move of his pack members, he still played an important leadership role. She didn't think he could pack up and leave for a month. He'd already been gone for too long—he'd said it himself.

She needed to go. So she replied to John's unasked question. "I'm going." What she didn't say, what her anger prevented her from saying, was that she wanted him to go with her.

He'd nodded, picked up his keys, grabbed his wallet, and said, "I'm checking in with the Pack. I'll be back tonight."

CHAPTER THREE

After Lizzie called Harrington to accept his offer, he'd instructed her to take whichever flight suited her schedule and just drop him a note with travel details. He would arrange for pickup on the Prague end. So she'd hidden herself away in her office and booked the quickest flight she could find. She was scheduled to leave for Prague the next night. With any luck she'd be able to sleep for a good portion of the flight to London. She hoped to arrive early in the morning feeling, if not great, then at least human.

Last minute, while she was still on the phone with Harrington's travel agent, she'd decided to schedule a layover in London. A long layover. She'd have enough time to make a local visit if she didn't hit any major travel delays.

And that left her with the rest of the day and all of tomorrow to pack, deliver the dogs, and regret the ongoing dissension between her and John. The time stretched out before her, seeming both too long and not long enough. She mentally girded herself for some errand running and travel prep. She didn't really want to think about John—so she wouldn't. *Right.*

First up, it was time to call her best friend, Kenna McIntyre. Probably past time. She was in on all the super-secret stuff—magic, Lycan, spell casters. Lizzie rolled her eyes. When had her life gotten so weird? Oh, yeah—when a spelled book mysteriously showed up in her mailbox. Someday, when she wasn't running around like a manic Chihuahua, she'd have to figure out who put that book in her mailbox.

Kenna was sure to be curious. Lizzie hadn't spoken with her in a few days. She'd given her a quick "hey, I'm-alive" call. She might also have hinted at a need for some alone time…or maybe not hinted, just said, "Don't expect to hear from me for a few days."

"Well, hello, sex kitten. How have you been?" Kenna said.

Lizzie swallowed. What should she say? *Really shitty, but thanks for asking?*

"I have an internship," Lizzie said, infusing as much enthusiasm as she could into her voice.

"Um, that's got nothing to do with sex and your hot Lycan. And it makes no sense—you already have a job." Kenna's voice turned skeptical when she mentioned Lizzie's current work. "And for someone who hasn't had any loving in ages, you should have sex on the brain, not a new job. Especially when you already have your own business."

Lizzie replied, "Harrington offered me a job at the Library."

"Way to avoid the sex question. Who knew you were such a prude?" Kenna teased. "But that is exciting that you'll be working in the Library. I know how much you loved those creepy books."

"Um-hm. But I wouldn't say creepy," Lizzie replied, knowing the other shoe would drop any minute now.

"What about John? You guys finally got together. Well, not that it took long—but it *seemed* like it took a long time. I mean, a lot's happened since he showed up on your porch. Is he going with you? Are you guys still together?" Kenna had started curious, but near the end she sounded worried. "Wait a minute—did that bastard break up with you after screwing you to Sunday?" Kenna was practically yelling into the phone. "I'm coming over there right now."

Lizzie couldn't help it, she laughed. Wildly, with no reservations. After a few seconds, left hand on her side pressing against the stitch she'd developed, gasping for breath, she said, "Sorry. It's just—oh, Kenna. Thank you."

"He did break up with you?" Kenna asked more cautiously.

"No. At least, I don't think so." Lizzie inhaled slowly, trying to catch her breath. "No," she said again but with certainty.

Lizzie had needed that. She'd allowed too much tension to build up around the questions facing her and John. They had issues. They were both mature—okay, maturish—adults. They'd had their own lives before meeting each other. It wasn't surprising those lives wouldn't immediately mesh and intertwine without complications. The question was—could she and John overcome the complications?

"But?" Kenna prompted.

"But he's not exactly happy with me right now. And honestly, I would seriously like to kick his ass." Lizzie chewed on her lip. She hadn't actually called to unload on Kenna. It was all a little too new to share. Normally she shared everything with Kenna, but the timing seemed wrong. All of her feelings were simply too new to take out and discuss.

"We'll sort it out," Lizzie concluded.

"Uh huh. While you're in Prague and John's in Texas. Let me know how that goes. Where is he now? He's not there, is he?" Kenna asked.

"He's out of town, visiting the Pack. So I'm sure he has

stuff—Lycan Alpha stuff—to take care of." Lizzie scrunched her nose up in annoyance. Even *she* thought she sounded defensive, so Kenna would definitely pick up on it.

It wasn't her fault John had picked up his keys and walked out the door after she'd announced her plans. Okay, maybe it was a little her fault. She'd started pacing at some point during the conversation, Kenna's agitation rubbing off on her. But she stopped mid-pace now. He hadn't yelled. He hadn't even looked pissed.

Weird. Weird enough that maybe she should be worried. *Well, shit.* Why hadn't that occurred to her at the time? Maybe she could have stopped and asked—what? "Are you plotting something nefarious, sweetheart?" Sure. That would have worked.

"How long do you plan to stay in Prague? I assume internship means temporary—or I would be begging you to take me with you. Life without Lizzie would be too boring for words. And everyone knows where you go, so goes adventure and mayhem." Unfortunately, Kenna wasn't wrong. Mayhem *did* follow her. The difference between Kenna and her was that Kenna thought that was interesting and exciting. Well, until someone got hurt—then it sucked.

"Humph. Only recently. But I'm only gone a few weeks. As for John—I told you, we'll work it out. It'll be like the blink of an eye. There and back again. Did I mention that Harrington has offered to act as my mentor while I'm there?" Be vague, deflect, cross her fingers. That was Lizzie's best strategy.

"Hmm." Lizzie could hear Kenna's disbelief in the hum of her voice.

"Uh, any chance you want to give me a ride to the airport tomorrow evening?" Lizzie made a last ditch attempt to divert her attention.

"Sure. And I'm visiting, of course," Kenna finally said. And that was as close to a stamp of approval as Lizzie would get.

As soon as she hung up, she made arrangements with Kenna's mom to take the dogs for the whole month. The few face-to-face client meetings she had scheduled over the next month she rescheduled as teleconference meetings. She wouldn't be able to accept any new clients, but she could manage maintenance on current accounts for the month. She spent the rest of the day catching up, trying to squeeze in a little work before her departure.

Later in bed that night, all of the thoughts and concerns she'd pushed aside for the day came rushing back. She'd meant to talk to John about Harrington's offer. He was her boyfriend, however new. She may not have agreed to be his mate in the sense that he'd intended it, but she certainly had meant to be his girlfriend. In her world, that meant having a civilized discussion about one's plans before haring off to foreign parts.

She blinked up at the ceiling. Taking a month to intern with Harrington was a big decision that would impact her relationship with John. Of course, she'd meant to talk to him. But then Harrington had pushed her buttons with his comment about her needing permission. And then John had made it worse by telling her to calm down, like she was some hysterical twit—but she kinda had been. Mildly hysterical, she admitted to herself, but not a twit. She was dealing with huge changes in her life, changes that were happening at an alarmingly fast rate.

John hadn't returned yet. Lizzie groaned and beat her pillow with the flat of her hand, venting some of her frustration in the guise of pillow fluffing. Her breath caught as she felt the choking press of tears at the back of her throat. And even that made her angry with him all over again. She didn't want to cry about him.

She *hated* crying. She sniffed. She wasn't sure how to fix this without ceding him an authority over her life she wasn't ready to give. She couldn't let him unilaterally decide the when, where, and how of their relationship. She was an adult, and she'd managed to live on her own, making her own decisions, for—well, most of her adult life. She was thirty-six years old, dammit.

Lizzie experienced a flash of reason and calm, and she admitted that she was doing exactly what John had done—making decisions that impacted both of them without consulting him. Well, that was assuming he didn't just break up with her. She punched her pillow again. Because it would be simpler for him to date someone who knew the rules of Lycan society. Someone who wouldn't embarrass him in front of his people. Someone who wouldn't have a problem being treated like a little girl required to ask her parent's permission before making every decision. She wanted to laugh at the absurdity of that image in this day and age. But she couldn't. In fact, all she could do was think about how much she hated that imaginary girl, the one who fit better into his life and might take her place. She curled up on her side into a tiny ball and tried not to cry.

CHAPTER FOUR

"I'm going with her." John sat in his uncle's living room, staring into the obstinate but well-loved face of the man who'd raised him. His uncle was far from pleased with the update John had just delivered.

"You need to get your priorities straight. Your first commitment is to the pack, not to some human woman who holds our society and traditions in such low esteem that she can't even be bothered to show up for introductions." Logan Braxton made this pronouncement in a scornful tone.

The former Alpha of the Texas Pack—his intimidating height, his physical strength, and his strong sense of pack loyalty undiminished since his retirement—was a formidable opponent. John had always been able to count on Logan as an ally, but perhaps not in this instance. This was much the same speech he'd heard when he first announced Lizzie as Alpha Mate three days ago.

"I understand your concerns. And you know my position. Lizzie and my alliance with her will both be advantageous to the pack in the long term." Sitting in his uncle's living room, only hours from leaving the country, he wasn't sure he would be able to sway Logan to a position of support before he left. But he had to try.

"And leaving now? That's a strategic error. You've just announced a new Alpha Mate and you've made a very controversial choice. A woman neither Lycan, nor known to the Pack. You fail to introduce her to the Pack, which hints at shame, embarrassment, or her disinterest in the Pack. And now, during this critical time, you plan to leave?" Logan crossed his arms across his massive chest. "You're begging to be challenged."

John replied with a hard look on his face. "So be it. I can beat any Pack member in a direct challenge." His pack owed him some loyalty for his years of service. He found it hard to believe he had so little support. Either his uncle was being a pessimist—always a strong possibility—or his position in the Pack was much more precarious than he had realized.

"I would look outside the Pack for a more serious challenge. And you know what that would mean," Logan said.

John sighed. An outside challenge would more likely mean a fight to the death, or serious injury. And the threat would be less predictable if it came from an outsider.

"Four to six weeks. I should be able to deal with some personal issues for four to six weeks without inviting outside threats. And the council is not without power. In my absence, the council should be more than equipped to handle anything pressing." John was tired. At times, the responsibilities of the pack weighed heavily on him, and now was one of those times.

Logan barked out a humorless laugh. "You know it's not that simple. This is a moment of transition, and that is when a pack is always at its weakest. You have to be strongest and ready for attack in these moments. And the council? They only have as much power as you and I have granted them. The idea is still a new one. It will be another generation or two before the council is so firmly seated within the pack's structure that it couldn't be ripped apart by the right combination of events." He gave John a narrow-eyed look. "I'm not telling you anything you wouldn't know under normal circumstances. This woman has blinded you; she's made you weak."

"And I think you're biased, because you never took a mate. The right match can make the pack stronger." John knew he was touching on a sensitive subject. Logan had lost the woman he believed was his mate when he was a relatively young Alpha. But Logan's persistent disapproval—when he hadn't even met Lizzie—was annoying. But it was no more than an annoyance, because it wouldn't change his opinion or his plans.

"I don't argue that point. I'm saying she's not the right match," Logan said.

"Enough. I've made my choice, and I'll make it work. Do I have your support?" John wanted Logan on his side, but he wouldn't beg. One thing he knew for sure, Logan would never do anything he thought might hurt the pack.

Logan sighed. "I support you, and I will continue to—so long as you continue to be good for the pack. And you're my blood." After a brief pause, it was clear he simply couldn't resist adding, "But sometimes you're an insubordinate ass."

"Likewise," John said with an amused glint in his eyes. "Keep me updated? While I'm in Prague, I mean."

John needed a few attentive eyes and ears within the Pack. Being far removed geographically meant that he would have difficulty gauging the mood of the pack. And he needed to know if a younger wolf was feeling emboldened by his absence. He could always come home and kick some impertinent whelp's ass—but only if he was kept informed.

Logan kicked back in his big armchair, legs stretched out in front of him. "Uh-huh. Need my help already, do you?"

"You're the best person to ask because you gossip like an old woman. Call it whatever you like—morning coffee, Friday night poker—it's still gossip." Logan deserved that, John thought.

Logan didn't even blink at the accusation.

"I'm telling you, you need to stay." Seeing John's expressionless face, Logan shook his head in frustration and said simply, "Yes, I'll keep you updated."

"I'll check in weekly, but give me a call on my cell if anything raises a red flag. You do remember how to use the phone, old man?" John cracked a small smile.

"You're an ass. I even know how to text, so don't give me shit," Logan replied.

The two men parted on good terms, but John knew he'd have to get his personal life in order quickly. If he took too long, a challenge might be the least of his worries. The pack may never accept Lizzie if he didn't resolve their differences and bring her home for introductions soon.

On the drive back to Lizzie's, John did some quick math to calculate the difference in time zones. He decided six in the morning was a great time to call the man who had loosed a hornet's nest on his and Lizzie's relationship.

"Harrington." The clipped tones of a very much awake Harrington came across John's cell. Ah, well. Pulling the guy out of his bed had been a petty thought anyway.

"John Braxton, here."

Harrington was silent just a hair longer than was polite. "I've been expecting your call. What can I do for you?"

"I'm flying to Prague. You've discovered a sudden need for a security consultant." John glanced at the time again. He frowned. Lizzie was probably already in bed. He hadn't intended to be gone so long from the house, but there had been some construction and an accident that had made traffic ridiculously slow.

"Have I? I've employed Lachlan McClellan's security firm to handle the short-term security needs of the Library," Harrington replied. His tone turned cautious. "I'm not certain if a consultant would be appreciated."

"Your problem, not mine. I hold you partially responsible for my current situation. So you'll do this for me, and I will consider your debt paid—in part." John considered this conversation a formality. He was going, and he was staying at the Library. It was Harrington's problem to sort out the various details and soothe ruffled feathers.

Harrington laughed. "You're a cheeky bastard." There was the muffled sound of movement in the background. "Done. But you'll have to deal with Lachlan. I hope, for your sake, he finds your situation amusing."

John raised an eyebrow at that. He'd have to do a little research on this security firm. Clearly, the man was some kind of magic-user, or Harrington wouldn't have hired his firm. Some kind that wasn't too concerned with Lycan.

"As long as he keeps himself to himself, we'll be fine," John said dryly, and he hung up. He was in a good mood. His plan was moving along nicely.

John still needed Lizzie's flight information, but he'd be damned if he let Harrington know he was in the dark. He'd texted Max earlier for the information, and there was a good chance he'd come through. Max Thorton had some serious connections. He was one of the few men John knew who managed to not only stay friendly with his exes but actually be friends with them. And he always knew a guy, or had a friend, who could do whatever he needed. He knew that many people, had that many connections. He was a handy guy to know and an even better one to be best friends with.

Next on the list, get back to Lizzie's. He'd planned to be back before Lizzie went to bed. Not that he knew what he was going to say—but at least he'd be there. And that was the question. Did he tell her that he was going with her? Pack concerns aside, it was an easy decision to go. Less so talking to Lizzie about it. And that summed up one of his issues—acting was sometimes easier than talking.

When he got to the house, it was dark, except for the motion light in the front. He let himself in with the spare key. The dogs hadn't barked at his truck pulling up. That was an improvement. Vegas, the pointer, greeted him at the door, but the yellow lab, Beau, didn't even get up. He just lifted his head and thumped his thick tail against his dog bed. After a rough start, John was now the dogs' favorite, second only to Lizzie and Kenna. And maybe Kenna's mother. That woman stuffed them full of tidbits and goodies every time they went to stay with her. He smiled. Lizzie grumped about having to put them on a diet when they came home from Mrs. McIntyre's house, but he could tell she wasn't really upset.

John kneeled down and gave Beau a chin scratch. Then he stood up and scrubbed a hand over his face. He quietly walked into Lizzie's bedroom—and it was hers, because they hadn't yet tackled permanent living arrangements. She was asleep, curled up with her arms and legs tucked close, like she'd been cold. She probably was. He liked it colder, so she'd cranked the air conditioning to make him more comfortable. He thought briefly about grabbing another blanket but discarded the idea. Shrugging his shirt off, he walked to the armchair in the corner of the room. After tossing the shirt in the chair, he reached down to unbutton his jeans—and paused. She was awake.

CHAPTER FIVE

Lizzie peered at John through her lowered lashes. Pissed or not, she couldn't help but see how the muscles in his back and shoulders bunched and moved as he pulled his shirt over his head. *Thank you, full moon.* Since she hadn't been sure he was coming back this evening, or if he did, where he'd be sleeping, she didn't really want to question his sudden appearance—in her room, almost naked. It probably didn't help that she had been in a deep sleep for a very short time when she'd awoken. So she was groggy and only half awake.

He must have removed his shoes before he came into her room, because he was barefooted. Lord, but she loved how he looked in jeans and nothing else. Bare feet and a bare chest, jeans slung low on his hips…there wasn't much that was hotter, except John in his bare skin. He paused after unbuttoning his jeans, head tipped down, fingers touching his zipper. She'd just been made.

But after that brief pause, he continued removing his jeans—slowly. After lowering the zipper, he tugged at the waist, first the left side, then the right, and the jeans fell to his knees. He leaned slightly, resting his right hand on the armchair and then, using the chair to balance himself, he leaned down to pull his pants off.

Lizzie's eyes followed the long line of his thigh up to the muscled curve of his ass—and stopped, lingering. She was pretty sure she sighed. Or exhaled. She'd made some sound that made it clear she was awake, watching, and enjoying the show.

"Hey," she squeaked. *Ugh. So not sexy.* She didn't mean to squeak. But just as she opened her mouth to speak—to fess up to her wakefulness—she got an eyeful of full frontal nude John. Who could blame her for squeaking?

"Hey." His voice rumbled, low and comforting, as he climbed into bed next to her. He pulled her close and whispered in her ear, "Traffic was bad."

Not exactly an apology, but it was good enough for her raging hormones.

Several sweaty and acrobatic minutes later—even John was panting from exertion—he held her snugly in his embrace and said, "I'm going with you."

Lizzie just nodded. She wasn't sure if it was because she couldn't catch her breath or because she didn't have anything to say.

When Lizzie woke up the next morning she realized she'd managed to sleep through John getting out of bed. No simple task, since she tended to drift towards warmth in the middle of the night, and she and John slept in a tangle of limbs. Her eyes felt scratchy. She blinked a few times. Ewww. More crunchy than scratchy. She rolled out of bed and headed to the bathroom, grabbing her cell off the nightstand as she went. Eleven o'clock? She stopped, turning to check the large picture window. John must have closed the curtains this morning when he got up. She grinned, thinking about their midnight acrobatics. Wait—eleven o'clock? *Dang it.*

The list of things she needed to do today started rolling through her head as she stared at the puffy-eyed, dark-haired woman in the mirror. Pick up dog food, drop the dogs off, clear out her garage so her car would fit, pack. One more look in the mirror and she decided it would all wait for a shower. She looked like crap.

Slightly less crunchy, Lizzie strolled into the kitchen after her shower. She raised her eyebrows at the scene that greeted her: Kenna sitting at her kitchen table looking uncomfortable, and John across from her with an inscrutable expression, both of them drinking coffee.

"Hi," Lizzie said tentatively. "Did I miss something?"

"Half the day, maybe?" Kenna teased. "Don't you have things to do? You're still leaving this evening, right?" As soon as the words left her mouth, she bit her lip and shot a quick glance at John.

John stood up and tipped his head to the garage. "I'll be in the garage making room for your car."

Lizzie tried not to look guilty. Her garage was a huge mess. She stored her business files, Christmas decorations, boxed up charity donations that were long overdue for delivery, and about twenty other different categories of little-used junk.

"If you think you can manage, and you don't mind…?" If a look could be disdainfully snarky, Lizzie just saw it. So maybe she was an idiot to ask a Lycan if he could manage shifting a few boxes around. And since the man was trying to give her some time with her friend before she left town *and* he was taking care of one of her list items for the day, she couldn't help but notice that he was trying.

"Thank you." She said it before he had a chance to change his mind. There was a lot of junk in her garage, and *she* didn't want to move it.

She and Kenna moved to her room, but not before

Kenna poured her a cup of coffee and spiked it with a large amount of milk and sugar. At the second spoonful, Lizzie had smiled. Now settled on the love seat at the end of the bed—thankfully cleared of miscellaneous clothes the day before—Kenna eyeballed her.

Lizzie took a sip of her coffee, and laughed. "I must look worse than I thought. You've doctored up my coffee like you do when something really bad happens. I'll be on a sugar high for hours."

"Hmm. Did you cry yourself to sleep last night?" Kenna asked, looking at her thoughtfully.

"Humph. No, just allergies. Though I might have briefly considered crying." Lizzie put her coffee on the dresser and busied herself yanking a suitcase out of her walk-in closet.

"But now you're okay?" Kenna asked.

"Now I'm okay," she confirmed. *Dang it.* Her suitcase was wedged between a box of scarves and an old photo album. She tugged a little harder. Her bag almost fell on top of her as she gave it a particularly good solid yank. Moving the bag to her bed, she unzipped it and started tossing clothes inside. "He's coming with me. I think."

Lizzie could see Kenna still on the love seat. Lizzie kept throwing clothes in her bag or shoving them back in her closet, debating how much to tell Kenna.

"You think. Last time I talked to you, you couldn't say with any confidence that you were still dating. And now he's going to Prague with you. You guys move fast." Her snort of amusement didn't fool Lizzie. Kenna was definitely worried about her and John. "Not that I'm saying that's a bad thing. I'm just having a hard time keeping up," Kenna clarified. "All right. You need to spill. John was gone yesterday—to see the pack? What's up with that? And he's back now. So you guys are good? But I'm thinking not, because there was some awkward going on in the kitchen. And how exactly does

John feel about this whole Prague thing? And how do you feel about him coming with you? Shit. Can he hear everything we're saying?"

Once Kenna took a breath, Lizzie laughed. "Exactly how much coffee did you drink while you were waiting for me?"

"Only two cups, so don't get all snarky on me. Besides, you can't talk to anyone else about this stuff. I'm all you've got." Kenna scooted her butt back on the love seat, making more room for her legs, and then she crossed her ankles.

"I doubt he can hear us this far away—and it's not like he'd be trying." At Kenna's skeptical look, Lizzie replied, "Not everyone is as nosy as you."

"I'm glad you buy that explanation," Kenna said, still with a skeptical arch to her brow.

Lizzie shook her head and rolled her eyes. "What else did you ask me?"

"The Pack," Kenna reminded her.

"Right. I don't know. He went yesterday and came back late last night. I'm not sure how much of the Pack activities I can talk about—but that's actually all I know. But I can tell you that John and I are in extended negotiations over my current perceived position within the Pack." Lizzie frowned. She hadn't actually thought about it like that until now.

Kenna sat up straighter. "So is this why your eyes are all puffy and you look like you're hung over?"

"Gah. Seriously? You're going to damage what little self-esteem I have, you evil wench. You know I have allergies." Since Kenna had poked and prodded her to date more and was always telling her how gorgeous she was, Lizzie couldn't help but grin at her evaluation today.

"So—no crying?"

Lizzie smiled. "No, I did not cry myself to sleep."

"Okay. Tell me about these negotiations. Who knew you

had a position within the Pack." Kenna seemed intrigued by the concept.

"Right? I'm still in the dark about how Lycan packs work." Lizzie raised an eyebrow at her friend. "If you hadn't shown up when you did, I planned to ask."

Kenna laughed and rolled off the love seat. "Got it; I'm outta here. I love you, too. I'm still driving you to the airport tonight?"

Lizzie hugged her tight. "Yes, please. I'd really like to see you again before I leave."

CHAPTER SIX

It had taken John about fifteen minutes of heavy lifting to clear out a space for Lizzie's car. Making enough room in a two-car garage for one Jetta wagon hadn't been that hard. Although, he thought as he looked around, she did have a lot of items that seemed to serve no immediate purpose. He saw several boxes labeled "donate" and made a mental note to take care of them when they got back.

Once he was done, he found a few boxes that looked sturdy enough to hold him and sat down. He'd give Kenna and Lizzie a few more minutes and take care of some pack business. He placed several calls, one to each of the Pack's Council members. His preference would have been to speak with them in person, but he simply hadn't the time before he had to leave for Prague. Except for his Uncle Logan, who was a Council member, a phone call would have to suffice.

During the latter half of his Uncle Logan's tenure as Alpha, John and Logan had developed and eventually created the Council of Elders. The idea was to create more stability within the Pack. And so far, it had. The Council had thrived for the last twenty-one years, nine years of which had been during John's tenure as Alpha. Most of the Council were ardent supporters, but not all. John rarely missed a Council meeting, and he wanted the members to know he wouldn't be missing the next meeting, scheduled in three weeks. He also always—almost always, he amended—updated the Council on any foreign travel. So he would be giving them his contact information in Prague.

Interestingly, most of the Council members had been open to discussing formalizing a relationship with the IPPC. Given the past reclusive and almost xenophobic behavior of the Texas Pack, that was a pleasant surprise. The groundwork that first Logan and now he was doing to yank the Texas Pack into the current century might actually be paying off. Now, if he didn't alienate too many members with his choice of mate, he'd be doing great.

An hour later, John was done. He was happy to build and maintain relationships with several senior, knowledgeable members of his pack. He even considered several of them personal friends. But sometimes the diplomacy and finesse required to further his goals was wearing. No—exhausting. But the head-bashing alternatives were less appealing. And he refused to rule by fear within his own pack. Respect, naturally, but not fear. His neighboring allies in Arkansas were one example of how governance through fear failed long-term.

He shook his head. The Arkansas Pack may now be his *former* ally. He'd finally spoken at length with Ben Emmerson, his top Enforcer. Ben had created such a mess in Jonesboro, Arkansas that John had attempted to schedule a meet with Arkansas's Alpha, Jared Warren, but he'd been rebuffed. Since Warren had a pack uprising on his hands, John wasn't particularly concerned that he was a direct threat to Texas. He had an eye on them—Jared and the volatile pack dissenters, because instability so close to home was always a concern. Christina Landford, known to her friends as Chris, was coordinating surveillance and reporting to John. Arkansas wasn't a pressing concern—yet.

He pinched the bridge of his nose. He might actually be getting a headache. Just a hair before Lizzie opened the door to the garage, something warned him of her presence—a scent, a sound—so he stood up and turned, the look of exhaustion wiped from his face before she stepped into the garage.

"Wow. That was quick." Lizzie was looking not at the open space he'd made for her car, but the shelves he'd assembled and the items tidily stored on them.

What else was he supposed to do once his butt got tired of sitting on a box? He'd puttered around and tidied as he'd spoken with the Council. And the shelves hadn't even required tools; they just slotted together.

"Hmm. I had to make some phone calls, so—" He peered at her. It hadn't crossed his mind until this moment that what he was doing might be considered invasive. It needed to be done, and he was standing around. He was starting to realize relationships held more mines and traps than pack politics.

"Thank you," she said and gave him a brilliant smile. All right, then. Apparently not the wrong thing to do. Maybe he'd ask next time. Who was he kidding? No, he probably wouldn't.

"My pleasure." He followed Lizzie back into the house. He eyed the kitchen table, laid out with sandwich fixings. He really had been preoccupied if he'd missed that just one room away. "I am ready for some lunch. Where's Kenna? And the boys?"

"Headed home. She offered to drop the dogs off at her mom's for me. She'll be back by later to give us a lift." She sat down at the table and started slicing bread. She'd hesitated just a fraction of a second before she said "us" but didn't glance his way.

He wasn't really sure what would piss her off at this point, but he figured full disclosure was his best bet. "I bought a ticket this morning."

She nodded. His nose wasn't detecting the acrid, sour scent of anger.

"Are you on my flight?" she asked politely enough.

"I am." Since there didn't seem to be an immediate danger of a fight, he figured he might as well eat. He was starving. After his first bite, he couldn't help but focus on the excellent ham, so her next question was somewhat jarring.

"Do I want to know how you have my flight information, since you didn't actually ask me?" Lizzie asked.

The ham sandwich would have to wait. His brow rose as he speculated on the right answer to that question. "Probably not, but I'll tell you." Damn, he was hungry. Hopefully that didn't impair his decision-making skills. "I had Max ask a friend to dig it up. I didn't want you to leave before we had a chance to talk."

She nodded.

"Why the long layover?" He'd mentally shrugged and bought tickets on the same flights, but a seven-hour layover is excessively lengthy unless she had an appointment.

She cocked her head to the side, as if considering her answer. "I made arrangements with Harrington to stop by Sarah's care facility. He said that she's still in a coma and may not recognize the presence of visitors. But since she was injured trying to save me, I wanted to visit."

"I'll stop by IPPC headquarters," he offered. He figured she'd appreciate a little space.

"Thank you." She gave him a quick smile and went back to picking at her food. Since Lizzie had recovered her appetite after the kidnapping, not eating was a sign—of something.

"We haven't—" he started.

"We need to—" she said, speaking at the same time.

He waited. She started chewing the corner of her lip, a sure sign that she was thinking really hard—or upset.

"We need to talk about what a mate is. What you—and everyone else—expect now that the magical world thinks we're mated."

He cringed slightly, but it had to be said. "Technically, we are mated." *Shit.* He could see the slight pink flush starting on her cheeks and moving down her neck.

He drew an audible breath. "I understand you had no idea what you were agreeing to. But the point is, I asked and you said yes. Technically, that makes it true."

"Okay." Succinctly said, but his nose picked up a combination of sharply sour and sweet odors. Fear and anger.

"As a human, being mated isn't much different than being married. You can walk away whenever you like. There's no repercussion—nothing to prevent you from leaving." John was hoping that might put her mind at ease.

She narrowed her eyes. "And you? What about you?"

"In theory, I can do the same—but it's not done." He almost laughed at the look on her face. Almost. "You're it for me."

"But—why would you…" she sputtered.

"Because I'm sure. As sure as I can be." This wasn't really a topic he wanted to linger on. "You want to know the expectations of a mate?"

"Yes." Lizzie frowned. "Yes," she said a second time, more firmly.

"Lycan have historically tended toward isolation—though that's changing. And Lycan also tend to think in terms of 'us' or 'them.' That means that packs frequently don't follow the same rules or have the same traditions." John looked at his sandwich and debated whether he could reasonably eat at this point.

She looked at his plate and said, "Finish your sandwich before you faint from low blood sugar."

Hey, he wasn't that bad.

Halfway through his sandwich, she brought up Harrington. "So Harrington was wrong? I mean, his assumption that I'd need permission to leave Pack territory?"

"Not exactly. Any area outside pack territory is basically the equivalent of foreign soil. Since Alpha Mate is a respected position within most packs, there are implications to crossing boundaries. In more traditional packs, an Alpha might require not only his mate but all pack members to inform him of travel and possibly even receive approval."

"Kind of like a visa? You're basically your own country?" Disbelief was strong in her voice.

"A little. Except someone like you—someone unfamiliar with Lycan boundaries—wouldn't know when you were entering another pack's territory or were on neutral ground. And I need to make some accommodation when you travel through or visit a territory," he said.

Her nose wrinkled slightly and her eyes narrowed in an involuntary wince. "It sounds very political."

This time he couldn't stop a sharp bark of laughter, though it held little humor. "Yes. It can be."

"Hmm," she said noncommittally.

"It's out there in the magic-using community that you're my mate—" He noted the look of disapproval Lizzie didn't bother to hide. "—so there will be certain expectations. Until we resolve our differences, some pretense of support in public would be good."

"I assumed." Lizzie grumbled. "I told Kenna it sounded a lot like being a politician's wife."

"Is that so terrible?" Her attitude was starting to grate. He would put up with politics and more for her.

She deflated, sinking lower into her seat. "No. I mean—what you've told me so far seems reasonable enough. I would do that and more to pursue what we have. But I also can't lose all control over my life. And you've made me feel out of control."

John realized now wasn't the time to point it out, but this wasn't just about him. Being kidnapped must have made her feel powerless. And not having a good understanding of her magic didn't particularly help. But pointing out the chaotic state of her life didn't seem advantageous to his argument or to her state of mind.

"You haven't eaten a bite since we sat down. Why don't you finish your lunch, and we can discuss it further later."

She nodded absentmindedly, staring at her plate. He'd managed to finish his sandwich as they spoke and was gathering his plate and glass when she looked up.

There wasn't any trace of doubt when she spoke. "I'm glad you're coming."

That was a start.

CHAPTER SEVEN

"You're it for me," John had said. *No pressure.* That was Lizzie's mantra as she finished packing and even when Kenna arrived to drive them to the airport. She wasn't sure what to make of the fact that John was stuck with her or no one. Although, she supposed Catholics had done it for years. And he had lived thirty-nine years without a mate. She really was grasping at this point. Regardless of which way she looked at the situation, he'd taken a risk. On her. Right—no pressure.

In an effort to deflect, she focused on something positive, something exciting. *The Library.* All of those spelled books. It made her head spin just to think that she would be able to dig around in a roomful of such amazing books and read anything that caught her eye.

And first-class air travel. That was something she could focus on, she thought as she stretched her legs out and wiggled her toes.

"Enjoying that leg room, I see," John said.

"Yes. I can't say I'm sorry you upgraded us, but I feel just the tiniest bit guilty." She saw him glance at her in mild amusement. "Okay, only a very tiny bit guilty." She was excited enough that the bumpy ascent of the plane barely registered.

John started to look green. Whatever it was about John's magic that imbued him with a higher metabolism, increased strength, improved senses, healing, and all the other Lycan goodies, it missed the mark with motion sickness. While Lizzie felt sympathetic, she couldn't miss the irony. And having suffered from airsickness herself, before her magic had been unblocked, she knew how completely rotten it felt. She inched just a little farther away from him. Airsickness had always made her feel claustrophobic. And since John took up a lot of space, she figured giving him a little room was wise.

Before they left, she and John had discussed the pack book. She hadn't had the time or energy in the last few days to begin pulling information from the spelled book. She'd been just a little distracted by John, and she'd also been recovering from some serious sleep deprivation after her kidnapping.

Now that she'd have some time, she could start delving into the Texas Pack's history. She figured the risk in traveling with the book was minimal if she was discreet. John didn't have a problem with it, and neither had Harrington. She'd even chatted with Harrington about detecting spelled books and had received her first mini-mentor session. She'd learned that a spell caster could use a special sensing ward to detect a spelled book, but they'd have to know to look.

It was past time she made the pack book a priority. The book had brought John and her together, initially. It was his search for the book that had brought him to her doorstep. She smiled, remembering the first impression John had made. Rude, pushy—and incredibly hot. All bulging biceps and determined persistence. She hadn't actually liked him all that much. She glanced at his very dear—currently tinged with green and quite pale—face. She couldn't believe how much her feelings for him had changed over such a short time. Well, except for the incredibly hot part. Those feelings were pretty consistent.

Given her recently acquired magic, she *finally* had the power to read the book. After two years trying to make something out of the shifting words, she was ready to kick that book's butt. Or maybe to ask very nicely if it would spill its secrets. Spelled books could be finicky about when, how, and to whom they gave their information.

Lizzie took a second to look around. Off-season, the seats around them were sparsely filled. The closest passenger was one row up and on the other side of the aisle, a young guy with headphones firmly planted in his ears and his eyes closed.

She ran her hand lightly down John's arm. She hated to disturb him, but his color was looking slightly better—and she needed a second opinion.

His eyes blinked open, slowly focusing on her. She'd told him on another flight they'd shared that when she used to get motion sickness, letting herself fall asleep for a few minutes on takeoff and landing would frequently take care of it. Apparently he'd decided to give it a try.

"I hate to bring it up—but have you considered Dramamine?" Seeing his color continue to improve, she moved her hand from his arm down to his hand. She briefly clasped his warm dry fingers.

"Doesn't work." He twined his fingers with hers. "The catnap might work, though. So far, so good. What's up?"

"I wondered what you thought about me using this time on the plane to do a little *research*." She raised her eyebrows, trying to hint that research referred to the book.

"Worst super-spy ever," he said dryly. Since it wasn't the first time he'd told her so, she wasn't shocked.

"And?"

"And—feel free. It's just a book." He leaned back in his seat, tipping his head back against the headrest and closing his eyes. His fingers remained clasped firmly around hers.

Lizzie decided a small nap before she started with the book wouldn't hurt. Especially since this was an overnight flight. If she didn't get some sleep, her visit with Sarah and making her connection would be rough.

Hmmm. She felt warm. She rubbed her cheek against soft cotton. And hard chest. She took a deep breath of—John. Her eyes popped open. Tipping her head back, she looked up into bright blue eyes. Lord, she loved his eyes. Not a washed-out blue or a gray-blue, but a richer color. She took another breath. John always smelled like cloves, minty toothpaste, and a unique musky smell that made her think of warmth and man. Clean man.

John hugged her closer for a brief second, and then he removed his arm from around her shoulders.

She looked down and saw he'd flipped up the armrest between them. And she'd gained a blanket at some point. After a jaw-cracking yawn, she came to the conclusion that she might have slept a little longer than she planned.

Before she had a chance to check the time, John said, "We have another three or four hours before we arrive."

She stretched her legs out, pointed and lifted her toes a few times, and rolled her shoulders. "Did I mention how grateful I am for my first-class upgrade?"

"You might have. It was purely selfish." John rolled the shoulder that Lizzie had used as her pillow. "I don't fit in coach."

Lizzie stopped stretching to admire his broad shoulders and tall frame. "No, I don't suppose you do." She frowned.

"Do we have shared assets? Because you seem to fling around first-class tickets and even private plane charters pretty casually. Am I rich?" She grinned at him.

That elicited a loud laugh. "Did you win the lottery? Or come into an unexpected inheritance?"

She let out a huge, put-upon sigh. "No."

"That's your answer then." John grinned, pulled her to him and kissed her so thoroughly she forgot what she'd been teasing him about.

She felt like fanning herself but settled for yanking off the blanket she'd been huddled under while she slept. "I'll be right back. I think I'll have a look at that research when I get back."

When she returned, she found John engrossed in what looked like work. He was a statistician and had his own market research firm. Since Lizzie had known him, he would periodically pull out his laptop or a stack of papers and work intently for hours at a time. Then the work would disappear and he'd never mention it. Since his job didn't sound incredibly fascinating and he wasn't keen on sharing the details of his work with her, she was okay with that. But, eventually, she should probably figure out exactly what it was a market research firm did. And what that had to do with stats.

He'd also pulled the pack book out of the carryon he'd stashed in the overhead bin for her. She almost had to laugh at herself. He could open every door, pay for every meal, carry her heavy bags, get things off tall shelves, and reorganize her garage. And she would smile and say thank you every time. She was a Texas girl at heart, and she enjoyed the fact that John was nice. He was polite. He was thoughtful. But then he'd do something completely asinine, like make an *important* decision without her.

She picked up the book and planted her butt back in her cushy first-class seat. Book in hand, her thoughts turned more serious. They had barely scratched the surface with the talk about mates earlier. She needed a handbook. She blinked, looked down at the book in her hand, and blinked again. She was a complete idiot. If not a handbook, she had a resource. Although, to give John some credit, it sounded like his pack—their pack?—had changed significantly in a positive way since the last entry must have been made in the book.

She ran her hand across the soft leather of the cover. It sounded like the book had gone astray before Logan's tenure as Alpha, and that had been forty or more years ago. Not a bad place to start. *When was the last entry?*

Lizzie glanced at John, and she nudged him with her foot. When he glanced up, she said, "You're sure—"

But before she could finish her question, John interrupted her. "Yes."

He leaned over so his lips were next to her ear. So close, that she could feel the soft exhalation of his breath with each word. "The plane won't explode if you use magic," he whispered. "And no one is popping out of the aisle to snag the book."

"Am I that paranoid?" She couldn't prevent the sheepish look that crossed her face.

"Hmm." And that noncommittal noise was all the answer she got. John was already typing away on his laptop. Diplomatic of him. There really wasn't a good response to that question, because clearly the honest answer was "yes." She mentally shrugged. Who could blame her after all the craziness she'd seen and experienced recently?

She'd always had magic, but it had been locked away. She hadn't known she had it, hadn't even known magic existed. So when it became paramount that she unlock and use her magic, she hadn't even a hint how to do so. With the help of Pilar—another kidnapped spell caster held by Worth—she reacquired her magic. Then Pilar had given her a crash course in how to use magic, or Magic 101, as Lizzie liked to think of it. Pilar had broken the process down into three easy steps. Primarily because they both anticipated she'd be under great stress when she would be using her magic. Not having grown up with magic, she'd desperately needed the Cliff's Notes version.

Step one was to reach inside herself and find her magic. When she'd first tried several days ago, she hadn't known what she was looking for and it had been difficult—like her magic was reluctant to emerge or was buried deep inside. Then her magic had practically dripped from her fingers—too accessible—and making her worry she'd create some kind of magical disaster. But in the last several days, she felt like she'd gotten to know that part of herself a little. Her magic was there, but it wasn't burbling like frothy champagne. Settling deeper into the roomy first-class seat, she hunted for the pulsing, glowing, warm bit of herself that was her magic. Eyes closed, she breathed out a small sigh of satisfaction as she found it.

Second, she had to create a clear mental picture of exactly what she wanted. The one successful experience she'd had trying to pull information from a book, she'd found that crafting the most precise question wasn't always the most productive option. It was more feeling than logic—so annoying. She wasn't getting any vibes, so she just asked what she wanted to know. *When was the last entry?* And then—step three—she pushed. Pilar called it exerting will, but it felt like a mental shove to Lizzie.

Lizzie's eyes popped open. "John?"

He stopped typing and turned to her. "Find something interesting?"

She nodded. "When did you say the book had gone missing?"

Small creases appeared at the corners of John's eyes. Worry or concentration—Lizzy wasn't certain which. After giving the question some consideration, he said, "It's difficult to say. Certainly, it wasn't in our possession in 1980."

"Wasn't that a little before your time?" At his confused look, she clarified. "It's just, you have such a specific time reference. And you were only around five at the time."

"My uncle assumed control in '79. The transition was not a peaceful one. I'm not sure of many details prior to that year." His responses were choppy with pauses between each sentence. He'd also become more distant as he spoke, his gaze drifting out the window.

Curiouser and curiouser. But if he didn't want to discuss it— "There's an entry from a little over two years ago."

His head whipped around. "What does it say?"

Lizzie closed her eyes, whispering the words as they came to her. "I can only hope as I pass along this beautiful burden that the book's next home will bring it closer to the Pack, it's one true home. I wish you everything that is good, Elizabeth, as you assume from me this gift, this burden."

She opened her eyes to find John studying her intently.

"I had no idea," she said.

He frowned in confusion. "About what?"

"Who had it before? That she knew me? Why she picked me?" She chewed her lip. "You just look a bit peeved, so I thought I'd assert my innocence and ignorance proactively. You know, cover my butt." Okay, she was rambling. He smiled. More than that, muscles taut with tension eased. "No need on my account. I like a bare ass as much as the next guy."

He'd pitched his voice low, and she was certain no one else had heard. She still blushed a fiery red.

CHAPTER EIGHT

Memories of his father, who was Alpha before Logan assumed control of the Pack, pressed in on John. But Lizzie—curiosity and concern practically vibrating off her—brought him back to the present. He couldn't resist teasing her. Or making her blush. His father was far, far in the past, and Lizzie was his Here and his Now. His smile widened.

"You know this means a—" She frowned in annoyance and lowered her voice still lower. "—*a person like me* was in possession of the book, at least for a little while, before it landed in my mailbox."

A single huff of a half laugh escaped. He couldn't help finding her efforts at discretion and secrecy laughable. She was terrible at covert ops.

"What's funny? That's big news, right?" She glanced down at the book in her hands. She fingered the worn green edges thoughtfully.

He wiped the humor from his voice. "Absolutely. Completely unexpected, in fact. It begs the question why she didn't return the book to the Pack, or seek us out." This was the first effort Lizzie had made with the book since she'd had access to her magic. It was an important first step. And it begged the question—"What did you ask it?"

As John understood the process, the spell caster—who the Lycan called Record Keeper—formulated questions, and the book responded. Or it didn't.

"I thought I might be able to use the book to answer some questions about *significant others* and their function in...your town." She shook her head at him. "I know. Don't start."

Since he had no idea what she was talking about, he was content to remain silent.

"But then I realized the information might be out of date since it wasn't clear when the book went missing."

He nodded. "So you asked about the last entry. Which happened to be about you."

"I get a sense of sadness from her. Maybe because she's letting the book go?" Lizzie looked troubled. "I didn't know these books could hold emotions."

John tried to keep his voice light, but probably failed. He'd done the math, if the book had disappeared in the seventies, then.... "Or you're getting some of her feelings for the Pack."

Lizzie shot him a quick glance. "Something I should know?"

"Probably." That didn't mean he was ready to talk about it. "I do know that Logan claims there were no Record Keepers affiliated with the pack before or during his tenure as Alpha, so that takes us back to the fifties."

"Eh. I'm not so sure." At his raised brow, she clarified. "Naturally, that could be the case. But isn't it also possible you didn't know? How would you know? You only guessed I was a Record Keeper because I had the book."

At least she'd stopped with the euphemisms. They'd

apparently progressed enough with her comfort level that they could openly talk shop. He did a quick sound check. They were surrounded by silence interrupted only by the slow, even breathing of a few sleeping people. That was the beauty of first class: you could actually sleep if you chose to.

"True. It wouldn't mean anything to anyone else." He grinned. "And no one else would have created such a massive electronic footprint searching for magic books."

"Can a girl not Google in privacy anymore?" She huffed in annoyance.

"No." He rubbed his chin. He'd need a shave when they landed. Maybe he'd grab a quick shower at the IPPC before he picked Lizzie back up at the care facility. "But a typical Record Keeper comes from a family who actually shares their history. You're an anomaly, not having known anything about magic."

"But it's possible she could have not known, or kept it a secret?" Lizzie persisted.

"Possible, but unlikely. And as for not knowing, you'd have known if some unknown relative hadn't put your magic to sleep when you were young." He flipped up the armrest between them so he could pull her tight against him.

He knew she didn't like the uncertain cloud that hung over her family history. She didn't know it, but he'd asked Christine to do some digging. John hoped that with a little more information about her family, Harrington—or one of his contacts—could pinpoint the magical branch. If someone had locked up his magic, he'd sure as hell want to know who —and why.

"That's true. According to Pilar, most children know before puberty but certainly no later than their early teens." She tipped her head back into his shoulder. "Even if she was very young and didn't know, that still doesn't explain how the book ended up with her. Maybe you're right, and she wasn't affiliated with the Pack and stumbled on the book."

He hoped that was the case. If she'd been a Pack member and left around the seventies, his father had been involved. And there had certainly been blood, as well as the rage and insanity that had always followed his father.

CHAPTER NINE

"I'm here to see Sarah Melton." Lizzie spoke with greater confidence than she felt. John had left her at the front door of the care facility, but only after she'd shoved him back into their cab. She could do this. And if she couldn't, she was an idiot for insisting John leave her at the door.

The nurse typed in the computer and asked her, "Your name?"

Lizzie paused a second—Harrington wouldn't dare. "Lizzie Smith."

The nurse didn't even look twice. "Here. I've got Elizabeth Smith Braxton listed as an approved visitor. Can I see your ID?"

Lizzie handed over her ID.

Harrington was an ass. She wasn't changing her name. No way. *She wasn't married.* It's a good thing John hadn't come with her, because she'd likely have thrown something at him. Even though it was Harrington who'd made the arrangements...yep, she'd still have blamed John. Sometimes, life wasn't fair.

Apparently, "Elizabeth Smith" on her ID was sufficient,

because the nurse asked her to have a seat and told her someone would be by to escort her to Sarah's room. So Lizzie sat inside a private long-term care facility, in a quiet and well-appointed lounge area, waiting to see a woman she'd never been introduced to, who might never wake up. A woman who had sustained her injuries saving Lizzie. The amorphous feeling of guilt that had hovered in the back of her mind for several days now clawed its way forward. She was responsible, if indirectly, for Sarah's condition.

As her escort appeared, Lizzie realized the inside of her lip was throbbing where she'd been unknowingly biting it. She followed the uniformed staff member into Sarah's private room. With a few quietly murmured instructions, Lizzie was left alone with Sarah. No equipment, no bandages, no visible sign of her condition at all. Just a slight, pale form on a bed.

Lizzie approached Sarah's bed, unsure of the right way to handle such a situation. *What the heck.* "Hi, Sarah. I'm Lizzie —the woman whose life you saved a few days ago."

She reached out her right hand and clasped Sarah's limp, pale fingers. Hanging onto Sarah's hand, she reached behind her and pulled a chair close, sitting down and making herself more comfortable. Very little was known about Sarah's condition, so there was no way to know if she was aware of anything happening around or to her. Since the experts didn't know, there was a chance that Sarah could understand. Lizzie owed her so much more than a conversation, but that was as good a place as any to start.

"Harrington arranged the very best of care for you." Lizzie looked around the room. "You have plenty of sunlight and fresh flowers. They're beautiful—pink and yellow and white. And you have a very pretty nightgown that's just like a dress, perfect for having company over." Lizzie smiled. "If you can call me company."

Harrington told her that a number of healers had evaluated Sarah but none could pinpoint the cause or provide a cure. The good news was that her condition was stable. She was breathing on her own. And there didn't appear to be any damage to her brain—though an extended amount of time in a coma, regardless of the cause, was problematic and likely to have a negative impact on her cognitive abilities upon waking.

"I'm sorry this happened, Sarah. I'm sorry I couldn't stop him sooner. If I knew how I did it, if I had known I could stop him, if…well, if things had been different, maybe you wouldn't have been hurt." Lizzie thought long and hard about her next statement, but she thought it was the right thing to do. "He got away. Worth got away. He was injured, but not so badly that he couldn't slip through a solid wall to vanish into a neighboring home and from there likely into another country."

Lizzie wasn't sure where her next words came from. But out they came. "We'll fix this, Sarah. Even if I have to go straight to the source, we'll figure out what's wrong and fix this." Once said, she couldn't unsay the words. As she thought of Worth—the source of Sarah's illness—her strongest memories were of his impeccable dress and manners. And, of course, of the last time she'd seen him, so far removed from his normal appearance. His face was bloodied, red oozing from every orifice. She didn't *want* to unsay the words.

The sight of Sarah's almost lifeless form stretched out on the bed brought back a vivid memory of Worth sucking her magic, her vitality away. Lizzie remembered the particular feel of Sarah's magic—spell caster magic— and how it was different from what she'd felt as Worth had begun to suck that same vital force from John. She shuddered. It was horrifying. It was almost as if Worth had slit open a vein and let their blood drain away—but something even more personal and vital than their blood had been stolen. Blood could be easily enough replaced. What Worth had stolen seemed to be unique. Lizzie thought of it as magic, but she couldn't really pinpoint what *exactly* he'd stolen. If it was only Sarah's magic, wouldn't she still be conscious but without her magical abilities? Lizzie feared Worth had stolen a piece of Sarah's soul as he'd sucked away her magic. If not soul, then something that made Sarah…Sarah.

Lizzie heaved a huge sigh and said, "I'm sorry, Sarah. I'm not really up on the metaphysical, and it's making my brain hurt to try to wrap my head around it all."

"Hmm. You're not the only one." Lizzie jumped at the sound of a voice—British, male, clipped, and clear. Thank goodness it was a man who had startled her, otherwise she'd have thought Sarah was talking back to her…and that she'd well and truly gone around the bend.

Lizzie turned to see a young man, maybe mid to late twenties, standing near the door. He was tall with a spare frame and a shock of unkempt orange hair. He also had the same type of visitor's badge on that she'd been given in the lobby.

"Hello?" Lizzie eyed him dubiously. He didn't *look* related, but you couldn't always tell. Maybe a brother? Oh, God—her boyfriend? She was having enough issues with guilt; she didn't need to meet Sarah's family or a boyfriend.

He stuck his hand out and said, "Hi—Lizzie, right? I'm Harry. One of Sarah's assigned healers. Harry, the healer." He grinned widely as he pumped Lizzie's hand enthusiastically.

"Um, hi, Harry the healer." Once she'd retrieved her hand, Lizzie said, "Can you tell me about Sarah's condition? Or is that confidential?"

"It's probably confidential, but I'm not a doctor and I

don't work for the facility. I'm one of Harrington's." Harry looked quite pleased with himself.

All Lizzie could think was Harrington's Harry, Harry the healer. He was a bit silly, but he certainly had brightened the atmosphere significantly.

She couldn't help but ask the obvious question. "You're one of Harrington's what?" Lizzie had stood as she shook hands with Harry, but now she sat back down next to Sarah. If he wasn't going to kick her out, then she might as well make herself comfortable.

"His people, his network." Harry lowered his voice. "His stash of secret resources."

"Harry, you're having a little too much fun with this. Are you a new recruit to the IPPC?" That was the only answer Lizzie could come up with for his peculiar behavior.

Demeanor more serious, Harry said, "No. I'm just someone Harrington outsources to occasionally when he has a particularly challenging problem. Playing at the cloak and dagger stuff makes it a bit more fun." He grimaced slightly and tugged on his ear. "Anything to lighten the load, right?"

"I take it you're not happy with Sarah's progress." Lizzie understood the need for a coping mechanism, and Harry's was a benefit to the people around him. He was fun.

Harry reached over to Sarah, sweeping his hand over her body about three or four inches above her prone form. Then he tucked a piece of hair behind her ear. "She's stable, which is excellent news." He tipped his head towards the door.

They both headed out to the corridor.

"There's a guest lounge on this floor. It should be empty this time of day." Harry was already briskly walking down the hall. He seemed to do everything with great energy.

Lizzie mentally shrugged and then followed him. She still had two hours before John picked her up. And just maybe she could get some clue as to what exactly had happened to Sarah.

Once in the room, she turned and asked, "You think she can understand what's going on around her?"

Harry raised his eyebrows and peered down a long, thin nose. "I hope *you* do, since you're the one who was holding a conversation with her." He sighed, assuming again the more serious persona of caregiver. "No idea. Not if she can hear you, not if she might recover, not how to speed her recovery, and not even if she's still there." He paused, a thoughtful look crossing his face. "Well—I do have *some* idea that she's still there. A glimmer every once in a while. Like the flickering of a bulb before it extinguishes."

"Were you lying when you said she was stable?" Somehow, the thought of Harry misleading Sarah, even an unconscious Sarah, made her really sad.

"No. Her condition is stable. The flickering has occurred several times, in no discernible pattern. Certainly not in diminishing frequency. I can maintain her general physical well-being with a small push of healing power every few days. I just don't want negative outcomes discussed in the room. No patient needs to hear ongoing chatter, based solely in speculation, regarding the various unpleasant outcomes she might face. I encourage visitors to talk to her, and I share what information I'm certain of." Harry looked very much the professional now, even if he wore tattered jeans and a T-shirt with a Marvel character splashed across the chest.

Lizzie took a quick, small breath. She wasn't sure why, but she kept catching herself holding her breath. She wasn't particularly excited to discuss that night with a stranger, as kind as she suspected Harry was. But if she wanted answers….

"Do you know who I am?" Before Harry could respond,

Lizzie plunged ahead. "Not my name. I mean, about that night? The night Sarah was injured?"

"I'm not an IPPC agent—not for lack of Harrington trying. I do, however, have the appropriate clearances. And I won't involve myself without all the facts. So, yes, I've read the reports. But a firsthand account might be helpful." Harry waited with no apparent impatience for Lizzie to decide what she wanted to share. He busied himself making a cup of coffee. Stopping mid-prep, he said, "Sorry. Coffee? Or Tea?"

That was a question she could answer. "Yes. Tea, please. Strong with a dash of milk." Once she had her hands wrapped around the thick, sturdy mug, she started to speak.

"I'm very new to magic. I didn't grow up knowing about magic-users, spelled books, Lycan. Not like all of you."

He shook his head slightly in disagreement. "It happens more than you might think."

"Well, the whole thing with my kidnapping and Worth being this super-villain, it came at a really bad time. I didn't —I still don't—really know that much about my magic. I didn't even know I was a spell caster or how to use magic until Pilar explained it to me." Lizzie paused in her story, looking up at Harry. She'd been staring at her mug thus far, hoping to stay a little detached from the story. "Pilar was also being held. She saved my life."

As her eyes were starting to burn with what promised to be the beginning of a deluge of tears, Harry interrupted. "I know Pilar. Her son is a menace. And I'm always happy to tell her that she must be at least partially to blame. He put bugs in my bed at school, and told Sally that I was in love with her." He paused dramatically. "I was *not* in love with Sally. I wasn't in love with any girl. Girls were disgusting."

At Lizzie's curious look, Harry said, "I was eight." He flashed a cheeky grin. "I grew into my love of women. It took me a whole four or five months after that, if I recall."

"Cute," Lizzie replied. "I knew Pilar had a daughter but didn't know about her son. What was he doing in England?"

"Attending boarding school, but that's a different story. The point is, I do know Pilar. I forgave her the bugs enough to speak with her after I saw her named in the report." He finally cracked a grin. "You'll be glad to hear her son turned out to be a good sort. Still likes his bugs but refrains from hiding them in bed linens. Or so I last heard."

Lizzie smiled weakly and sniffed a tiny bit. "I'm not usually quite so emotional. It's just recently, with everything that's happened—" Lizzie frowned, suddenly distracted by another thought. "Could that be tied to my magic somehow?" With everything that had happened over the last few weeks, it was no surprise that she hadn't stopped to analyze this one small piece of information.

"No doubt. From Pilar's description, your magic was locked up in a way that is contrary to your very nature as a magic-user. You would have seen the greatest effect in times of peak stress or emotion. It wouldn't surprise me if you had an unusual physical reaction to stress."

"Gah." *That explained a lot.* "Passing out? Throwing up?" Lizzie clarified.

"Sure." Harry, now sitting on a sofa across from Lizzie, scooted a little farther away from her. "Uh, you look angry."

"My magic was all tied up in some bizarre ward that no one completely understands, with a side-effect of making me puke and pass out at the most inconvenient moments. My magic is unlocked and the problem is solved, right? Uh, no. Now I blow up people when I'm super stressed. And by the way, when Pilar explained how magic worked, it didn't seem that was possible. That a person could do something unintentionally—like what I did to Worth."

"Okay, slow down. First, your magic has only recently been unlocked. It had been forced into an unnatural, dormant state. Whenever a magic-user is under stress, the adrenaline that surges makes it easier to access our magic. Basically, it's as if the magic has pulled to the surface. When your magic tried to respond to the adrenaline surge, it was blocked, resulting in—"

"Throwing up and passing out," Lizzie supplied.

"Yeah, I can see how that would be inconvenient. You need to give your body time to adjust. I suspect that you have a heightened response to adrenaline, and that your magic practically drips from you in those moments. That should go away over time. As to your second question—you are not practicing magic unless you assert will and give the magic a place to go and something specific to do." Harry seemed awfully sure of his words.

"Does that mean that I willed Worth to start bleeding internally? Because that's what happened. I don't remember thinking anything specific, like, 'I want you to die,' or 'please bleed from your eyes.' I just thought 'no.' I wanted him to stop." She looked at Harry intently. This was important. She needed to know that her magic was controllable. That her magic couldn't escape wildly at unexpected moments.

"What was he doing?" Clearly he already knew, because he said earlier he'd read the report. And it seemed he'd also spoken with witnesses.

"Wait a minute. If you've spoken with other witnesses, why hadn't you contacted me already?" Lizzie rather thought she was the *key* witness.

"Harrington's orders. He thought you'd already provided what information you could and that further questioning might be detrimental to your recovery," Harry responded matter-of-factly.

Huh. She was recovering? If there was one way to keep Harry away, it was to assert Lizzie would be harmed by the questioning. Healers were funny that way.

"Uh—I feel fine." Close enough, anyway. Lizzie blinked a few times. *'K. That was weird.* Since when did Harrington worry about her getting better from an emotional trauma? He didn't seem the sort. She gave her head a tiny shake. "So, Worth. He was pulling something from Sarah. I know it was partly her magic, because it *felt* like spell caster magic. But that wasn't all that it was. Did they tell you about Moore?" The thought of the dry husk that had been Moore's remains, or all that was left of him after Worth had finished draining him, created a sour taste in her mouth and made her stomach churn. She quickly took a sip of tea and banished the image.

Harry nodded. "And I examined him. But I'm not particularly good at analyzing the dead. Especially the very dead. There was nothing of him left—his magic or his energy—by the time I saw him."

Lizzie raised her eyebrows skeptically when Harry said "very dead." She nibbled on the corner of her lip. "A person can be more or less dead? I thought dead was—well, more of an exact thing."

"Hmm. It's more complicated than that." He was clearly about to wave away the question. Then he looked more closely at Lizzie, and she suspected—as usual—her emotions were clearly written across her face. Frustration, confusion. "Okay—long story short. Magic is a kind of energy. When a person ceases to live, their magic and any other energy that is associated with them—some call it soul—doesn't simply extinguish. It fades away over a period of time." He held up a hand forestalling a question that was about to burble from Lizzie's lips. "Don't ask; I don't know where it goes. Chat with your pastor or preacher, whatever you people have in Austin, Texas."

"Now you're just being intentionally rude." Lizzie eyed him askance.

Harry grinned. "Perhaps. But here's an even more interesting factoid for you. How long it takes for the energy to fade, that varies by individual. For some people, in rare cases, it's so slow that their physical body ceases to exist and only the energy is left. When the energy persists beyond its tie to the physical body, well, you get what might be considered a ghost."

"You did not just tell me that ghosts are real. Are you a lunatic?" She eyed him askance. "Do I look like I need to know about ghosts right now? I could have done just fine without that tidbit. Now I'll be worried about the ghost of Moore coming to haunt me every time I enter the Library." Lizzie shivered.

"I can ease your mind on that count. And if you were paying closer attention you'd know, he's exactly the ghost you'll never encounter. I suspect that the persisting energy that creates a ghost is exactly what our evil genius stole from Moore. And what he tried to steal from Sarah. Except, in Sarah's case, he didn't completely drain her," Harry said.

"You still haven't explained how I made something happen that I didn't *will* to happen. Pilar gave me a down and dirty explanation of how magic works: find the magic in yourself, decide what exactly you want to happen, and will it to happen. I never imagined or asked for what actually happened."

"You did—imagine and ask, that is. You imagined and willed a cessation of Worth's forcible and unnatural manipulation of spirit energy, or magical energy. Whatever it's called, it is perhaps one of the most powerful types of energy. I suspect you snapped the connection between Worth and his victim. The injuries to Worth were simply a side effect—a whiplash of the momentarily uncontained energy, perhaps?" His voice became less serious, the tone lightening. "Problem solved. Absolved of all guilt. Et cetera." Lizzie doubted this was Harry making an effort at piety. More likely he was just poking fun at Americans.

"It's not quite that simple. If I actually felt guilty for hurting Worth—and don't be mistaken, *I do not*—then you would *not* be helping." Harry might be a fabulous healer, probably was in fact a fabulous healer, but he would be a terrible therapist. She reminded herself, he *was* a fabulous healer, or Harrington wouldn't have put him on Sarah's case.

"Ah. But now you know your magic wasn't wild," Harry said.

Lizzie sighed. He was right. Maybe not such a completely horrible therapist. "Thanks." And she meant it more than she knew how to say. "The possibility of unpredictable magic was driving me nuts. Uh, not literally crazy. You know what I mean."

Harry laughed. "I do."

"And if I see red sparkly stuff when I'm upset?" Lizzie asked tentatively.

"Sounds better than being sick or fainting to me. But that's your call." Harry was kicking back in the sofa, long lean legs stretched out.

Lizzie digested that for a minute. Apparently red sparkles were not dangerous. *Huh. Who knew?* It seemed freaky to her.

They both drank their tea in silence as Lizzie digested the information Harry had shared.

After a few minutes of contemplative silence, Lizzie sat up straighter and her face took on a firmer cast. "How do we fix this, Harry? How do we make Sarah better?"

"Give her back what Worth stole. If that's even possible. I've never heard of a spell caster—or any magic-user—doing anything like this before. But who knows what our history holds?" Harry gave her a significant look.

Brow crinkled in confusion, Lizzie thought about some

other evil, nasty spell caster hurting innocent victims in some other time. *Disturbing.*

"Or where we might find information about our history." Another glance her way.

When Lizzie just looked at him in confusion, he sighed and said, "Really? No ideas?"

"Oh. Oh! Sorry," she said sheepishly. She wasn't at her best. An international flight, her first successful interaction with the pack book, meeting the woman whose illness she was at least partially responsible for, and learning that she wasn't a ticking time bomb of wild, uncontrollable magic. She'd had a big day. Harry needed to cut her some slack. "I'll talk to Harrington about digging through the Library just as soon as I arrive. But I would have guessed they'd already done that, right?"

"Ask Harrington, but I don't think they've had enough time to make good progress. Even if IPPC is actively working on it, another set of eyes won't hurt. Has any magic-user ever stolen energy, magic, life force from another? Is there any record of a magically induced coma? What's the best recipe for lemon cake?" Harry winked at her. "You know the sort of questions."

"I do. Thanks, Harry. It's been…interesting. And informative." Lizzie flashed him a grateful smile.

CHAPTER TEN

After her chat with Harry, Lizzie had said a quick goodbye to Sarah, reiterating her promise to fix the mess that Worth had created, then made it outside just as John was pulling up in a cab.

A yummy-smelling John, clearly showered and shaved, leaned over to kiss her in greeting. *Great. He's the one with an amazing nose, and I'm the one who hasn't showered. Not cool.*

As his lips brushed against hers in a PG version of a typical kiss, she thought—what if they couldn't work out their differences? What if it was all too hard? What if she couldn't do whatever it was a mate did? And then he was helping her into the cab, and the moment passed.

John climbed in after her. "How is she?"

"She's the same, still stable. I did get a chance to meet her healer." She settled herself more comfortably into the cushions and watched the confusion of wrong-sided traffic outside the car window. It was mildly disorienting. Tuning out the rush of traffic, she turned back to John. Her voice firm with a strong sense of purpose, she said, "We have to figure out what's going on with Sarah."

John shifted in his seat. When he spoke, his voice was wary. "I assume that's what her healer is doing."

Anything even hinting at Worth's involvement was guaranteed to put John on guard. Lizzie knew he didn't want her near anything dangerous, and that was doubly true for Worth. Her brain stuttered to a halt, finally catching the contradiction she'd overlooked the last two days.

"You didn't want me to go to Prague." She spoke slowly and deliberately as her brain did the math.

John looked at her like she'd lost her mind. "No," he agreed.

"Not because it would split us up—because you're here." She looked at him as she slowly put the pieces together.

He didn't say anything. He just waited for her to finish sorting through her thoughts.

"I thought you were mad because I didn't discuss it with you first." She narrowed her eyes at him.

"I was, and you should have."

She snorted. When he raised his eyebrows and gave her an impatient look, she conceded. "We should have discussed it." After a brief hesitation, she added in a small, slightly sheepish voice, "Thank you for coming with me. I know it's hard for you to get away. Although—"

She'd been about to comment that he'd barreled ahead with his plans to join without ever discussing *that* with her. But she wanted him here, and at some point, she needed to learn to pick her battles more wisely.

He waited for her to finish her thought. It was incredibly annoying. It was like he knew she'd fill the silence. If she were a skeptical soul, she'd say it was a deliberate tactic to get more information out of her without disclosing anything himself. *Hmm.* She eyed him suspiciously.

He returned her look with a calm expression.

Her eyes narrowed. "I'm on to you."

"I have absolutely no idea what you're talking about," he replied casually.

"Never mind." She shook her head. That was a conversation for another time. "But back to Prague—"

"I wasn't aware we'd left that topic." When she shot him an accusatory look, he just grinned.

"You don't want me in Prague because of Worth. Because I'm closer to him and to the investigation." And why she hadn't realized that before now, she had no idea.

"Of course." He glanced out the window then back to her. "That's surprising?"

"You couldn't just say that? I feel a little like an idiot." She was annoyed to see they were almost to the airport.

"It didn't occur to me that I needed to," he told her matter-of-factly. He looked at her and must have seen her bewilderment. "You didn't think twice about Worth when you received the offer." That wasn't a question, and his tone was resigned.

Maybe they needed to focus more on communication in general. Because as much time as they'd spent together in the last few days, they hadn't discussed any of this. Granted, they'd been busy with other things. She pulled herself away from thoughts of sex on the sofa, the kitchen table, her office floor…what the heck had they been talking about? That's right—Worth and John's irrational fears.

She frowned. "Why would I be worried about Worth? The Library should be safe now. IPPC controls access, and security is ramped up. And Worth is who knows where, probably still recovering."

"Do you have no sense of self-preservation?" He was clearly exasperated.

Of course she did, but before she could pursue that thought, they arrived at the airport. She'd think about what a condescending ass John could be, and then—once she was less annoyed—she'd consider if maybe, just maybe, she'd glossed over some concerns when she'd made her decision to come to Prague.

A lengthy line through security and a quick board onto their plane later and Lizzie was wiped. She needed to learn to pace herself, but she wouldn't have missed the visit with Sarah for anything. She felt a responsibility towards her that she couldn't shake. Actually, that she didn't want to shake. Sarah had fought for Lizzie, and now it was time they fought for Sarah. She yawned. But not right this very second, she thought as she closed her eyes and rested her head against the headrest. John had power napped through takeoff, woken up, and encouraged her to get some sleep for the remainder of the flight. She decided that was excellent advice.

She and John had been in the air for a few hours when she woke. He must have felt or heard the change in her breathing and guessed she was awake, because he spoke before she'd even opened her eyes.

"You're awake?" John asked.

Her nodding head rubbed softly against the fabric of his shirt. She blinked half-awake eyes up at him and let out a grunt of disgust. He looked nothing like a man who'd been traveling for almost twenty-four hours. He had a little stubble, but otherwise he looked fresh as a daisy. She rubbed her nose against his shirt. And he smelled lovely. She gave a little growl of annoyance. She'd had a look in the bathroom mirror earlier, and she'd looked worn out, frumpy, and mussed. And that was two or three hours ago, before she'd had a nap. *Great.*

"What?" he asked.

"You look annoyingly handsome and showered and not rumpled." She narrowed her eyes at him. "And you smell wonderful," she finished in an accusing tone.

He chuckled. "Thank you. And you look and smell as lovely as you always do."

She had to laugh. Because he actually meant it, the poor confused man.

She excused herself to make one last quick run to the restroom. On the way back, the seat belt sign flashed on. They were almost to Prague. And that little light, accompanied by a crisp British voice announcing their impending arrival, brought a crushing rush of worry, almost panic. Her chest felt constricted, her clothes too tight, and the aisle incredibly small.

Prague, the city where she'd first met Worth, where she'd been held prisoner by him. Would being in the house so soon after her kidnapping be too difficult? And her new job. Was she qualified? Could she do the job? And the Library, with its floor to ceiling rows of magic books. Would she be able to wade through them and find anything to help Sarah?

Dang it. Why couldn't she catch her breath?

She stopped next to John's aisle seat, her breath coming in short puffs, and waited for him to shift slightly so she could get around his bulky frame to her own seat. Looking down at him, the tightness in her chest suddenly eased. Her lungs filled, and she took a slow, easy breath. And that's when she realized that the mere fact of his presence made all of those questions fade. No, that wasn't quite right. The questions were still there in a big jumble in her brain, but the worry and panic those questions had caused, was fading.

She must have stood in the aisle too long, because he asked quietly, "Are you all right?"

"Yes." Her voice was confident, because she was. She was just fine. Right now, in this moment, everything was okay.

CHAPTER ELEVEN

One of Harrington's men picked up John and Lizzie at the airport. They maintained a comfortable silence for most of the car ride. Then the buildings turned less industrial and more historic, signaling their impending arrival. Within a mile or two of the house, John could feel the tension in Lizzie building. He took her hand in his and raised it to his lips, giving her knuckles a quick kiss.

She blinked in confusion and then she laughed—at his intentionally, overtly gallant gesture or at herself for her intense reaction as the house loomed closer or both, he wasn't sure—but the tension broke. She grinned up at him. Then she slipped her hand around so she was clasping his hand. He could still feel her nerves, smell her anxiety, and it tore at him.

He didn't have the right words, so he chose not to say anything. Apparently, that was just fine with her, because she didn't let go of his hand until they pulled up in front of the rich wine colored residence that housed the Library. As his eye followed the line of the house, higher than the neighboring row houses, he couldn't help but think it looked like a dollhouse with its intricate trim.

"Lizzie. Good to see you again. Your trip went well, I trust." Harrington smiled in greeting but didn't offer to shake her hand.

Wise man. John wasn't feeling particularly charitable toward the man who had yanked his mate to foreign soil and possibly closer to danger.

"Very, thank you. What floor are we on? Shocking, I know, but even with the negative memories, I liked the room I was in last time." She grinned.

Bravado or the truth, either way, he wasn't staying in the room she'd been held in less than a week previously. He gave Harrington a clearly warning look.

Looking unperturbed by John's mild threat, Harrington responded. "I have you and Braxton, along with a few security staff on the second floor. Ah, third floor by American standards."

"Fine," John replied without inflection. Taking hold of Lizzie's elbow, he steered her toward the stairs when she might have stayed another moment to chat.

Lizzie looked over her shoulder, "Which room?"

"The Rose Room, to the right of the stairs." He smiled politely. "Braxton."

When John turned around, Harrington handed him a key.

"The guest and staff rooms are on floors two, three, and four. The basement, ground, and first floors are all public or for staff use and have varying levels of security. You're cleared for all areas." Harrington spoke to John's back, but Lizzie had stopped to listen attentively.

"Thanks. Oh—what about meals?" Lizzie asked.

"Dining is on the ground floor. There's information in your room with the times and menu for the week," Harrington replied.

With a quick nod of acknowledgment, Lizzie headed up the stairs.

"Braxton. When you get a moment, I'd like to speak with you."

John nodded, but he didn't stop his progress up the stairs.

After reaching their room, conveniently marked with a plaque stating "Rose Room," John waited long enough to see that Lizzie was comfortable and that their bags arrived. When the man delivering their bags had gone, Lizzie practically pushed him out of the room.

"We just got here," he said.

"Um-hm. And that's why you're dragging your feet? I think it's interesting he wants to see you right away even though I'm the employee."

"Ah. Technically, I'm contract labor." At her skeptical look, he replied, "I don't seem a good investment as a security consultant?"

She smothered a laugh. "Whatever got you in the door, you're the one he wants to talk to. Get your butt down there so you can come back and give me the scoop." And she smacked him on the ass on his way out the door.

That tap on his ass made him pause and consider spending the next hour in a much more enjoyable pursuit than maneuvering and posturing with Harrington. As he wavered on the threshold, her next words pushed him out the door at a good clip. In a quiet and much more serious voice, she said, "He might have an update on Worth."

He tracked Harrington down in his office, a smallish room located on the ground floor, near the back of the town home. He'd thought the house was six or seven thousand square feet, but every time he turned around he discovered another small room or a corridor he hadn't known about. It must be at least three times that size. The windows of the office looked out onto a small courtyard.

Harrington sat behind a simple, elegant desk with few frills. He'd closed his laptop when John entered the room, but hadn't stood.

"The surrounding town homes?" John asked as he looked out over the small, manicured space. There were walls separating the courtyards of each town home.

After a brief pause, Harrington responded. "Anything attached or in the row has been purchased. We're working on some of the closer homes, as well."

Finally standing, Harrington walked over to the small cart and picked up a carafe of coffee, raising it slightly in question.

"Yes, thanks. Black," John said. Abandoning the view for a love seat with a small table, John sat down, leaned forward, and rested his forearms on his thighs. "So—Worth? Any news?"

Harrington walked over with a mug. Accepting it, John waited patiently while Harrington fixed a cup of tea for himself. This wouldn't be good news.

As soon as he was seated, Harrington said, "Worth's location is unknown. We suspect he's still recovering from injuries, but our healers aren't certain. Our healers are baffled by both the coma-like state Sarah is in and the condition of his dead associate's corpse. Correspondingly, they don't have any knowledge of how Worth's condition would be impacted by the stolen magic. One presumes improved, otherwise why do it?"

"And the residences IPPC discovered during Lizzie's kidnap investigation?" John asked.

Harrington grimaced. "Liquidated. In the last week, he's sold most of the properties. Each was sold for cash well below market value."

"How is that even possible in such a short time?" John shook his head. "Never mind. With enough money and preparation—I get it. So he's flush with cash and found a new place, below the radar, to recover."

"Likely," Harrington agreed with a slow dip of the chin and a pensive expression. "We'll keep our eyes and ears open, but at this point we're waiting for him to appear on the grid. A financial transaction we can trace, a public sighting, even a similar medical case or missing person filed in the magic-using community. If he continues to siphon magic from others, there will be victims."

"How important to Worth does IPPC think the Library is?" His voice was neutral, but his thoughts were on Lizzie now sharing the same building as the Library.

Had she walked back into Worth's sights by accepting this job? And if she had, the man in front of him would regret offering her this position, temporary though it might be.

"It's likely Worth cleared out the important texts as soon as he discovered them. We've found some interesting works and the collection has immense value, but there haven't been any particular books or section of books that stand apart. None that address Sarah's condition, for example. Or how Worth may have caused it. So either he removed valuable texts as they were uncovered, or we haven't gotten to them yet."

Harrington seemed thoroughly unconcerned with the threat to Lizzie. Because he perceived none, or because he didn't care? As helpful as Harrington had been in the past, his motivations—beyond furthering the scope and effectiveness of IPPC—had always been murky.

"You're still reviewing the contents of the collection?"

Harrington nodded. "Hmm. We have some of Worth's notes, though there's no way to tell how complete they are. And Heike Schlegel. She was one of the women working here. The first, actually."

"You're kidding. Wasn't she a part of Worth's gang?" Lizzie would not be happy.

"If by gang, you mean employee—then, yes. She was under contract with Worth to do some translation. She may have been willfully blind regarding Worth, but she didn't know that Pilar and Lizzie were being held against their will."

"No one can be that blind. She must have known—" John stopped. Known what? That her boss was ambitious, immoral, maybe a criminal? In fairness, he wasn't sure that would stop a good number of Lycan that he knew and respected from taking on a job. "Didn't she have some idea he was harming other magic-users?"

Harrington's brow lifted in question. "How? The kidnapping was the only questionable act she may have had knowledge of. The Library? Perhaps morally questionable to keep the contents from the magic-using community but, technically, his property. He purchased the house with all its remaining contents intact." He allowed a small, wry smile to escape. "I suspect the former owners were aware of the garden furniture and window coverings but perhaps not the collection of magic books. Regardless, contents were included with the sale."

"She shared a house with two kidnapped women. Even if her only offense was stupidity, she's certainly a potential security risk." John didn't want this woman watching Lizzie's back. Hell, preferably nowhere near her back.

"IPPC and the Library's temporary security both cleared her. And—" Harrington paused significantly. "I'm vouching for her." Harrington's tone made it clear he believed that sufficient to allay John's concerns.

And that was simply not the case. He'd keep an eye on this Heike woman.

"Tell me about your temporary security." John cocked his

head and narrowed his eyes. He couldn't quite pinpoint the source of the oddness, but the few members of the team he'd met thus far shared certain unique undertones to their scent. A scent that was unique enough he'd been unable to link it with anything else in his experience. So whatever they were, he hadn't encountered it before.

"The men are…unique, but very effective. The CEO is a personal friend. Given that the need was urgent and IPPC resources are currently stretched thin, he was happy to lend a hand. He and his Clan will stay until we have a secure system in place."

"Clan?" Interesting word choice, John thought.

"Clan, crew. The men assuming security staff roles until we hire permanent staff." Harrington waved away John's question. "I'll introduce you to Lachlan McClellan, the firm's CEO, at dinner this evening."

"And Heike? She'll be at dinner?" At Harrington's nod, John replied, "Have you told Lizzie that Heike's on staff?"

When Harrington just lifted an eyebrow, John sighed.

CHAPTER TWELVE

After freshening up, Lizzie and John had both gone down to the basement Library. Where they were currently, as she contemplated John's news bomb.

Heike. On staff at the Library. Lizzie wasn't sure how she felt about that. Why couldn't Harrington have hired Pilar? Lizzie would trust Pilar with her life. In fact, she already had. It was in large part due to Pilar's tutoring that Lizzie had managed to emerge unscathed from a magical battle against Worth. Well, maybe not a battle. But she did walk away whole. She wasn't as certain Worth could say the same.

Heike. Lizzie sighed. She didn't have any *proof* that Heike was involved on a deeper level with Worth's plot, just suspicions. Had Heike played some greater role? Or had she really just been an employee who believed she was working for an eccentric collector? And even if she hadn't been involved with the kidnappings—Lizzie didn't like her. Or trust her.

They were alone inside the Library. Only staff were allowed unescorted access. Good thing an intern was considered staff, because Lizzie found the security men to be just a little out of step in some way. She wasn't sure why. If she had spidey senses, they'd be ringing a loud alarm. *Weird.* She'd have to ask Harrington about them.

"Are you okay?" John asked. Apparently, she'd been silent too long, processing the news that Heike was not only in the building but was to be her coworker for the next several weeks.

"Hmm," Lizzie said noncommittally. *Not really* was the honest answer. But she could hardly say that without sounding petty. *Hell.* It made her *feel* petty. As far as she knew, Heike had been a grunt. Brought in to translate titles and get enough of a feel for the books to categorize them. Not so very different from Pilar and herself.

"Lizzie," John prompted.

Except for the kidnapping part. She sighed again. Right—the kidnapping bit was actually a big deal. Not so petty, then.

"Okay. I'm not thrilled. Even less thrilled that Harrington would conveniently leave out the name of the staff he hired, knowing our history." She should be a little more wary of Harrington. She had suspected he had a sneaky streak, and she'd guessed his priorities were IPPC first, second, and third. She huffed in frustration—at herself. She should have asked.

They sat at one of three tables that were oriented in the center of the room to roughly form a triangle. Lizzie flipped through the notes in front of her. If she understood the process correctly, Harrington's new librarian, Emme, had started by first reviewing the notes the three women had made while Worth had been in residence. Except Lizzie hadn't really made any notes. She'd just barely managed to sort out how to use her magic, when her rescue had begun. She'd only interacted with one book, *The Witch's Diary*.

She had a strange, slightly uneasy feeling. Like an itch but of the magical, rather than physical, kind. And then she realized she knew exactly where *The Witch's Diary* was located. A shelf directly behind her, low and to the left. *Okay—that's creepy.* She had her first official mentor topic to discuss with Harrington. Would every book she opened create some kind of connection with her? If so, this temp job was going to be a little more challenging than predicted.

Lizzie rubbed her dry, itchy eyes that seemed unable to recover from the transatlantic flight. She looked up at John and realized she'd been lost in her own thoughts for a perhaps embarrassing amount of time. Or maybe just a rude amount of time. "Sorry. I'm not very good company right now, am I?"

"There's no right answer to that question, so I'll pass," he replied while flipping through one of the books on the table.

"I'll take that as 'you're horrible company but I'm too nice and too worried about upsetting you to say.'" She smiled softly at him. "We didn't discuss the particulars before, but the healer I met in London, Sarah's healer? It seems he's the main one in charge of her care. Maybe the only one." She shook her head. "It doesn't matter. The important part is that he's some kind of healer whiz kid."

"Does he think Sarah might wake?" John said.

"He's not sure. They really have very little information about her condition. He was very informative about *my* condition, however." At John's quick glance, she added, "I'm fine."

His eyes narrowed slightly. "What did this healer have to say about you?"

"Feeling nauseous, passing out, all of those odd reactions I've had to stress—you remember, I passed out when you told me you were Lycan?"

"I'm not likely to forget. Not my preferred response to revealing an intimate detail about myself." Was that a small wince from John that Lizzie detected? If so, it was gone in a flash. He said, "And you guessed. I just confirmed."

John had a small smile on his face. She'd bet money he was remembering the moment her ass hit the floor. She wrinkled her nose in annoyance. She still thought he should have caught her. What kind of guy let his future girlfriend hit the ground with a splat after a faint? Although, she had to admit that there had been no inkling at the time that she would actually be his future girlfriend. And she didn't actually *know* that he'd let her splat, per se. But she had come to firmly planted on the tile.

"If I were into violence, I'd punch you in the arm right now." Lizzie raised an eyebrow. "Be glad I'm enlightened."

"What? What did I do?" he said, but he was grinning. "Okay, small confession. I did catch you as you—gracefully—sank to the ground. No bruise on your beautiful tush afterwards, right? Although—" He paused in consideration. "—that seems to have been a one-time thing. I assumed it was the shock. But you've had more than your share of high stress, shock-inducing situations since then. And your reaction recently hasn't been—ah, to pass out. Your healer had some insight?"

She'd pay money to know what his real opinion was of her recent reactions to stressful situations. She hadn't missed his quick mental edit. *Hmm.*

"He did. He theorized that there's a medical, or rather a magical, reason for them. Something to do with bottling up my magic way too long," Lizzie said. She shifted her weight in the chair. "And now—what I thought was wild, out of control magic—is just easy access to my magic. Bottle it up too long, passing out. Unleash it after being contained, and it —burbles out."

"And that information is helpful?" John looked a little skeptical. *Party pooper.*

"That part not so much. But he said it would likely even out. And he also said that my magic is definitely not wild."

"So—really easily accessible?" he asked.

"I'm paraphrasing. Until everything evens out, I have to be a little more careful about practicing magic. But I'm not a ticking time bomb."

"And Worth?" John was asking because *she* was worried about what had happened with Worth. He'd made it clear he was never afraid of her, her magic, or what she might accidentally or intentionally do.

"Apparently, I didn't hurt Worth directly. I just severed the connection." Lizzie spoke with confidence. She may have some doubts, but it made sense. And she truly didn't believe, in her heart of hearts, that she'd willed into being the damage caused to Worth. She was ultimately responsible for it, yes. But that was an important distinction in her mind.

John tipped his chair back and closed his eyes. Watching him balance on two legs of the chair, Lizzie thought she might be getting a glimpse of adolescent, pre-Alpha John. A little silly, less serious, less weighed down by responsibilities. Probably because he wasn't thinking about what he was doing. He was concentrating on remembering the events of her rescue—and his, she was sure.

"Recoil." John opened his eyes, and the chair legs came down with a thud. "You cut it, and it snapped back at him. But why not me? The connection was between him and me. Why him, and not me? I felt nothing but stronger once the connection was destroyed. No backlash or recoiled magical energy."

"Because it was your magic?" Lizzie guessed. "It belonged with you?"

"Perhaps." John nodded his head in assent, but it was clear his concern remained. "Not to look at a gift too closely, because this is really excellent news, but—"

"I know. The red, sparkly lights? All good."

"That was never a concern." At her annoyed look, he

modified that statement. "That was never my concern. I was thinking about whether it was repeatable. If it could be used defensively." After registering her reaction, he seemed to decide against discussing it further.

His response highlighted the very different world views and priorities they each had. She'd been primarily concerned about hurting someone by accident. And he was more concerned about her ability to protect herself.

He gave her a searching look, then said, "I bet Harrington has a liquor cabinet stashed somewhere."

She walked over to his chair, biting the inside of her lip. "I think it's incredibly hot that you're plotting how I can use my new wicked cool skills to defend myself against bad guys."

He lost the slightly guarded look he'd assumed and grinned. "Hot, huh?" Pulling her closer, he ran his hand down her back following the line of her spine until he reached the curve of her ass. He cupped her ass in both hands, and before she could blink, she was straddling him.

"Are you sure—" she began.

"Always," he growled into her throat. His mouth was pressed into the hollow between her clavicle and neck, directly above a pulse point.

She wondered distractedly why John loved that part of her neck so much. But before she could consider it, he bit her lightly. She immediately shoved closer, aligning her body with his. She turned her head and he caught her lips with his own. After a kiss that left her gasping for breath, she pulled away and briefly rested her forehead against his shoulder. She blinked, seeing the book-lined shelves.

"Crap. We *cannot* have sex in the Library." She huffed out a breath in disgust. Why the hell weren't they in their room? Where she could—

He laughed. "Why not?"

"Um. It's the Library. No public sex—we talked about that

one already, remember?" She grinned when he snorted out a half laugh at that. She'd talked. He'd never agreed.

"And," she continued, "it's the Library."

"You said that already." But he was slowly lowering her feet to the floor.

"It's worth mentioning twice." She kissed him on the cheek. "And you've distracted me from my research."

"That's all you—you said hot." He stood up, shaking the wrinkles out of his shirt.

Lizzie looked at the abandoned notes in front of her. "Damn. There's a chance that something, some small piece of information, in the Library can help Sarah. I'd like to at least develop some kind of strategy for approaching all of this information before dinner."

Glancing at his cell, he said, "Too late. Dinner's in half an hour."

Lizzie huffed out a small puff of air in frustration. "After dinner then, and before bed."

After a quick recap of dinner logistics—where, when, who would be there, and appropriate dress—John left to grab a quick shower before the meal. How was he always finding time to shower and she was running around like an idiot hoping to catch a second to brush her teeth. She sighed.

Up to this point, Lizzie had forgotten about *The Witch's Diary* and the odd feeling it had given her earlier. But once John had left the room, there it was. That odd, itch-in-the-middle-of-the-back feeling. Lizzie tried to remember how exactly she formed a connection with the book originally. She had felt an awareness. Not human, just…something. She turned toward the wall where she thought the book was shelved. And she let it reel her in. She kneeled down and ran her finger down the spine.

Yep, that was the one. The newly hired librarian must be

shelving all of the books that had title translations completed.

She didn't really have time today to delve into the diary, much as it appealed to her sense of adventure and her curiosity. But, wow, this book was wicked weird. She debated, then decided, a few quick questions. She hunted back in her memory and remembered. She'd addressed the book, much as she'd address a person.

Here goes.

"Um, hi. I'm in a bit of a time crunch right now. I've got to help a girl who's really sick." A thought popped into her head. Surely it couldn't be that easy? "I don't suppose *you* know anything about magically induced comas?" Dang. She forgot. Find her magic. Done. Think about what she wanted to happen. Well, that's what this conversation was, right? Done. Apply will. Um, probably done. She still didn't have tons of practice, so the success of the last part was somewhat debatable.

She waited a few seconds. Last time, the answer to her question had popped right into her head. But all she was getting was a kind of low-level static. It was something. The book wasn't ignoring her. Maybe that was a "no" in spelled book speak.

She felt incredibly foolish, but she continued. Magic, question, and will; steps one, two, and three. "So I'm hunting for information about this magically induced coma. Specifically, how I can reverse it. This really bad guy—" TMI. Be specific. Be clear. "How do I reverse a magically induced coma?"

More static. Maybe more specificity was needed. "How do I reverse a coma caused by siphoning off a spell caster's magic?"

Not witch magic.

Whoa. How cool was that?

"Does the diary contain information that will help wake up the coma patient?" Lizzie wanted to pursue the whole "what is witch magic" line of questioning, but now wasn't the time.

Silence. Not even static. *Crap.* Maybe she made a mistake. She rubbed the spine with the tip of her finger. "I'm sorry. I have to focus on the coma question right now. But later—" She sighed. It was like talking with Sarah all over again. She was speaking to thin air. After initiating the conversation, she couldn't help but say goodbye—even if she felt silly. "I'll be back."

CHAPTER THIRTEEN

Dinner had been uneventful enough. Heike had been as she was before, polite but uninterested. As far as Lizzie had seen, Heike experienced no twinges of guilt or feelings of awkwardness. The fact that her coworker, Lizzie, was a woman whose kidnapping she'd played a part in—indirect though it might have been—didn't cause Heike any apparent concern.

Lizzie had requested a meeting with Harrington sooner rather than later. Hence their meeting after dinner, scheduled even though Lizzie was still struggling to overcome the symptoms of jet lag. The squishy sofa she sat on threatened to put her to sleep if it didn't swallow her first.

"I wanted to talk to you about Sarah. Actually, more about what we can do for Sarah." She declined Harrington's silent offer of coffee with a quick shake of her head. She still needed to squeeze another two or three hours out of the day, but coffee would have her bouncing off the walls all night. Then she'd never get over her jet lag.

"We've made every effort to ensure she's receiving exceptional care. Did you find it lacking in some respect?"

Harrington inquired as he seated himself on a much less squishy love seat.

"Not at all. Actually, the opposite. I met Harry during my visit. He seems quite knowledgeable. Fabulous, in fact—and not even a little bit modest." Remembering her encounter with Harry brightened her mood. Not easy in such challenging circumstances. But he was that guy—the one who just made you want to smile.

"And meeting…uh, Harry, that made you think—what, exactly?" Harrington prompted, bringing her back to the conversation at hand.

"Sorry," she said with a small shake of her head. "Is doing some investigative work to determine what caused the coma, and see if there's a way to reverse it, does that fall within the scope of my internship?"

"Absolutely. We can't know what's in the Library, helpful or otherwise, without additional organization and cataloguing. But I've already given Heike instructions to look for any connection to Sarah's condition as she translates the texts. I envisioned you doing the same." He brushed off a bit of invisible—to Lizzie—lint from his trouser leg. "Anything else?"

Harrington had basically just given her free range to investigate. Thoughts of unfettered access to the Library flitted through her head. But there was one gnat.

Lizzie chewed on the corner of her lip. "Heike," she said in reply to his question.

Harrington waited politely, face impassive, for her to verbalize her concerns.

"After everything she did…I don't understand how you can hire her to work here." Again, her teeth started to worry the corner of her bottom lip.

"And what exactly did Ms. Schlegel do?" Harrington asked.

Since it didn't appear to be a rhetorical question, she replied, "She worked with Worth. Mad genius, kidnapping Worth. She must have known something was wrong with Pilar and me—and she did nothing."

"Employment and disinterest. Ms. Schlegel—Heike—is my employee. I'm satisfied that she's a good candidate for IPPC." Harrington paused, looking down casually at the spot where he'd removed the lint. "If that isn't sufficient, then perhaps we should discuss the suitability of *your* employment here."

Well, shit.

"You asked," Lizzie grumbled. Gah. Now she was sounding a little juvenile. Time to be a grown-up. *Dang it.*

Harrington didn't deign to respond to her mumbles. When it was clear she wasn't going to add anything else, he said, "Do you have any other questions?" Harrington was clearly impatient to move on.

Lizzie was happy to drop it. Working with Heike didn't sit right. But Harrington had a point. She'd had a job, one that she'd fulfilled well by all accounts. And neither she nor Pilar had actually confided in Heike. She hadn't invited late night girl chats, but she and Pilar could have said something to her. In a pinch, Lizzie wouldn't trust her. But they were surrounded by security men. And their work seemed safe enough. That would have to be good enough for now.

Lizzie shifted to a less flammable topic. "I'll meet with the librarian at some point? To get an idea of how the cataloguing will work?"

"Emme Roberts holds the position. She's out for a few days, an unexpected personal matter. If that's all, I have some business I need to see to." And she was dismissed.

It wasn't until she was out the door and walking down the hall that she realized—nothing about her mentorship had been discussed. She may have alienated her mentor by implying she didn't trust his judgment. *Great.* That had been a big part of the reason she'd come, initially. Well, that, and her knee-jerk response to being told what she could do, as well as, where, when, and with whom.

But that had all changed when she met Sarah. Sarah, who was lying, half-dead, in a hospital bed because she'd tried to save Lizzie. Because Lizzie had been just a little too slow to stop Worth. *Well, okay, Harrington. Fire me as your mentee. I'm still here for Sarah.*

And that little bit of righteous sass got her all the way to her room. At which point she sat on her bed and decided she wasn't actually that sassy, and having a mentor would be *really* helpful. *Dang.* She needed to work on her "take that," *snap*, attitude. She was polite. She liked to be liked. She generally followed the rules. She was pretty terrible at this sassy thing.

After a quick shower and a rushed prep for bed, Lizzie checked her cell for the time. It was past time to crash for the night. The Library staff had moved dinner late just for her and John. Then she'd met with Harrington. And now it was past her bedtime. *Sheesh.* Bedtime—she felt like a kid. She'd planned this whole acclimation schedule so she'd be over her jet lag as quickly as possible. But she'd been feeling like a night owl recently. Add to that, she'd planned to have a look at the translation paperwork and get a feel for the Library before she went to bed, and the decision was made. Besides, she'd sleep better if she had a plan of attack, she told herself. After waiting a few minutes, she decided to leave John a note rather than waiting for him. She slung a robe over her jammies, shoved on some flip-flops, and slipped out the door.

And almost ran into a very large, very broad, very solid green-eyed man. Green eyes? *That's odd.* Before she could think beyond the fact that it was too dark to discern something like eye color, Mr. Green was backing up several steps, head tipped slightly to the side. By the time Lizzie had recovered from her near collision, he was standing a good five feet away.

"Lachlan? Lachlan McClellan, right?" They'd been introduced very briefly at dinner but hadn't spoken beyond a brief "hello." And Lizzie wasn't exactly great with names.

"Lizzie Smith," he said, and dipped his head in acknowledgment.

Lizzie offered him a wide, open smile, one that seemed to take him aback. Seeing him cock his head slightly to the side, Lizzie thought she must have confused the poor man by providing such a friendly response.

"My name," she said by way of explanation. "It's just—you're one of the few people here who calls me Lizzie Smith." Lizzie remembered that when she'd been introduced, only her first name had been used. She hadn't thought about it at the time, especially since the tone of the late dinner had been casual. But perhaps that omission had been intentional. An attempt to keep the peace between her and John.

"Ah, I see." And from the intonation, Lizzie knew immediately that Lachlan was up to date on the drama that was her love life. Another bonus for the Alpha Mate—no privacy in her personal life. "Then Lizzie Smith it is, until you tell me otherwise. Deal?"

"Thanks." It was nice for her opinion on this whole name mess to be a factor. Lachlan was the first one, so far, to even consider what she preferred. The magical community assumed she'd take John's name. From what she'd learned it wasn't even really a Lycan tradition, just a casual assumption made by semi-strangers. *Grrr. She wasn't married.*

It belatedly occurred to her that she might be stirring the pot. "Although, I don't particularly want my…uh, John upset with anyone over something so small."

Lachlan's chuckle rumbled up unexpectedly, deep and sexy. *Huh. Where did that come from?* She wasn't into him at all. Weird, spidey-sense feeling; visible-in-the-dark green eyes; unwanted sexual attraction. Something was up with this guy. Lizzie casually backed up a step.

"I'm not worried about your little wolf, Lizzie Smith. But I appreciate your concern," he said, the amusement still evident in his voice.

Okay. She wasn't sure where to even start. Offended that he'd just called a Lycan, her Lycan, a little wolf—like John was a little ball of fluff? Worried she was in the hall by herself with him? Glad that such a scary guy was on her side?

Lachlan was an enigma. He was in charge of security. He was clearly some kind of magic-user—she suspected a kind she hadn't met before—and he seemed a good sort and likable. Yet, he set off her creepy alert. She mentally shrugged and filed him away with the five hundred and thirty-three other odd things she couldn't easily explain. That list was only growing now that magic had taken up residence in her life.

Deciding that she didn't need to figure out Lachlan right this second, she opted for retreat. "I'm just headed down to the Library for a bit. Harrington said he'd cleared it through security."

"No problem. I'll just walk you down." He motioned to the stairs.

"Not necessary," John said, coming up the stairs.

Lizzie jumped. Only a little bit—but still embarrassing to have been startled by her own…whatever he was. He was like a damn cat. She gave him a hard look, one that he simply accepted and returned with a bland smile.

With an odd little formal quarter bow to John, Lachlan said, "Of course." He turned to Lizzie. "Good evening, Ms.

Smith." Turning back to John, he said simply, "Braxton." And continued along the corridor.

And there went the bland look John had worn. She *knew* the Smith comment would piss him off. It was a small enough thing, accepting a name that wasn't really hers. Maybe she should—wait, what was she saying? That actually wasn't a small thing. Not a small thing, at all.

And the sass was back.

"I'm headed to the Library," Lizzie said as she passed by John on her way down the stairs.

"In your nightgown?" John raised an eyebrow as she paused next to him on the stairs.

"I'm not wearing a nightgown—" And before Lizzie could comment on her jammie choice for the evening, John had lifted her, wrapped her legs around his waist, and kissed her breathless.

"Um, that's not what I meant," she said, panting a little in between words.

With his hand supporting her bum, he could hardly have missed that she was wearing something under her robe. In contrast to the nothing that he'd clearly pictured.

"I'd be lying if I said 'no problem.'" She could feel his smile, since his mouth was pressed against her neck, nibbling and licking his way to her ear.

As soon as she felt his tongue on her ear, she made a squeaky, startled noise. Seriously—she knew it was coming, so how did he manage to make her scream like a teenager every time?

"We're on the stairs. In public, basically," she mumbled between pants.

"Really?" She could just hear the leer in his voice, the degenerate.

She smiled. She was sure he could hear the laughter in

her voice when she said, "Yes, you letch. Really. What is it with you and public places? This is basically my office."

It was cute but a little inconvenient. Because he was ridiculously difficult to resist. And she *did not* need Harrington running into the two of them screwing like bunnies on the stairs. Her situation was hard enough without *that* being thrown in the mix.

He hesitated a moment, then reluctantly, slowly lowered her to the ground. Her body slid against his in a way that made her mind wander to the joys of public sex. Really, it wasn't such a bad idea.

Once he saw that she had her balance and wasn't in danger of tumbling down the stairs, he discreetly shifted his erection. Jeans, no underwear, rigid cock...ack. That could not be good.

"Ah, sorry about that," Lizzie said diffidently.

He grinned. "No problem."

She tugged his arm slightly, indicating her readiness to head down the stairs. "What's with the fuck-me-now kiss?" She avoided his gaze, concentrating on the stairs. She still couldn't look him in the face and say "fuck." Baby steps.

"Are you complaining?" He was so laughing at her.

"Never mind. Forget I asked." She tried to keep the sheepish tone from her voice, but she couldn't help that she embarrassed easily. She was quickly and quietly making her way down the stairs while she spoke.

She was starting to weigh the risks of public sex versus Harrington interruptus. She was even reconsidering her views on public intercourse. Before her thoughts traveled too far afield, they ran into another security guard.

"Library," John said in explanation of their late night appearance.

The guard just nodded and kept walking.

When they reached the Library door, both tried to speak

at once and stopped. After a small pause, Lizzie spoke up. "I'm just planning to stay a little while then head to bed."

"You think you'll be at least half an hour?" He looked a bit fidgety.

That's when Lizzie realized he'd been cooped up on a plane all day and likely had been tied up at IPPC in London too long to go for a run.

"Plenty of time for you to catch a run." She tried to act nonchalant when she said, "I bet there are a few security guys who usually catch a late night run."

He gave her a crooked smile. "Worried?" He reached out to tap the tip of her nose, but she ducked. "I'll be fine. See you in a bit."

By the time Lizzie walked into the Library and settled into a chair, she'd decided she was only going to stay long enough to review the librarian's notes outlining the new organization and filing structure of the Library. She'd read through some basic notes, a few lists of proposed topic-related categories, and was reviewing a sketch of the Library with shelving options penciled in when she realized she'd stayed a little longer than planned.

She was tired and more than ready to be done for the night. She was especially edgy that evening, but she didn't think about why until much later. Pent up sexual frustration, sitting in the same seat in the Library for a long time, or jet lag? Whatever the reason, she screamed like a little girl when she heard a loud thump directly behind her.

CHAPTER FOURTEEN

She was in a house full of magic-using security guards, most of whom likely had super-hearing. So it was no surprise when, seconds later, one of the guards appeared. Before she could do more than scream, jump, retrieve her heart from her throat, and turn around—not necessarily in that order—the guard was there. Dougal, Fergus, Tavish? She couldn't remember who was who, and they all had Scottish names.

Huh. She hadn't realized before, but the Scottish-named guards didn't all have Scottish accents. *Weird. But irrelevant. Focus, Lizzie.*

"Ms. Smith, you're all right?" the guard asked. He was moving to the area where the sound had originated. Lizzie noticed three very large books splayed on the floor.

Nodding, Lizzie decided it seemed like a good time for an inventory. As she was making sure all her relevant bits were in working order, including her sanity, John ran through the doorway.

After pinning her with an intent stare and then scanning

the rest of the room, John turned and spoke to the guard. "Everything in order?"

Lizzie tuned them out. She was trying to figure out why she was so shaken. It looked like a few books fell off the shelf. Big deal. She was a badass, evil-dude-fighting wench. Something like a little thud shouldn't have been problematic. She sighed. Well, at least she hadn't blown anything up, or done any spur of the moment, halfway-accidental magic. *Bonus.*

"Stop," Lizzie shrieked, as she saw the guard kneeling next to the displaced volumes.

"Ma'am?" The guard looked puzzled but unoffended. He stood up slowly, taking a cautious step back.

"Sorry. Just, ah, maybe you shouldn't move the books." Lizzie made her way across the room, never taking her eyes off the splayed texts.

The guard nodded, looking amused, and said, "I wasn't planning to."

"What are you thinking?" John asked.

"I'm not really sure." Lizzie was only half listening. Her eyes squeezed partially shut, as she peered at the books on the floor. "That is definitely text," she mumbled to herself. She turned to John and the guard. "Can you see writing?"

"Ah. That's actually not as unusual as you might think." This surprising statement originated with the guard.

Lizzie turned to him, smiling, and said, "I'm so sorry. I seem to have forgotten your name."

"Tavish, ma'am," he replied.

She was still inspecting the open books. She distractedly tapped John's leg and murmured quietly, "Cell?"

She smiled up at him when he produced his cell without question. She'd left hers in their room when she'd left in such a hurry earlier.

Tavish explained as Lizzie took several pictures of the books on the ground.

"Years ago, when books were difficult to come by, spell casters would use whatever was on hand as an anchor for their recordings. It's common to see empty journals in use today, but actual books were once used. And scrolls—but that was some time ago." Tavish finished and waited for her to complete her round of photographing.

Lizzie nodded her understanding. It was only recently that she'd learned the books themselves didn't house information. The books were anchors for a spell that allowed information to be recorded. So a massive tome might hold a very small amount of information and a slim volume a great deal more. She liked to think of them much as she would an Internet site. Each site had its own limited quantity of data that you could either search or read sequentially. She had, thus far, only encountered spelled books that were clean journals, no books with printed content.

Speaking of printed content— Lizzie dropped down to the ground next to the books. As she tried to decipher the pages, the typefaces foreign and hard to read, she wondered how Tavish knew so much about spelled books. He wasn't a spell caster. Of that she was sure. She mentally shrugged. He was a guard for a Library of magic books. Of course, he knew a little about them, she told herself. But she did make a note to revisit her concerns about the guards and all of their peculiarities with Harrington, in the next few days.

John, silent through her prolonged investigation of the books, was finally showing signs of impatience. "You've got several pictures. And I know you're tired. Can we tackle this tomorrow? We know the room is secure." John looked to Tavish for confirmation.

"Against physical and magical attack," Tavish agreed.

"I hate to point out the obvious, but if the room is secure —who or what knocked the books down?" Lizzie said.

"We'll look into it in the morning. After we've gotten a

little sleep." John tipped his head encouragingly toward the door. "Let's go."

"You're totally trying to get me out of here so you can come back and consult with security—with Tavish—aren't you?" Lizzie's tone was only mildly accusatory. She was starting to get that a protective streak was part and parcel of the package that was John.

"Will you leave if I agree and say I'm sorry?" John asked.

She snorted. "Sure. But only because I actually *am* tired. Exhausted, to be truthful. That red-eye flight is catching up with me. You wouldn't have heard me scream like a little girl, otherwise." She hoped.

Lizzie didn't comment when John dropped her at their room and immediately left. She knew exactly why he was in such a rush. And she hadn't needed an escort to the room—but he said it would make him feel better. She was learning that it was easier to agree with the little things.

Once she was alone, lying in bed awaiting sleep, it occurred to her—why was she convinced that something or someone had manipulated the books? Why would she think the scattered books had some hidden meaning? She didn't consider herself even a little prescient. She closed her eyes and tried to bring herself back to that moment. Entering the Library. Sitting down at the table. Settling into a chair. Time had passed. And then—there had been someone there. She'd had a sense of someone in the room with her. Not something she'd consciously registered at the time. But, nonetheless, it was there. She was there. A faint presence. And *that* was why she was convinced the books had been knocked down. *Damn.* Now she'd never get to sleep.

CHAPTER FIFTEEN

Bleary-eyed, Lizzie blinked down at her scrambled eggs. Jet lag, crappy sleep, whatever the reason, she was wiped and it was the beginning of a long day. She gave the coffee carafe a hard stare. Maybe today was a coffee day. She was wrapping her head around the need for a stronger, caffeinated beverage when a woman's voice interrupted her thoughts.

"Would you like a cup?" Lizzie turned her bloodshot eyes to the surprising source of that question.

"Morning, Heike. Yes, I think I would." She peered up at Heike, her pixie-cut blonde hair neat and her delicate features looking fresh and well rested. Heike, at least, looked ready to conquer the day.

She reached over and poured two cups. Handing Lizzie one of them, Heike said, "I thought you might do some damage to the pot, the way you were staring at it. That, and you look like you could use it this morning."

Lizzie smiled wryly. "Rough night." Lizzie cocked her head. She couldn't remember ever having a casual, civil—normal—conversation with Heike. Was that one of the reasons she'd not trusted her? She'd never connected with her on a personal level? Even if so, it was Heike who had been abrupt to the point of rudeness during Lizzie's earlier stay at the Library.

"I heard some noise, but Ewan told me it was nothing." As Heike spoke, a very faint blush washed across her face and neck and then was gone almost as quickly. If Lizzie hadn't been looking direct at her when she spoke, Lizzie would have missed it. *Interesting.*

There was one obvious reason that Lizzie thought might cause a blush. "Ewan is one of the security team, isn't he?"

Heike nodded and immediately took a sip of coffee.

Not wanting to try the strange truce that seemed to be developing, Lizzie let the question of Ewan drop. She floundered for a moment, trying to conjure another—preferably neutral—topic but coming up blank. She'd always admired people who could think on their feet. That wasn't a trait Lizzie had ever claimed, unfortunately.

Work was just making its way to the surface of her brain as a relatively safe topic when Heike spoke. "Ewan and I recently started dating."

She didn't seem particularly excited to share the news. Downright reluctant, in fact. Why bother then?

Heike cleared her throat. "I'm not good at small talk." *You think?* "But I'm trying to practice. Ewan says it gets better with practice." Heike seemed uncomfortable with her revelation but quite determined.

Damn. Now Lizzie felt guilty for her snarky thoughts. And a little angry. She should be able to snark and judge without guilt. Heike owed her that. But it was apparently not meant to be, because guilty was exactly how Lizzie felt.

Striving for a light tone, Lizzie replied, "True. It does take some practicing. I'm hardly an expert, but I'm sure we can manage a little morning conversation about our plans and progress in the Library."

"Work counts?" Heike looked relieved.

"Um, sure. Why not?" Lizzie needed to get up to date on the project. She just would have preferred the person updating her to be anyone other than Heike.

By the time John came by the breakfast room, she and Heike had managed a halfway civil and relatively unstrained conversation. Shockingly.

"When do you start for the day?" John asked after eying her empty plate.

"As soon as I can get to the Library." Obviously, something was up.

"I'll walk you," he said and pulled her chair out.

When they stepped into the Library, John asked her, "Is there any reason you didn't think the books had been carelessly placed on the shelf? That they'd fallen on their own?" When Lizzie didn't immediately reply, he said, "Tavish and I made the same assumption that someone or something had pushed them."

"Funny you should mention that." She hadn't really planned to discuss the presence she thought she'd sensed. Surely, if it was real, she would have noticed it at the time? It was only afterwards in the middle of the night, alone in her room, that she'd thought someone else had been in the Library.

What the hell. "Late last night, I kinda had the same thought. Weird that I was so startled. Weird that I immediately assumed something was wrong when they fell. And weirder yet that I was so sure the position or content of the books meant something. So, I tried to replay exactly what had happened."

She paused. Really, it was a crazy thought, right?

"And?" John prompted.

Lizzie wrinkled her nose a bit. *What the hell—why not?* "I felt like someone else was in the room."

"Why didn't you tell us last night?" John asked.

"I was already in bed," she said, a little defensively. "And, um, I didn't actually believe she was really there. All the more reason for me to expect someone else to believe she was just a figment of my imagination."

Lizzie peered at John, looking for some reaction. "You don't seem particularly surprised." Her tone was light but laced lightly with suspicion. She knew something was up.

"Hmm," he responded noncommittally. Then he said, "She? Are you sure?"

Lizzie frowned thoughtfully. She hadn't actively realized that the presence she sensed was female, but in articulating the events for John—well, apparently she was a woman. "Of course, I'm not sure. Once the sun was up, I thought I'd imagined the whole thing."

"Unlikely. Tavish had a few thoughts that he discussed with me last night." He held his hand up defensively when Lizzie inhaled a quick, huffy breath. "Hang on. Nothing that couldn't wait until this morning. And I knew how tired you were. Better at least one of us get some sleep."

Lizzie snorted. "And that's part of our problem. I didn't sleep well at all. I kept wondering—why would I realize there was a presence only afterwards, as I replayed the events? Why not immediately? Because I sensed her with my magic? And I don't always understand how my magic works—we can all agree on that. Or because she wasn't really there? Because I was editing the events in my memory after the fact?"

Now she was on a roll. Her voice wasn't escalating in volume, but the intensity was increasing as she spoke. "If you had any useful information and had thought to share it, it might have given me a little peace of mind. But you assume that you can make decisions for me. And that you know what's best. And that you can protect me." Her voice had finally risen slightly near the end.

Crap. Her pulse was beating a rapid tattoo, her breath coming a little faster. When did she get so pissed off? She gulped, trying to catch her breath. When had that happened? She knew everything she said had been lurking in the background of their relationship. Of course, she knew. And she knew she was upset, but she hadn't realized how deeply those feelings ran until now. She blinked, trying to clear the blur from the angry tears that were gathering. Apparently, this was the last straw, and she was the camel.

John's eyes burned. "Did it ever occur to you that it kills me I wasn't able to keep you safe? Did you even think for a second what that feels like? To be helpless in the face of mortal danger, not only to myself but also to my mate? I didn't ask for the feelings I have for you. They just are. And I can't change the need to protect what's mine. That's who I am. An essential part of what makes me who I am. What do you want from me?"

He was pissed. Violently pissed, if the throbbing pulse at his throat and clenched jaw were any indication. She'd poked at something raw—his inability to protect her. But Lizzie wasn't sure she cared. She thought there was likely a compromise, a middle ground where they both could be who and what they needed to be. But she was in no state to consider where that place was. If he was this implacable.... If he continued to view her possessively, like a piece of steak he had to hunker over and protect from the world.... If he had no desire to compromise....

How had this conversation devolved so quickly? She wanted to scream. Or to cry. This situation was so frustrating. He was so frustrating.

She took a slow, almost even, breath. "I'd like to know

what you and Tavish discussed—" Another breath. "—but not now. Maybe later." And with that last statement, she got up—slightly light-headed as she rose to her feet—and walked out the Library door.

Thoughts racing, she headed for the garden. She needed a quiet moment. A few minutes of silence, green plants, blooming flowers—surely that would help? She felt lost. And she very much needed that feeling gone before she saw anyone else.

As she sat on the garden bench, slowly and rhythmically swinging her legs back and forth under the bench, a few things settled in her mind. She couldn't remember the last time she'd been this angry with anyone, because no one had ever brought her emotions as close to the surface of her skin as John. Her emotions were so strong the effects were physical. He made her feel—more. More anger. More passion. More fear. More alive.

She sighed. She wasn't sure that was a good thing. She'd blamed some of her emotional excesses on the stress she'd been under lately. Some to her newly unlocked magic. Both were certainly in part to blame. But John was different. She hadn't lost her temper with Kenna, her parents, or her clients. It was John that brought out the extremes, good and bad.

Was she willing to live a life so filled with emotional excesses? She'd always considered herself more interested in contentment than joy. Happier to avoid the excruciating downs, even if it meant missing some of the thrilling highs. Kind of boring, now that she thought about it. She frowned. But not in a *bad* way. Hmm.

And the flip side— as strong as her emotions for John had been, apparently the same was true for him. Because he had already considered her his mate a short time after they met.

She hadn't missed John's admission that he had considered her his mate as the battle between the rescue crew and Worth had unfolded. She hadn't become his mate in truth until after the fight on the flight home when he'd asked and—ignorant of the underlying meaning of his question— she'd accepted.

At the time of her rescue, Lizzie knew John was special. And that he considered her—well, at least worth the effort of a rescue attempt. She smiled a little at that. She'd been certain he'd come for her, because that was the kind of man he was. The kind of man he is and likely will always be. She huffed out a quick, angry breath. But just as he could be counted on to act the knight in shining armor, he could be equally relied upon to push and shove at her personal boundaries and sense of independence. Her stomach was tightening just thinking about the issues raised by the two sides of the singular coin that was John.

She looked around at the green, flowering plants, at the tiny fountain, and she focused on the sound of the moving water. That was supposed to be calming, right?

Ten minutes later, she left the garden feeling slightly more at ease. At least she wasn't light-headed anymore. It had helped to calm her nerves—once she'd picked something specific to focus on. She'd discovered that trying *not* to think about something or someone was a complete bust.

Revisiting her to-do list. That was an excellent plan. If she focused on any one of the several other pressing tasks she needed to complete, she might just manage to get her mind off questions she wasn't ready to answer.

She started ticking off items on her mental list: the pack book, magical coma research, her graphic and web design clients— *Ha.* She had just the thing. Checking an item completely off her list would make her feel worlds better. Hopefully. The only item on her list that she could easily complete in minutes was a call to Pilar. And, bonus, she'd wanted to speak with Pilar for a few days now.

She'd intended to quiz a spell caster about the difference between her experiences with the pack book and *The Witch's Diary*. Outside of the fact that she wasn't sure Harrington was still her mentor, he didn't have the particular skill, reading magical texts, necessary to make him a good source. He might have second-hand knowledge, but given the ambiguous state of their relationship—why bother when she could likely get better information from Pilar? Heike—well, she just didn't trust Heike.

With the time difference, Lizzie figured a late afternoon call would be morning in Mexico. She wrote a quick text and scheduled it to go out around four o'clock: *Have a book question. Call when you get a second? Lizzie*

Before she did anything in the Library, she wanted to know what the heck Tavish had to say about last night. And she wanted a look at the pictures she'd taken—just in case she could actually discern some kind of meaning or message there.

Perfect. A plan of action always made her feel better. Next stop, Tavish.

CHAPTER SIXTEEN

After running Tavish to ground in one of the parlor rooms on the ground floor, Lizzie interrupted him reading a book.

"You're off this morning?" Silly question. She knew he was because she'd run into his boss a few minutes earlier. It was Lachlan who'd pointed her this way.

He raised his dark blond brows.

For all she knew, he and his boss communicated psychically, and Lachlan warned him she was headed this way. Every time she thought she had a handle on the weird that was her life, she'd run into something—a presence that wasn't physically there, for example—and she'd be a little freaked out all over again. Psychic communication wasn't out of the realm of possibility.

Tavish quickly erased those thoughts with his practical response. "I thought you'd be sleeping late, recovering from jet lag this morning. How can I help you?"

"John mentioned you had some thoughts on the falling books?" He didn't need to know she was avoiding John for the moment—just until she was in a more reasonable frame of mind—and that was why she was here asking Tavish questions instead.

She cocked her hip, resting it against the armchair next to her. Maybe if she acted casual, he wouldn't realize she was actively avoiding John.

"Ghost." At her startled and confused look, he clarified. "Remnant energy, left after a magic-user dies?"

"Ah. That really happens? A healer explained it to me, but it seemed theoretical. Or I assumed it was." What were the chances? This house. Her. She just had to be the one to witness something freaky. *Awesome.*

"They're not common." Tavish made the statement with great authority. Then he gave her a sheepish look. "I've been around awhile. I'm older than I look."

Lizzie had learned that you didn't ask what kind of magic-user a person was. It was considered rude and intrusive. If they wanted you to know, they told you. So, curiosity on high alert, she had to bite her tongue to keep herself from asking—how old? And—what are you?

Since Lizzie constantly got grief about her overly expressive face, it was no surprise when Tavish said, "It's killing you, huh?"

"A little bit." She made a corresponding hand motion indicating a small quantity. "You guys do kinda stand out. With your Scottish names and accents that are almost anything *but* Scottish. You and Ewan sound American. I guess Lachlan sounds a little Scottish?"

He chuckled at her question. "Only a very little."

"And now, you're telling me you're an old man, even though you look like you're in your thirties. Can you blame me for being curious?" Lizzie wasn't touching the weird feeling the security guys all gave her initially. That would definitely enter seriously rude territory.

"You forgot to mention the scalp-crawling sensation

when you meet us," Tavish added. Damn, maybe he was psychic. And oddly, he didn't *look* like creeping people out routinely bothered him.

"Uh, maybe more a slightly unsettled feeling." Lizzie cast a half-worried glance his way.

"Ha." His sharp bark of laughter cut through some of her discomfort.

"We're dragons. You should feel unsettled." Then he winked.

"Huh," she said. Then she sank slowly into the chair across from him. "But you—" She stopped herself, biting her lip. She eyed him curiously. Starting again, she said. "Um—" She didn't realizing she'd held her breath after that "um," until she took a quick, short breath.

"Spit it out. Scales? Fire? There's always a question about fire." He was leaning back now, one arm resting against the back of the sofa, his book forgotten next to him on the seat cushion. He appeared completely at ease.

She finally registered his casual pose. The guy had to get sick of people acting like idiots when he said "dragon." *Shit. That was really cool.* She was looking at a dragon. "Ha. Yes, fire is an interesting topic. Actually, I was trying to do the math of you being, well, not dragon-sized."

She winced a little. Maybe that was a stupid question. Clarifying, she said, "Lycan stay the same size."

"Right, but I'm no wolf." He smiled. "I told your mate I sensed a ghost when I entered the room. Very briefly—then nothing."

Clearly, that was all the dragon scoop she was getting for now.

"John seemed surprised when I identified the presence as female. I'm not at all certain, but it's possible," she said.

"That's helpful. There's likely a tie to the house. Or maybe even you. Has anyone mentioned the house was owned by the Kovars at one time?" He cocked his head slightly, bringing attention to his face—and green eyes. They *all* had green eyes, she realized. Well, Lachlan, Ewan, and Tavish.

What was the question? Oh—Lizzie nodded.

"Any relation, by chance?"

"No." She frowned. "Why would you ask?"

"Seriously? Smith, Kovar? Same name. Immigrants frequently Americanized or translated their names. To better fit in. You're American. I thought you guys were all into your roots. Don't you know where your people come from?"

"My people come from Texas, as far as I'm concerned. So, the Kovar name? You're sure it's the Czech equivalent of Smith?"

He looked at her condescendingly and refused to answer.

"Huh." She felt like she was saying that a lot. But really, he needed to stop dropping unexpected news on her if he expected her to keep up. "It's a really common name. I'm sure there's no connection. Didn't you say that the ghost could be tied to the location?"

"Certainly. But then why present herself to *you*? No one else has had an experience with her. I checked with Heike and the other guards. None of the Dragon Clan sensed her presence."

"Dragon Clan?" She was like a puppy with a butterfly, except her shiny, fluttery distraction had green scales and played with fire. Maybe. No, she wasn't skimping on that mental image. Definitely flames. And horns. Definitely horns. Okay, the green scales were negotiable. Ooooh. Purple dragon. She was contemplating a particularly nice shade of deep, rich eggplant when she caught Tavish's eye.

He gave her a mildly exasperated look.

Damn. Focus. "Sorry. So the falling books incident was the first ghostly experience in the house that anyone knows about? Maybe this was a wrong time, wrong place thing."

"Maybe." But he sounded skeptical. "And by the way, Smith isn't actually a common name among the few spell caster families in America." Before she could ask, he added, "Or Great Britain."

She'd been told the Kovars were powerful spell casters. And she'd been warned that it was possible she would become quite powerful, herself. She wasn't an idiot—or willfully blind. She knew enough to ask if strength of magic was a heritable trait, and she'd learned it could be. Was that proof that maybe the Kovars were her ancestors? It seemed so farfetched. The world was a big place. She wouldn't just stumble onto her relatives—would she?

With each passing day, the magic-using community seemed to grow both larger—she looked at her new dragon acquaintance. And smaller—she thought of her possible connection to the former Library keepers. She wasn't sure how she felt about that. Well, okay, dragons were definitely cool. She knew how she felt about *that.*

CHAPTER SEVENTEEN

Lizzie clicked her laptop shut and settled more comfortably on her bed. Google hadn't yielded much in the way of family history for the Kovars. Apparently, important spell caster families weren't particularly excited about press and notoriety, now or back in the day. The Kovars either kept a very low profile, or time had erased much of their lives. Well, there was also the distinct possibility it was there but in Czech. She'd have to get out the big guns and go chat with Emme, Harrington's librarian, about how to do some better online research. But Emme wasn't expected back for a few days yet. Maybe she'd check to see if there were local sources—a historical society, perhaps?—that she could utilize in the interim.

The identity of the ghost was important. If the ghost had limited means of communication, knowing a little more about her would surely help in understanding her. *Crap.* How much could ghosts actually understand? Or even think? Maybe there was no communication happening. Maybe she was reacting to the stimulus around her.

She fluffed the pillows on her bed, crossed her legs Indian

style, and then picked up her phone and hunted through her contacts. *Eureka.* She dialed.

Silence greeted her, so she prompted, "Harry?"

"Just a moment," a sleepy, feminine voice murmured on the other end of the phone.

After some rustling noises, Harry came on the line. "Harry, here."

Hmm. To comment and apologize, or to completely ignore? She said, "Hi Harry. It's Lizzie Smith. Do you have a moment to answer a few questions?"

"Absolutely." The tone of his voice changed, sounding more excited. "Have you found something?"

"Sorry, not how you mean. I think I found a ghost. Or, rather, she found me." She could hear noises in the background, like Harry was moving around. At the mention of a ghost, he'd stopped.

Lizzie just realized that she might have put him in an awkward situation if he was with someone who wasn't in on the whole "magic's real" thing. "Are you someplace you can speak freely?"

The background rustling and movement picked up again. "Sure. Grizzie's cool."

"Grizzie?" Lizzie just couldn't help herself.

"Sorry. Griselda. Terrible family name. Something we share and commiserate about over large quantities of cheap booze every once in a while."

Harry wasn't bad, but she had other things to worry about. "Griselda is a great name. But about my ghost? I was calling to pick your brain about ghosts in general."

"Are you sure? They're not very common. Maybe I put the thought in your head. If I did, I apologize." After "common," his words were muffled. Pulling a shirt on, if she had to guess.

"Tavish, one of the security guys, confirmed. He seemed

pretty sure." Lizzie didn't know if Harry had the dragon down-low, so she didn't comment.

"Ah. He would know. I'd forgotten Harrington brought the Clan in to cover security. If Tavish is there, he probably knows more about ghosts than I do," he said.

"You sounded pretty knowledgeable when we spoke before, and, um—"

Harry's soft laughter interrupted her. "And I'm way less scary than a dragon. I get it."

"Eh. Scary isn't really the right word. Tavish was incredibly nice. Maybe, intimidating is a better description. So what *do* you know? I'm looking for the basics. Can ghosts think, reason, remember their previous lives?" Lizzie hadn't yet decided which was scarier, an unthinking entity acting without reason? Or a thoughtfully plotting ghost with an agenda? They both seemed like dodgy prospects.

"Yes, yes, and yes—but I'm uncertain as to the extent. For example, does Aunt Martha know she's an aunt and that she's called Martha? Most likely. Does she remember the tulips you brought her last May before she passed? No clue. And I also have no idea how much of a plan a disembodied bunch of energy might have. Do they have the same worldly concerns as us? No idea." Harry covered the phone with his hand or tipped it away from his mouth, and Lizzie heard muffled goodbyes, and maybe a kiss?

"Any idea why she'd be quiet and then pick me to make a bunch of noise over? And is there any way to know how long she's been there?"

"Best bet? Do some research. I'd gamble she died in the house. Did Tavish have any thoughts about why you'd been the recipient of your ghost's affections?" He was starting to sound a little more with it. She could even hear kitchen noises in the background. Running water. China rattling.

"Tavish thought it was possible there's a family connection. But that seems to be reaching. I can't imagine I'm a relative."

"He got that idea from somewhere." Harry paused, waiting for answer. Or, hell, maybe he was busy tying his shoes. What did she know?

"Let me restate. Where did he get that idea?" he said somewhat shortly.

Maybe he was a bit snarky when his sex life was tampered with. She couldn't blame him. But how was she to know he'd still be in bed in the middle of the day? Let alone with a woman? She made a small, exasperated sound that she hoped didn't travel down the line. *Dammit. What was the question?*

"Same last name. Well, similar last name. Kovar is basically Smith in Czech. But who translates their name when they immigrate? Wouldn't you just Americanize it? That is, if you changed it at all." She wasn't sure why she was so set against being a long lost daughter of the Kovar family. But every time it came up, her response was immediate and unequivocal denial or avoidance.

"I know the American school system leaves a lot to be desired, especially when it comes to European history. But your school even fails on American history. Troubling," he said.

"I'm guessing that means it was a common practice?" Lizzie was never too good to admit she was wrong…or ignorant. Even if it made her feel like an idiot.

"It was," he affirmed.

"Shoot."

"Why does it bother you that you might be related to one of the big spell caster families?" Harry's voice expressed only a very mild curiosity. More like he was pointing out the oddness to her, rather than actually caring about the answer.

"Well—" She thought about it. "They lost the Library.

That makes them kinda irresponsible, right?" Though true, she wasn't sure she was bothered by the fact that the Kovars, her potential long lost relatives, had lost control of the Library; there was surely a story there. So why was it so hard for her to believe they might be a part of her family tree? "Whatever, this may be irrelevant. I'm probably not related, anyway."

"It certainly would be easy enough to check. Genealogy.com, or even a call to your parents. It's worth a little time to check it out, just in case your ghost has a special connection to you." As Harry spoke, Lizzie heard the scrape of a chair being moved.

"Do you have any other good information on ghosts?"

"Try a Ouija board. To communicate, I mean."

"You're kidding me." An exasperated burble of laughter escaped before she could control it.

He sighed. "I don't mean that you literally need a Ouija board. But try to give her access to letters and a way to point that doesn't involve moving anything heavy. How did she make herself known to you? You just sensed she was there?"

"She knocked three really big books off one of the Library shelves." Her voice turned slightly defensive. "It was late at night. I was jet-lagged." True confessions time. "The sound, uh, well, it scared the crap out of me. I might have screamed like a little girl. Really loudly."

Harry was apparently not above sniggering over the misery of others. Once he was done having a laugh at her expense, he said, "Have you seen or felt your ghost since then?"

"No. I haven't. And I think Tavish would have said." Lizzie tried to wrap her brain around the logistics of a disembodied cloud of magical energy manipulating physical objects. "Okay—I totally don't get it. How did she move the books?"

"No clue," Harry started, only to be interrupted by an

annoyed exhalation from Lizzie. He continued, "But, my impatient and rude girl, weight has to play a role. Your ghost may be tired. No telling how long she'll need to recoup before she can try again. Or her sense of time is different from ours. Or you're just incredibly dull, and she wandered away to find more entertaining fare. Either way, try to give her a means of communication that is lightweight."

"Got it. Any other words of advice?" Lizzie stole a glance at the wall clock. It was almost lunchtime, so she needed to wrap up. She'd forgotten to ask if lunch was buffet style, like breakfast, or a sit-down meal.

"She didn't throw the books at your head?" he quizzed.

"Uh, no." Confused, Lizzie tried to figure out where that came from.

"Lovely. Scratch murderous ghost off the list. You might have found a helpful ghost. Hit her up for some friendly advice about Sarah's condition." *That* was his advice?

"Why did I think you'd be helpful?" she muttered.

"Because I'm an accommodating, helpful sort. And you're not terrified to grill me. Till next time." And he hung up before she could say exactly how helpful he *hadn't* been.

She smiled. Okay, she admitted to herself, he *was* an accommodating, helpful sort. And that *was* why she'd called him. And though he hadn't oozed happiness to hear from her—she barely knew the guy and didn't expect him to—he'd been pretty darn cool given what she'd interrupted. Or suspected she'd interrupted.

Off to lunch. Then she was making a Ouija board.

CHAPTER EIGHTEEN

John was in a piss poor state of mind. And he had a security meeting shortly—great. Being reminded that his mate had saved *his* life wasn't particularly helpful. She wouldn't have escaped Worth without the rescue attempt he'd spearheaded, but when push came to shove—she'd pulled his ass out of a world of trouble. He had only to look at Sarah or Moore—Worth's other victims—to have a full understanding of that truth.

And it was more than just who had saved whom. He couldn't seem to be himself without rubbing up against Lizzie's sense of independence. Even the little things bothered her, though she made an effort to hide it. Maybe that was part of the problem. They were glossing over the issue like it didn't exist, letting the small things slide, and it was all piling up.

He stalked up the stairs. He'd grab a shower before his meeting. No time for a run, and he needed to get his head on right before he met anyone else.

While he headed up two flights of stairs, he contemplated Lizzie's introduction to the Pack. They needed to present a cohesive picture when they arrived in Texas. To look like a fully integrated unit—at least as observed from the outside in. Weakness between them would cause untold problems when he introduced her to the Pack. And if she was perceived to be anything less than fully supportive of his role—well, Texas was progressive, but they weren't that progressive. And the Pack would be actively looking for faults. After the delay in her introduction to the Pack, it was inevitable.

He'd been more than a little naïve—or maybe just optimistic—when he'd asked Lizzie to be his mate. He certainly hadn't anticipated the complications. *Fuck.* He stopped throwing his kit together, toothbrush in hand, and he closed his eyes. They hadn't even discussed living arrangements. He'd desperately like to opt out of that conversation.

He grabbed his kit and headed to the bathroom down the hall. He laughed without any humor. All this stress over how to work things out with the Pack. That was assuming he and Lizzie got right with each other. Hardly a certainty. He was who he was, a mated Alpha. Progressive pack or no, he was still a man who wanted the people he cared about and was responsible for to be safe. And in Lizzie's case, he felt a sometimes overwhelming desire to protect this fragile person who was becoming so dear to him. And, he couldn't forget the lust. *God.* Always there at a slow burn, but occasionally all consuming. He cranked the shower a little colder.

Independent, convinced she was invincible, more concerned for those around her than for herself, Lizzie invited trouble. *Damn.* One minute he wanted to shake her until her brain started working properly and the next he wanted to fuck her. It was an unsettling and unpleasant combination. Lust, a desire to protect, a sense of possession, and a variety of other emotions mixed together and butted up against her complete lack of common sense and her decidedly negative reaction to the suggestion that she might need help or be unable to handle everything alone.

Shower over, he wrapped himself in a towel and grabbed his stuff. Most of the time, he was a reasonable guy. He even managed to be reasonable with Lizzie—sometimes. But he couldn't constantly be on his guard that something he would say or do would set her off. That wasn't any way for either of them to live. Throwing his kit on the bed, he rubbed his hand over his face. He may love her, but no one should live like that. He'd made his choice—impulsive though it may have been. And he stopped. He *had* made his choice. And he wasn't an impulsive man. That, in and of itself, was another factor to consider.

When he finally arrived at the security meeting with Lachlan, he was hardly in a better frame of mind. He felt like there were too many questions, not enough answers, and someone was playing a massive joke on him.

All of those thoughts, the chaotic swirl of turmoil and emotion drifting around in his head—hell, in his gut, maybe his heart—well, that's what he was blaming. Because normally he'd have more sense than to pick a fight with a dragon. Lachlan was an unknown entity, so starting a fight would be foolish in the extreme. The goal of the meeting was for Lachlan to bring John up to speed on the security team rotations, educate him about the wards that Harrington and his staff set including their limitations, begin plans for hiring full-time, permanent security staff, and set a deadline for the handoff to the new permanent security staff. They got so far as reviewing the staff names and roles, and that was enough to set John's hackles up.

"Is there a reason that you've got Tavish assigned specifically to Lizzie? That she's his primary duty?" John asked.

"Your little mate likes trouble, and Harrington specifically requested we ensure her safety. I owe Harrington a debt, paid only upon successful completion of this project. Would you have me rely upon a single wolf to secure her safety? Given the uncertain state of your relationship with the girl, I thought an alternative plan feasible." Lachlan's eyes burned green for a moment. When he began speaking again, the glow faded. "Such a tiny human girl. I see why you don't trust her to keep herself safe." Sarcasm dripped from his words.

John could feel a low growl rumbling deep in his chest. What the hell did he mean? Lizzie *was* a tiny human girl. But John was pissed so he didn't dwell on the strangeness of Lachlan's comments. And he looked like a good candidate for a brawl. Especially since he was the only one around. Never mind the three inches and at least thirty pounds of muscle that McClellan's CEO and Chief of Security had on him. And he'd heard something about fire…S*hit. He was an idiot.*

His intent must have been clear. Or perhaps that growl had rumbled just loud enough for dragon ears. "I know you're accustomed to being the baddest wolf in the room. Trust me when I say this—you will not win." After a pause, Lachlan said, "And I have no desire to fight a man over a woman, like two dogs over a bone."

John stopped. Okay. That was a distasteful image. And not one that he wanted to leave this room. Lizzie would go ballistic in her current frame of mind. He rubbed his face. *Shit.* If Lachlan wasn't trying to pick a fight, what the hell was he doing?

"If you repeat that comment to Lizzie, I don't care how big you are or what kind of fire you have, I'll find a way to kick your ass." Seriously, Lizzie would lose it. *Two dogs over a bone?*

Lachlan laughed. A huge booming sound, that came from his belly. "If you're alive to do it. Your tiny mate packs a punch."

What the fuck? This guy was impossible to follow. He was

done with this. "Say what you mean. I've had enough of guessing and miscommunication for one day."

"Wolf. You're no fun." Lachlan sighed. "Your woman can protect herself. You're currently lacking a partner, not another responsibility. You do the math."

John cocked his head. "She's human."

Lachlan looked at him with pity. "She's not *only* human."

John looked at Lachlan's retreating back. Presumptuous, condescending SOB. And odd. Tavish came in almost immediately. So quickly, John would be surprised if he hadn't passed his boss in the hallway.

"Sorry I'm late. Where's Lachlan?" Tavish asked. Apparently they had missed each other.

"Gone," John said curtly. "Can you give me the rundown?"

"No problem." Tavish didn't even blink over the fact his boss had come, gone, and failed to impart any of the relevant details of the meetings.

The two men discussed business and set a tentative plan in motion to begin the hiring process for long-term staff. John had some contacts within the American Lycan community, and he even had a man or two in mind from his own pack. Tavish would run it by Lachlan before getting the pieces moving.

After they'd wrapped up, he couldn't help but recall Lachlan's implied criticism. "One last thing. I think Lachlan... never mind," he said, shaking his head in annoyance.

Tavish eyed him sympathetically. "Lachlan's been giving you advice?"

John's curiosity was piqued. Did he cruise around doling out unsolicited advice routinely? "Yes."

Tavish nodded knowingly.

"So?" John prompted when Tavish didn't continue.

Tavish sighed. "Lachlan is like a friendly cousin to Loki."

"Sorry?"

At John's impatient look, Tavish clarified. "He can be a mischievous ass. It's also hard to know what his motivations are. Frequently, they're convoluted and the end result is his own amusement. What was the gist?"

"The point seemed to be that Lizzie can take care of herself." He stopped, trying to recall what exactly Lachlan had said. "I need a partner, not more responsibility—I think."

"Love and relationships? Pay attention. He's actually quite good when it comes to relationships." Tavish rolled his shoulders. "Don't ever take investment advice from him, though. Or race tips." After a second, he added, "Actually any sports tips. And don't listen to any weather predictions."

John laughed. Then he saw the dead serious look Tavish shot his way. "Seriously? You're not kidding?"

"No, not kidding."

Huh. "Thanks for the heads up." And that was about all John could manage, because really—all he'd learned was that Lachlan was a nut job who gave horrible advice, sometimes on purpose, about almost everything—except love. He snorted in disgust. *Enough. That was three minutes he'd never get back.*

John excused himself to place a call to Max. The call was overdue, and John had endured more than enough dragon freaky shit for the day.

"Where the hell have you been? I expected a call when you landed." Max's tone was shy of angry, but certainly not as light-hearted as his usual self.

"Since when are you my nanny?" At Max's grunt of annoyance, John took pity on him. "Look—I appreciate your help. Both in getting me Lizzie's flight info and in keeping an eye on things with the Pack. I've just been busy."

"I don't suppose that has anything to do with our curly-headed caster?" Max ventured.

"She's not ours; she's mine. And you know it does." John

made a note to check in with Logan. He hadn't received an update since he left. "I'm guessing you have pack news?"

Max was human, but he was also friends with half a dozen Texas Pack members. And friendly with twice that number.

"You need to get Lizzie back. And plant your ass in Texas for the next few months. Once this current adventure is over, don't leave." Max paused. "Hang on." A little background noise, a few shut doors, the electronic ding of a car door ajar, and the soft hum of an expensive engine. "There's talk of a challenge."

John should have known. This whole mess with Lizzie made him look weak. "Internal or external?"

"Both. There's a line forming." Max's tone was grim.

Fuck. "Who?" John asked.

"Does it matter? Get your ass home. And bring your woman." Max chuckled, but John wasn't sure there was any humor in the sound. "Just make sure she agrees not to start a civil war on arrival."

"I've only been gone two days. Logan said nothing of a specific challenge when we last spoke."

"But he warned you trouble was coming, didn't he?"

John thought back to the conversation. "He warned generally that a challenge could result. But my impression was that no one was rushing to be first. He had no names. I'm sure of it; he would have said."

"It's been a while since you've beaten the shit out of anyone. Memories fade. And the Council—actually, I'm not sure what's going on with the Council. Come home." Max snorted. "And if you need a little help getting your problem out there sorted, let me know. I could use a break myself from some bullshit here in town. Cracking heads and shooting people may be just the thing to brighten my mood."

John laughed. "Thanks for the offer, however self-serving

it may have been. We're having spirit issues. No guns required. I'll keep you in mind if that situation changes, though." After a short pause, John asked, "Are you all right?"

"Yeah, I'm fine, just frustrated and annoyed. Kenna's driving me nuts. What's with your spirit issues? Actually, I don't want to know. I'm assuming everything's all right unless you call for reinforcements. And I'll keep you updated if the situation escalates here." John could hear the indrawn breath of pending speech, but Max hesitated. Then—"Something's not right, John. There shouldn't be this much of a reaction—this much dissent—traced back to your absence. Even factoring in Lizzie, your mate announcement, and your apparent refusal to introduce her to the Pack, it's still—off. The faster you're home, the better."

"Thanks." John ended the call with a sense that another little piece of his world was crumbling. Lizzie, the Pack—what else did he have? If his business manager gave him a call and said all their accounts had cancelled their contracts, he wouldn't be particularly surprised.

He dropped down into one of the chairs. Papers were strewn across the table from his meeting. He sat in that chair for ten minutes. Not thinking about Lizzie. Or the Pack. Or his business. Or this security job. He just needed a moment to simply be.

After about ten minutes, he straightened, packed away the papers, clicked his laptop shut, made a mental note to razz Lachlan and Tavish about their reluctance to use electronic documentation, gathered everything together, and left the room. He'd catch a quick bite, then try to get started putting a preliminary list together for the new security staff. He was in control. He had a plan. He was ready to take care of business—Pack, Lizzie, and security.

CHAPTER NINETEEN

Lizzie looked down at the large piece of paper spread out on the parlor table. She'd coopted Tavish's favorite parlor for her craft project because it had a huge table and great light. Google was definitely her friend. Not having dabbled in spiritualism or been into ghosty, ghouly stories as a kid, she didn't actually know what a Ouija board looked like. So, after lunch, she'd found a description of one online. She could have run into town and bought one. Turns out, they were readily available in stores and even looked like a children's game board.

Since she needed a simple means of communication, she made her own. She'd gathered together some supplies and planted herself in one of the many parlors sprinkling the huge house. Looking down at her handiwork, she felt a stout sense of accomplishment. Good thing she Googled. She'd have left off the numbers, otherwise. And they seemed handy.

She grinned at her makeshift board. She'd taken an old serving tray from the kitchen and covered the bottom in thick paper. It rested evenly on its handles when turned upside down, presenting a stable, flat surface for the paper and the small pebble she'd planned to use as the planchette. She wasn't sure how good her ghost's motor skills were, so she'd made the board with large letters and numbers, none touching the others. A bit like a large print Ouija. She giggled.

Tavish appeared in the door. "What's so funny?"

"Large print Ouija?" Looking at the politely blank expression on Tavish's face as he walked into the parlor, she cringed inwardly. *Not funny.*

"Sorry. I've been at my craft project a little too long." She waved her hand in the direction of the paper. The big letters in purple marker looked foolish now, with Tavish examining them.

"Good plan with the big letters. She may not have particularly good aim." Peering down at her, he added, "Have you considered she might have intended those books as a warning, or, perhaps, a weapon? Rather than a means of communication?"

"No. And I'm going to continue not considering it. That's what I have you security types for, right?" She grinned at him.

But her grin hid her worry. Of course, she was concerned. She was dealing with a ghost. A disembodied ball of energy. Not even the experts were sure what type of energy. Or what a ghost could do. Well, if you considered Harry and Tavish experts.

But if she were to dwell—on the potential for malicious intent, on the possibility that the books *were* intended for her head—then she wouldn't have the courage to investigate. Or the courage to work in the Library at all. She was already getting a slow start with her internship because of this darn ghost.

The most troubling aspect was that she'd been unable to

find any pattern to the books' placement—and after having such a strong feeling that they were a message, not finding one was both galling and concerning. She'd studied the photos and the books themselves. Nothing. Well, almost nothing. Two books were in French and one in German. Did that mean something? Two philosophical texts and one religious. And that meant what? There was no similarity in the content of the exposed pages. *Argh.* It was enough to make a girl start picking at her cuticles.

She looked at Tavish and decided there was no time like the present. Especially if the present involved a badass, scaly bastard who could surely kick some ghost butt, standing about three feet away. "Let's do this." Well, she *sounded* confident.

"Right now?" At her firm nod, he said, "Okay." He seated himself at the card table where Lizzie had constructed her improvised Ouija board.

"Um, how?" Lizzie looked at Tavish hopefully.

He smiled. "I haven't a clue. What happened last time?"

Lizzie closed her eyes, imagining that night. "I walked in the door." She scrunched her eyes more tightly closed, trying to remember. "Ugh. It was just yesterday."

"No problem," Tavish said in a quiet, relaxed voice. "Backup. What happened before that?"

"I came down the stairs. With John. We'd, ah, whatever, on the main stairs to the ground floor." She could feel the heat in her face. She was incredibly glad not to be looking Tavish in the face right now. "Then he escorted me to the Library door."

She relaxed as the night came back to her. Her voice quiet but confident, she said, "I opened the door after saying goodnight." She smiled, remembering the kiss John had given her. He'd been disappointed she wasn't coming right to bed, so he'd wanted to leave her hot and bothered. She was guessing the idea was that she'd hustle up to bed quicker.

"I sat at the table to the right, my back to the wall. Worked for I'm not sure how long. And that was it."

"So the books fell behind you?" When she nodded, he asked, "In between the wall and where you were sitting?"

"Right. I didn't see anything, and I was distracted enough that it frightened me quite a bit."

"Hmm. I remember the scream. Like a teenage girl seeing her first snake." He grinned.

"Smartass. And by the way, I've seen grown men squeal like babies over snakes. Let's not discriminate." Lizzie's scalp itched in a creepy-crawly way. Snakes. *Ick.* She felt a quick shiver run across her body. Rattlesnakes might be right up there with ghosts for creepiness.

"So—I was focused on the notes I wanted to review. That's why I was there," she reminded Tavish.

"In the movies, they always just ask the ghost to make itself known." She paused, trying to come up with a less embarrassing version of that scenario.

Yep. Not happening. "Excuse me, lady ghost? Are you here in the room with us?"

She tried closing her eyes, then she realized that wouldn't be helpful, because then she couldn't see the board.

"We brought a board for you to use. If you want to speak with us." She realized sticking with a question was a good idea. "If you're here, move the stone to 'yes.' Please." She figured it never hurt to be polite. If she was lucky and really nice to the ghost, maybe her ghostly visitor would consider not throwing books at her head.

How about a personal connection? "What's your name? If you're here, please spell your name with the stone."

She looked at Tavish. "I feel ridiculous."

He nodded complacently. "You look ridiculous."

"Well, you don't have anything better," she said crossly.

"Hmm." He picked up her stone, rolling it for a second in his fingers then pocketing it. He gathered her board next. "Let's go."

"Where—well, damn. Why didn't you say something earlier?" She was miffed but mostly with herself.

"You seemed pretty determined. It was cute." He winked at her.

What a shit. They both headed in the direction of the Library. The only location they knew the ghost to have visited. A ghost who most likely had some special connection with this house. And if location was important, as both Tavish and Harry had said, it was possible the ghost was tied not just to the house, but specifically to the Library. Tavish really was a shit. He could have saved her that embarrassing little scene. *Ugh. Stupid men.*

Once they arrived, Lizzie realized that, of course, they'd be interrupting Heike at her work in the Library. *Someone* was working at making a dent in the translation and cataloguing. Harrington had expanded the work area to include both the Library and the large main basement area. So when Lizzie and Tavish stepped into the basement from the stairway, they immediately entered the work area where Heike had stationed herself.

"Hi, Heike. Sorry to bother you. We'll just pop right through to the Library proper. I'll close the door so we won't disturb you," Lizzie said.

"Investigating the ghost phenomenon?" She looked curious, but only mildly so.

Lizzie was surprised. Why hadn't she realized that Heike would be informed? They hadn't discussed it at breakfast, but she would have heard something by now. Likely from Ewan.

"Yes." Inspiration struck. "You can join us, if you like." Not exactly a warm invitation, but that's as good as it was getting for now. Harrington would have to settle for that.

Apparently, Heike was on board with a continued truce, because she seemed to consider the matter thoughtfully, rather than dismissing the invitation out of hand. "No. I don't want to chase your ghost away. But I'll keep half an ear open." And she smiled ever so slightly at Lizzie.

Lizzie returned her smile, tentatively. "If you hear Tavish squeal like a little girl, come save us." She shot Tavish a quick look and raised her eyebrows at him.

"You know Tavish is..." Heike began, but stopped suddenly and glanced at him.

Lizzie saved her. "Fire-friendly and slightly older than he looks. Yes."

Heike nodded.

Tavish hustled Lizzie into the Library. She sat down at the same table she'd occupied earlier that day. She wasn't comfortable with her back to the wall with the falling books, so she chose a seat opposite, facing the suspect wall. She took a few calming breaths, and asked what she thought was the most relevant question.

"If you're here, can you tell us who you are?"

Lizzie had placed the little stone on the corner of the board. Slowly, the stone moved from letter to letter. K-O-V-A-R

Holy shit. "Holy shit," she said. She briefly made eye contact with Tavish, and she could see a low glimmer of green in the depths. He nodded once slowly. She took that to mean, yes, ghostly presence in attendance. *Ya think?* And after she calmed down just a bit and paid attention to the room—the way it felt now versus before—she could feel it, too. The feeling that if she turned suddenly, she'd bump into someone. The feeling that she'd almost, but not quite, caught a glimpse of someone outside her peripheral vision. The feeling that someone's eyes were on her. She made a mental note. *This is what a room with a resident ghost feels like.*

Next question. "Why are you here?"

K-O-V-A-R

By the time she hit the "V," Lizzie was thinking that maybe her ghost could only spell one word.

"What—" she stopped. Her ghost was still working.

L-I-B-R-A-R-Y

Lizzie thought for a minute. "You're here because you're a Kovar, and the Kovars protect the Library." Of course. She was an idiot sometimes. Very occasionally clever, but today —a bit of an idiot.

The pebble moved to the "yes," then popped up about an inch, then back down again. And again. Three times total, her ghost said yes. An emphatic ghost. Okay.

"Why are you still here? In the Library?" Lizzie asked. She looked over at Tavish. They really should have consulted on their questions beforehand.

Tavish nodded encouragingly. He must approve of that one.

The pebble lifted in the air several inches off the board, hovered very briefly, then shot straight at the wall, impacting with a loud crack as stone hit wooden shelves.

Holy cow. "That was creepy, right?" She probably shouldn't say things like that in front of her ghost. *But—wow.*

Tavish nodded. His silence was becoming noticeable. Probably a wise choice, since her ghost was communicating freely with her. Wouldn't want to scare her off. *Ha.* After that stone throw, they should be more concerned for their own safety.

"I'm sorry. Did I say something to make you angry?" Might as well bring it all out into the open. Politely, she thought, eying the stone.

The pebble rose from the ground near the shelves slowly,

and Lizzie tried her damnedest not to flinch as it moved in her direction. But there was no force, and the pebble very softly landed on the "no" word.

That was vastly confusing. Though good. Maybe.

She considered her next question. She still didn't know which Kovar she was dealing with. If she was going to do some research on her ghost, then a first name was vital. And a time frame. A time frame would be really helpful.

"What is your first, your given, name?"

M-A-T-Y-L-D-A

Lizzie clapped her hands in excitement. Oops. Don't scare the ghost, Lizzie, she told herself. But how exciting! Her ghost had a name.

"When did you die?" Lizzie asked.

The pebble remained still.

"What year did you, um, become how you are?" Maybe she wasn't supposed to use the word "die"?

The pebble didn't move.

Lizzie frowned. As she tried to think how to reword the question, the pebble moved to "no."

"You didn't die?" Lizzie guessed wildly. Although how was that possible? Unless her ghost was not only emphatic but also a bit of a philosopher and didn't consider herself dead in her current state.

The pebble pinged on the "no" word with a slight amount of force. *Crap.* She was annoying her ghost. That wasn't good.

"You're not dead?" Totally nonsensical, but she had to ask. Heck—maybe she could astral project. That was a thing. She'd seen it in the movies.

D-E-A-D

What the... "So—you *are* dead?" She was confused as hell now. Looking at Tavish, she saw he was just as perplexed.

Yes

Gah. "How did you die?"

Nothing. Then the pebble jumped up and landed in on "no."

She looked at Tavish, thought through what had just happened, and decided maybe she had an idea. "A delay followed by 'no' means a bad question, right?" Her question was directed at Tavish, but Matylda jumped right in.

Yes

Tavish smiled and quietly said, "There's your answer." Lizzie was glad he found some humor in this. She was just frustrated.

As he spoke, Matylda started moving the pebble.

W-H-E-R-E

"Where?" Frowning, she thought back to her last question. Surely they were still discussing death? Death seemed like it would be an important point for a ghost.

In an aside to Tavish, she quietly said, "We need to write down our questions. I can't keep track."

He mouthed a response.

Aha. "Where did—" before Lizzie could finish with "you die," the pebble had hopped cheerily over to "yes." And yes, it really was a happy little bouncing motion to the "yes" word.

Good job, Tavish. She tipped her chin in acknowledgement.

Before Lizzie could get excited that she'd stumbled on something to make her ghost happy, the pebble stilled and there was a loud thud. Five books had fallen to the floor. Smaller ones this time. *What the hell was with the books?*

Lizzie's phone rang. She couldn't believe that she had enough signal in the basement to get a call. Glancing down, she saw it was Pilar. She quickly silenced her phone. She'd call her back in a bit. Pilar would certainly understand once she got even a hint of this story.

"Matylda? I don't understand. Are these books important?

Do they explain where you died?" Then Lizzie realized something. Why was Matylda concerned with location? "Where" was the one answered question, the one piece of relatively certain information. They'd all decided that the "where" must be here in the Library. That Matylda was likely tied to a particular location, the house, and even more specifically, the Library, because she'd died here.

"She's gone." Tavish shrugged. "I can't feel her presence any longer."

"Great. We have a weapon-wielding ghost, and she's the one who's afraid of a little phone noise. Although, phones are modern, so maybe any technology is scary?" Lizzie was still trying to work through the question when Tavish interrupted her.

"Or she exhausted herself pulling five books from the shelves to the ground," Tavish guessed.

"And the phone noise was a coincidence? Maybe. Most important question of the hour—why is Matylda fixated on where she was killed when that is the one thing we know? Well, think we know."

"Because we don't know?" Tavish picked up the books, scanning the open pages quickly. "I don't think the content matters."

"What?" Lizzie was still scratching her head. Metaphorically, at least. Hadn't she sworn to work on her quick-thinking skills? This whole ghost experience had been a near epic fail on the quick thinking. She really needed scripted questions.

"The content of the books?" He raised his eyebrows as he snapped shut one of the books and held it up. "Not important. Did you not notice how carefully your ghost placed the pebble on the board?"

"Yes. Except when she hurled it at the shelf. It was hard to miss the terrific cracking noise of the stone smacking the shelf. Otherwise, yes, she was very precise."

"If the content of the book was important, why not dump a book on the ground and flip to the relevant page? She understands us. So language doesn't appear to be a problem. She can spell—her name and a few words, at least—so one assumes she can read. And the caretaker of a Library, magical or not, I would assume could read. Probably multiple languages."

"Maybe the books themselves are the message? Or the titles of the books?" Lizzie asked.

"Maybe. But two of these books are empty of text. If she can read the spell, maybe, but that seems improbable." Tavish didn't look convinced.

"How long do you think before she comes back? Or can come back." She was doing the math in her head. "I guess there's a question of ability and desire. Maybe she thinks we're idiots and is throwing her ghostly hands in the air," she added.

"Sixteen hours since her last appearance. She interacted more, maybe tired herself more? But we also don't know how long she's been lurking in here, waiting for you to come back." He was a little quicker with the math than she was. Or more focused.

After examining Lizzie for a moment, he said, "I don't think our ghost would be so easily put off by a little incompetence. I'm guessing she's back as quickly as she's able. Even with as little at her disposal as she had, her enthusiasm was clear."

Lizzie pulled a half grimace. "Are we that incompetent?"

"Hey, she was talking to you. Don't include me." He grinned. He really was pretty laid back. For a guy who could probably breathe fire.

"So, what? I camp out here?" Lizzie started thinking about

the logistics. Why not? She could even start working. And she'd give her ghost, Matylda, an opportunity to grab her attention.

"Up to you," he said.

She thought about her mental to-do list, tallied up the important and not so important parts, then said, "Yep. It's a plan. I need to make a quick call to a friend and the reception down here is sketchy. So I'll just run upstairs, make my call, and bring some food down."

"My unsolicited security advice is to have someone with you at all times when you're in the Library proper. First, you'll appreciate the extra set of eyes when she does come back again. And second—" He gave her a serious look. "—she pitches a mean book and an even meaner stone. It's a good safety precaution."

Lizzie wasn't that obstinate. Why did everyone think she wanted to run off into danger and conquer the world? She wasn't all that brave. And certainly not stupid.

She gave him a squinty-eyed look. "Stop with the judging. I never said I didn't want help, did I? You've obviously been talking to some folks with some incorrect info." And she had one good guess who that was. Okay, two—make that three. Damn, maybe there were a few people around who thought she was incautious. But they were wrong.

"You didn't trade yourself to a bunch of kidnappers to save your friend? Or stick your hand into the equivalent of a magical meat grinder to stop Worth from hurting your boyfriend?"

Oops. She did do *that*. But she was a complete weenie. Really.

She chewed the edge of her lip, avoiding Tavish's more than likely amused face. "But I don't lack all common sense."

"Prove it." He nodded toward the door. At her confused look, he reminded her gently, "Your phone call?"

CHAPTER TWENTY

"It's so good to talk to you." Lizzie could hear the smile in Pilar's voice.

Shifting the phone briefly to sit snugly in the crook of her neck and shoulder, Lizzie used both her hands to open the heavy door out to the patio. "It's been a little busy, or I would have called sooner."

"And you have a question now," Pilar said.

Lizzie wrinkled her nose up in consternation. "I do. I'm sorry. That's horrible, isn't it?"

"Not at all. It's exactly what my children do, and they love me dearly. They even send a text telling me to call like you did." Her merry laughter tinkled across the phone line.

"And how old are they?" Lizzie planted herself on one of the benches. This might be the only outdoor time she'd get until tomorrow. She couldn't predict the length of her ghost vigil.

"Younger than you." Pilar laughed again. "You're young at heart, darling, that's all."

"I'm sorry I couldn't pick up earlier. I was having a ghost encounter."

Pilar snorted. Elegant, polite Pilar. Picturing that made Lizzie smile broadly. Apparently ghosts weren't regular fare for her, either.

"How did that work out?" Pilar asked.

"Still working on it. My question was about a weird experience I had with one of the magic books. I just wanted to be sure it's safe to leave out on the Library shelves."

"No problem. I'll help if I can," Pilar said. And she would. Pilar had been a rock during their shared kidnap experience. "Doesn't IPPC also have a full-time spell caster? Someone besides you that also has a language talent?"

"Heike."

"I see." Pilar's tone was neutral.

"Maybe not. She's…she's different, Pilar." Lizzie sighed. "Or I think she is. She's trying, anyway. And we don't really know what was happening in this house—between her and Worth. Or so Harrington reminded me quite forcefully."

"But not your first choice for a prickly problem," Pilar extrapolated.

"Not my first choice," Lizzie agreed. She peered up at the clear sky. The sun was muted at this time of day. The garden was truly lovely. "And I've wanted to check in for the last few days, to see how you're doing."

"My daughter is safe and doesn't seem to be suffering any lingering ill effects. Now that everything has turned out all right, she sees it as a grand adventure. And, of course, I never discussed the details of my stay with her." She summed up the entire experience with a succinct and completely motherly comment. "She's well, so I'm well."

Pilar's daughter had been held to ensure Pilar's cooperation during her captivity, and Lizzie's parents had been threatened. She didn't know until after Worth fled that her parents were unharmed. It had been an incredibly stressful and traumatic event for both women.

"Tell me about this funny book," Pilar said, getting back to the heart of the call. Lizzie suspected that Pilar was changing the subject before they both became maudlin over their shared experience. Something neither would enjoy.

"I'm not entirely sure it's funny. I've really only worked with the pack book and the one Library book I managed to translate before the rescue attempt."

The Witch's Diary?" Pilar hadn't been there when Lizzie had been put to the test, trying out her newfound magic for almost the first time in the worst possibly circumstances—in front of Worth. All while knowing that she or her parents might suffer horribly if she failed. Not how she would have envisioned using her magic for the first time.

"Right. I'd forgotten you debriefed with Harrington afterwards. That came up?" Lizzie wouldn't have thought one small book would have been noteworthy amidst the post-rescue chaos.

"Briefly. I didn't notice anything too odd, other than a reluctance on the part of the book to share its secrets. Just a moment." Lizzie could just barely make out the rumble of a masculine voice in the background.

"Sorry. My husband was just heading out for the day." She paused, likely orienting herself back to the conversation. "Right—a reluctant book. Otherwise, nothing unusual."

"Okay. That right there. That is supremely creepy, just so you know. Books don't have emotions or a consciousness—do they?" Lizzie thought of all the shelves and shelves of magical books in the Library.

Pilar chuckled. "I can see you thinking twice about heading into a room full of spelled books. No, they don't. Not like you mean. But a spell is interactive. It was created by a person and can reflect that person in small ways. I've also seen books that interface well with one person and not another. When the book's spell wouldn't immediately reveal the knowledge it held, I assumed my magic didn't work well with it, but I've no idea why. What exactly was your question?"

Lizzie huffed out a frustrated breath. "That book *is not* reluctant. It's more like an affectionate puppy, begging for my attention. Well, a really creepy, affectionate puppy. I feel like I have a connection with the book. When I walk in the Library, I can feel where it's shelved. Is that normal?"

"Having an awareness of a spell once you've identified it is actually very normal. Remember when I explained wards to you? And when you looked for them, they became visible to you?"

Lizzie nodded. Oops—she'd forgotten she was on the phone. "I do."

"Think of the connection you've made with the book in the same way. Now that you've had some interaction with the spell, you have an awareness of it. The difference, in this instance, is that the awareness is not a visual one like it was with the wards." Pilar's voice had begun to echo about halfway through.

"Did you just walk into a tunnel?" Lizzie asked.

"No. You're on speakerphone. I'm doing some kitchen prep for lunch and dinner. Both of the kids are home," Pilar said. Lizzie could hear the contentment in her friend's voice.

"Oh! Remind me later to ask you about Harry." She shook her head, thinking about the phone call earlier today with him. He reminded her of a naughty little boy who was always into some mischief.

"Sure." There was the hint of a question in Pilar's voice. Then she returned to the subject at hand, the snick of her knife audible in the background. "Any other concerns about the diary?"

"I guess not. It's just strange that it seems to call me, and yet the pack book—that I've had for years—doesn't seem to have any effect on me." Lizzie wondered if that was an omen of things to come. She wasn't getting off to a stellar beginning with the Texas Pack, having not actually made it out to meet them yet. A little more than an oops, more like a massive social gaffe, if not worse.

"Think of your connection as a tie to the spell, not the book. Remember, the physical book merely anchors the spell. And it's the magic creating and maintaining the spell that either speaks to you or doesn't." The chopping sound in the background was getting faster. Pilar must be a whiz in the kitchen.

"So I'm not connecting with the Witch of *The Witch's Diary*? I'm connecting with the spell caster who recorded that witch's thoughts?"

"Close. You're connecting with that caster's magic." Pilar's chopping halted for a few seconds then resumed. "I know next to nothing of witches, but it seems odd that a witch and caster would work together." Her voice was thoughtful.

"Hmm. That's a question for another day. I have enough problems and questions that need immediate attention. If something isn't marked urgent, it's moving to the end of the line. Now that I'm relatively certain the diary isn't going to wreak havoc on me or the Library, I can cross it off my list for now. My ghost is definitely on the priority list. And then, Sarah." Just thinking of Sarah made Lizzie worry about the diminished focus on Sarah's magically induced coma. But her ghost was more pressing.

"So—there are some murmurings in the magical community that you've become John's mate. You're making the international gossip circles, Lizzie." Pilar didn't seem particularly concerned that Lizzie was making Lycan news. Her tone was very matter-of-fact.

But Lizzie couldn't adopt Pilar's blasé manner. "Good lord, that can't be good. I've been viewing this whole mate thing as a political position, and this proves it. Why else would I be of any interest, but for John's position?"

"I'm not sure who would disagree with you." Pilar's calm assessment didn't put Lizzie at all at ease. "There are very discreet noises of you being rejected by the pack, or refusing the position of Alpha Mate."

"And where the heck do people get this stuff?" She still couldn't believe anyone cared about what was going on in her life.

"Probably just assumptions made because you haven't met the Pack." Pilar dismissed such silly assumptions and went right for the interesting stuff. "Who's this Harry fellow? A new fan?"

"Cute, like I have a string of admirers. John would love that. Harry is the healer in charge of Sarah's care. And apparently a good friend of your son's. They went to boarding school together." Hadn't she just been thinking the magic-using community was by turns extremely large, then very small? This was one of those odd moments. Pilar lived in Mexico, but her son had attended boarding school in England—where he'd met a healer—who was now caring for a woman—who'd helped save Lizzie's life. How many degrees of separation was that?

"Ah. You mean Alistair Harrington." Pilar laughed. "I hadn't realized he was going by Harry. I suppose it makes sense. He's never been fond of his given name."

"Harrington—as in, our Harrington? IPPC's Harrington?" Lizzie was appalled. She'd practically interrupted the kid having sex. Perhaps that was a mild exaggeration. But still... awkward for him to be related to her boss.

"His nephew," Pilar clarified.

Lizzie winced. *A nephew? Really?* "I don't think so. I had a conversation with Harrington about Harry. He didn't say a word."

"Harrington's nephew is a healer, a very powerful and creative one. He's a great choice for handling Sarah's unique condition. And he went to boarding school with my son. They're still friends." Pilar took an audible breath. "He checked in with me. You know, afterwards, when I was home. He wanted to get as much information as possible for Sarah's treatment."

"That little twit. He didn't say a word about Harrington." Lizzie sighed. Typical. The interconnectivity of the magic-using community would eventually cease to surprise her, she was sure.

"In Alistair's...or Harry's defense, he's not particularly close to Harrington. Quite the opposite, in fact. I think there was some kind of argument they never resolved, or a falling out."

"I think I know what their argument might have been about." Lizzie remembered Harry commenting on Harrington's efforts to bring him officially into the IPPC's fold. "I'm not sure why I'm so annoyed, other than I'm tired of being the only one who doesn't know what's going on."

Pilar had taken up her chopping again. "It'll take some time, but until then—you've got friends who can help and answer questions."

"Thanks so much for your help, Pilar."

"No problem. Why don't you go ahead and plan to check in with me every day or two, just for the next few days," Pilar said.

"It's a date," Lizzie confirmed before she ended the call.

She was just about to consider herself sufficiently recharged to face the beginning of her ghost vigil, when the source of at least thirty-four percent of her stress ambled through the patio door.

CHAPTER TWENTY-ONE

"I hate to say this, because I am *not* running away—but I was just coming inside." Lizzie eyed John suspiciously.

"To start your ghost hunt?" he asked. He didn't look particularly worried. Or pissed. She peered a little closer. He actually looked calm, maybe even well rested. *Damn.* Had he grabbed a nap, she wondered grumpily. As if there was time for that...oh, he's Lycan. She forgot he didn't need as much sleep as her. *Bastard.*

"Not exactly—more a ghost wait. I'm planning to hang out in the Library, do some work, and see if the resident ghost happens to stop by while I'm there." Lizzie glanced at her cell. "And my dinner should be about ready to pick up. The kitchen folks were kind enough to make a tray."

"I understand you're spending a lot of time with Tavish," he said.

Lizzie thought about it. Had she been? Then she looked at him. "You're jealous? Seriously? Please tell me you're not."

"No. Well, not in the way you mean. If you needed help, I'd rather it be me." He shrugged.

"Tavish just happened to be on duty, and then I found out about his—" Lizzie looked up at John.

"His handicap?"

She raised her eyebrows at that. "Um, right. Because he's—?"

"Mammal-challenged?" John asked.

Lizzie just shook her head at that.

"Are you telling me he's a reptile? Because you've obviously never met the man, if you are." She stood up and headed to the patio door. "Let's head to the kitchen. My phone call was a little longer than I planned, and I'd like to get back to the Library quickly."

He opened the door for her, ushering her through first. "I'm saying if he breathes fire, has scales, and likes shiny objects, then he's not a duck."

Lizzie waved his ridiculous comments away. "You're just jealous that he can cook his own dinner in three seconds flat. The relevant point is that he and the rest of the Clan have been around awhile. And know a little about ghosts." She considered for a moment, then she said, "Do you want to keep me company in the Library while I wait? Tavish made a big fuss over me not being there by myself."

They'd just about reached the kitchen, but she stopped before entering. Turning to him, her tone accusatory, she said, "He totally filled you in. Asked you to keep an eye on me so I wouldn't be alone in the Library, didn't he?"

Calmly, John replied, "Yes."

"Am I twelve? I heard him. I have no desire to be thwacked on the head by a flying book. Or to bleed profusely, with no one in sight to help me. Geez."

"He told all of the security staff. And suggested a rotation so you'd never be alone in the room." John nodded toward the kitchen door, indicating they should continue. "He's doing his job."

She wrinkled her nose in consternation. "I'm a little sensitive where you're concerned. So if I'm overreacting, I'm totally blaming you."

A small, surprised laugh rumbled from his chest. "Sounds about right."

John insisted on carrying the tray. She didn't protest, because it was a lot of food. A lot. She looked again. *Ah.* The kitchen staff had planned for two. She sniffed in annoyance, then stopped herself. She'd normally appreciate it. It was just her recent hypersensitivity to being managed, to having decisions made for her, to having so many people—other than herself—concerned about her welfare.

Really, she thought, even if she was in a completely normal relationship, she'd be having a hard time giving up some of her independence. The fact that she was in a relationship with a sometimes control freak who was part-time alpha-macho made it harder. Could be worse, she thought. She could have fallen in love with a full-time controlling alpha overachiever. As it was, John tried really hard to be reasonable, even though she knew it wasn't always easy for him to see her side.

Once in the Library, food laid out on one of the three tables, Lizzie checked that her board was still in place, her pebble on top. John pulled something from his pocket and placed it on the board.

"Any objections?" he asked as he picked up the pebble and closed his fist around it.

Lizzie looked at his replacement, and shook her head. Apparently, Tavish hadn't spared the details of their earlier encounter. Because John had brought a small plastic poker chip to replace her stone.

He tucked the pebble into the front pocket of his jeans. "I thought about a cotton ball, or something made of cloth, but then our temperamental ghost couldn't throw it very far.

That might frustrate her. But this is slightly better than a pebble, and it should slide well."

It did, Lizzie saw right away. Because as soon as John placed the chip on the board it moved.

Yes

"Holy crap," Lizzie said. "It's only been an hour."

The chip slid back and forth over "yes."

As Lizzie was trying to suss out what that meant—maybe she was impatient?—John grabbed pen and paper. Lizzie made a guess.

"Can you only stay a short while in this room?"

The chip hopped on the "yes" word.

"Shoot—I haven't had time to prepare questions," she said frantically, looking at John. "I thought I'd have more time."

"Hey. Take a breath. If we have more questions, my bet is, um, Matylda?" A quick tap of the plastic chip on "yes" was the response. "Matylda will come back again."

The chip hopped up and down on "yes."

"Were we wrong? Did you not die in the Library?" Lizzie was concerned Matylda found the question of where she died upsetting, but something about her death was clearly important.

The chip moved toward "no" but never reached it, then it slipped back toward "yes." It moved back and forth between the two words.

Shit. What did that mean? Lizzie was not good under pressure. She was definitely brainstorming questions the second Matylda left, so she'd be prepared next time. "In this house?" she guessed.

Yes

"Is the location important? Should we spend time on this?"

The chip jumped up and down on "yes." Then it moved

rapidly to the letters. She glanced at John to see if he was ready, but he was well ahead of her.

S-A-R-A-H

Lizzie read the letters aloud as Matylda moved the chip so John could record it.

"Where you died has something to do with Sarah?" she asked.

The chip moved very slowly to "yes" but never quite made it.

"Not quite yes," she narrated for John. Lizzie thought frantically. "The place you died has something to do with Worth?"

The chip stayed near "yes" but moved a little further away. "Less accurate," she said quietly.

"The place you died…." Sarah was in a coma. They needed to figure out how to get Sarah out of the coma. "The place you died has something to do with a coma? With Sarah's condition?"

The chip moved slowly to yes.

She looked at John and saw he was catching everything. Okay. In the house, but not exactly the Library. But not excluding the Library. Freaking riddles. "Is the place you died near the Library?"

The chip hopped up and down on "yes." Then it moved to the letters.

F-A-D-E

"Fade? I don't understand."

The chip raced through a series of letters. Y-O-U-K-O-V-A-R-F-A-D-E

And then the chip sped through the air, impacting with the bookshelf.

"I don't understand," she said quietly, shaking her head. She was almost in tears, her frustration was so strong. Matylda was gone. Lizzie was learning to read both the feeling of her presence and her absence. She pushed out a rapid, angry breath.

John looked at her. "She's gone, I take it." He retrieved the chip. Or, more accurately, the pieces of the chip.

She nodded once, jerking her head. Pinching the bridge of her nose, she tried to keep herself from bawling. *Gah.* This was ridiculous. She had resources. They'd tear apart the encounter and dig up some kind of meaning. And she'd have more questions, better questions next time.

"Okay. The first thing we do is to sit here and come up with the questions we want to ask if"—she corrected herself firmly—"*when* she returns." She'd noticed that John's note-taking had been more than Matylda's spelled-out words.

"She must like a dramatic exit. Tavish said she did something similar last time. Threw the pebble. Dropped some books." He grabbed a bite of food while simultaneously clearing a spot to work. Wise man. They'd have to eat while they worked.

Then his comment sunk in. "She threw a pebble at the bookshelf. The same bookshelf as today. She knocked off several books. From the same bookshelf. And the night she startled me?" She frowned when John grinned at her understated description of the teen horror scream she'd let loose the night before. "Watch it, buddy. That night, the books came from the same bookshelf."

Lizzie ran to the door, poking her head out into the main basement room. She was in luck. Heike was back from dinner and tidying up her workspace for the evening.

"Heike. Can you help us?" Lizzie asked. "And do you know if Harrington is still in the building? He'll want an update on this."

"Sure. He's here. Do you want me to find him?" she asked, surprised. Likely because Lizzie was asking for her help.

Lizzie debated briefly, then decided Heike's insight might

prove useful. Looking at John, she said, "Do you mind? I might need Heike's expertise with the books."

"No problem." He turned to Heike. "No one should be in the Library proper alone. That includes you. You're familiar with the buddy system?" When she nodded tentatively, he continued. "Good. One of you leaves to go to the bathroom, the other waits in the main basement room."

Heike nodded. Her normal impassivity appeared to be breached. She looked a little worried. "What's happened?"

As John headed out the door, Lizzie explained. "Our resident ghost may have a little anger issue." Lizzie brought her up to date, both on the content of the exchanges and the violence with which the ghost had responded at times. "I think there's something going on with the bookshelf itself. We've been focused on the content of the books she's knocked off the shelves. But Matylda seems focused on a particular set of shelves. Each session is so short, I don't think she can clearly spell out the 'where' that is so important to her. And as her time starts to end, she gets frustrated. Or maybe spelling is harder because there's more movement and it wears her out faster."

At some point during the conversation, Heike had dropped into one of the chairs. She didn't look upset or overwhelmed, just a little tired.

"What do you think?" Lizzie asked.

"I think we need to move all the books," Heike said with grim determination as she stood up and approached the shelf in question.

"I was hoping you'd say that. Do we need to keep them in the same order?"

Heike cocked her head, thinking. Then she turned to one of the tables and picked up a clipboard with a laminated diagram of the shelves. "No. These have all been screened for basic content, but none have been thoroughly reviewed, categorized, or grouped yet."

Emme, the librarian, was still creating a unique numbering system for the Library. So even books with translated titles that had been roughly grouped together into categories hadn't been labeled yet.

"All right then. Let's do this," Lizzie said, making the final decision. And the two women started moving the books.

CHAPTER TWENTY-TWO

Heike and Lizzie were about halfway done when John returned with Harrington. Harrington raised his eyebrows slightly and patiently waited for an explanation.

Lizzie explained her theory about "where" being the important message Matylda had been trying to convey. Harrington said, "Let's get the rest down. It can't hurt to have a look."

They decided to empty the shelf up to the point at which it joined another series of shelves. It didn't take long with three of them working. Harrington was busy studying the notes from the encounter.

When they'd finished with the books, Lizzie said, "We need to have a series of questions prepared. She's caught us unprepared twice now. I'm sure we can make more efficient use of her time if we have a list."

Harrington nodded briefly. "As soon as we've examined the shelving."

Walking to the shelves, Harrington began by examining the seams visually. An hour later, the four searchers were frustrated and stumped. No mechanical triggers could be found. No false shelves. No encoded message on the shelving. The shelving itself couldn't be removed without tools. Harrington—rumored to be excellent at warding—hadn't spied a ward.

Most wards could be easily seen. The caster had to attach the ward to some physical object, and it was these points of attachment that were most easily detected. Unless the caster used sophisticated methods intended to obscure the ward—a reasonable assumption in this case. Even then, a talented caster—like Harrington—could identify a hidden ward. So long as the caster actually *looked*.

Harrington had looked. Then he'd utilized this opportunity as a teaching moment for Lizzie. "You're here to learn, so learn."

What followed was a minor dissertation on warding that Lizzie was still trying to wrap her brain around fifteen minutes into the lecture.

She wrinkled her nose. "Couldn't you give me the Cliff's Notes version?" When Harrington responded with a disdainful look, Lizzie altered her approach. "Maybe I can summarize, and you can tell me if I've got it."

"Certainly." Harrington settled into one of the chairs scattered around a worktable.

"Okay, so first I find my magic. Then I formulate a clear picture in my mind. In this case, since I'm looking for warding on a large, solid object, I should create a net that drapes like fabric. I then envision that net covering the surfaces that I'm scanning. Any contact between the net and a ward will create a reaction." Lizzie stopped to gauge Harrington's reaction. Mostly to see if her magic-made-easy explanation would pass muster.

Harrington gave her a bland look and said, "Try it."

So she did. She carefully crafted a fine mesh net—but not too fine, because that needlessly ate up too much magical juice, per Harrington. Then she mentally cast that net over the now bare shelving. The push, or application of will, that drove the cast she accomplished with a hefty shove.

That shove was apparently a small miscalculation. In the moment her cast took hold and became visible, it was clear she'd made an error. Harrington's sensing wards had a bright glow—hers was blinding. Something she could clearly see from her vantage point on the ground. The moment she'd pushed, she'd felt a recoil strong enough to land her on her ass.

As she blinked and tried to determine where she'd gone wrong, she registered Harrington's quiet laugh in the background.

"I'll work on the assumption that you knew that wouldn't actually be dangerous," John spoke in a quietly clear voice.

Lizzie blinked dazedly at the bright light, now slightly faded. Since she wasn't looking at John, she could only guess that he was directing that comment at Harrington.

She looked at the hand Harrington extended to her, narrowed her eyes, then grasped it. Once on her feet again, she asked, "Okay—where did I go wrong?"

"Finesse is preferred to power when casting a sensing ward. Especially when a caster has your power and chooses to cast over such a large area." He raised his eyebrows at her. "Which I was trying to explain when you became bored and decided to hurry the process along."

Rather than addressing his criticism, she decided to move their search along. "I didn't see any wards."

"You wouldn't need to see them, because any ward near the bookcase would probably have singed you given the wattage you employed. And if there was a trap, you would certainly have triggered it." Disapproval rang in his voice.

"But you knew there weren't any traps." Lizzie blinked at her ward again. It was finally assuming the same glowing quality of Harrington's wards rather than the brilliance of an interrogation spotlight.

"I knew there weren't," Harrington agreed.

John and Heike were discussing methods for checking the interior of the wall, whether the shelving should be removed and, finally, if the wall should be knocked down.

At this last pronouncement, made by John, Lizzie piped up. "Have you considered, maybe, that I'm wrong? We've looked, and nothing is there. And it's not like I'm sure." Her tone became exasperated. "You can't tear an entire wall down. Especially not based on a guess."

"We can. But you shouldn't have to." Lachlan had stepped into the room so quietly that his statement was the first indication Lizzie had he'd joined them.

She was surprised it had taken him so long to investigate. At one point, they'd made a racket knocking on walls and shelving, listening for some small change in the sound.

"What exactly do you suggest?" John asked.

"No suggestions. I'm merely stating a fact. If there is something behind the shelving— and I suspect there is— there had to be a way to get to it. Did your ghost give no message hinting at the answer?" Lachlan raised his dark eyebrows.

Harrington responded to the question, which was a good thing. Lizzie was certain his familiarity with the notes would be more valuable and yield a more accurate picture than her muddled recollection. "F-A-D-E. She repeated it, so I assume it has some significance." He lifted his gaze from the paper in his hand to Lizzie. "Any idea what that means?"

"I haven't a clue," Lizzie said. She caught Lachlan out of the corner of her eye—a broad grin, flashing white teeth, and a mischievous twinkle in his eye. He was certainly entertained by the unfolding events.

"What's so entertaining?" Lizzie wasn't about to miss out on the joke.

"Fade. It's an archaic term for something known more commonly today as teleportation. Very rare and found in only a few caster families." Before Lizzie could wrap her head around the existence of yet another freaky magic ability, Lachlan began pointing out the various possibilities. "There's an exit or a passageway only accessible from the Library via teleportation—fade, if you will. Or, perhaps a secret chamber used to house prisoners. Perhaps our ghost is no Kovar, but a prisoner left by the Kovars to die within the walls."

"Seriously? Do you try to sound creepy and weird? Or does it just come out that way?" Lizzie was surprised that thought had escaped and not stayed firmly in her head. But really. The guy was giving her massive chills. Just the thought of a dead body trapped in the walls. Slowly starving. Dying of dehydration. And all while inside what was likely a tiny cell. *Ick.*

Lachlan seemed unoffended. He'd lost the grin, but still looked faintly amused. Who was this guy?

Ignoring Lizzie, Harrington commented dryly, "Of those, I'd opt for an exit. Strategically it makes sense that there's another way out." He followed that train of thought to the next logical conclusion. "And if that's the case, then the other message from the ghost is a pronouncement and a command. You, Lizzie, are a Kovar. And as such, should have the ability to fade. Or so the ghost believes." He turned to her, waiting for a response.

"Tavish thought it not unlikely that I'm related." Lizzie scrunched her nose up. "But I haven't had time to look into it. My parents wouldn't know, so we're talking research. And I haven't even had time to do a simple online search. I've been busy," she said defensively. Sounding a little huffy, she added, "I could really use an assistant, these days. All this magic stuff is really time-consuming."

"Not really," Heike said. "I think it's just you."

Lizzie frowned at Heike. Was she calling Lizzie a trouble magnet? Because this crazy drama stuff found her, not the other way around. She had slowly been softening toward Heike, but she'd have to seriously rethink her position.

John looked concerned. "There's a flaw here that no one has considered. If Matylda wants Lizzie to fade to the location, how can that happen? Even assuming she is a Kovar, and even assuming that the talent has remained true throughout several intervening generations—she can't teleport somewhere she's never been and can't see. That would be suicidal."

"Shit." Lizzie dropped down into one of the chairs. She'd bet she was pale. She *felt* pale.

Every head in the room turned to her. "*Worth* can teleport. If it's really that rare, and I'm actually a Kovar...." A nasty thought intruded. "Please tell me I'm not related to that, that—" She felt sick.

John was pushing her head down in between her knees. Lizzie could have sworn he was on the opposite side of the room no more than a second ago.

"What are you doing?" It came out muffled, since she was speaking to the floor.

John's hand lightly massaged the back of her neck. "You're white as a sheet. And seeing you pass out once was more than enough for a lifetime, thank you."

She hadn't realized that she'd gone all clammy. But a slight swoosh of air passed by, catching on her damp skin. Goose bumps popped up immediately. She tipped her head slightly to the side. Tavish had joined them, hence the mild draft as he'd opened the door. *Great. More witnesses.*

Hadn't John mentioned passing out? Nuh-uh. "I don't do

that anymore. My magic's all in harmony now, or whatever Harry said. You know what I mean." Her protest was mild at best. More an explanation than a protest, because his warm hand on her neck, his body close to hers, was making her feel less like she wanted to puke her guts up. *Wow. That was romantic.* She might keep that thought to herself.

"Uh-huh." The gentle but firm massaging on her neck didn't stop.

Heike interrupted her thoughts with a no-nonsense observation. "We don't know. These conclusions are simply conjecture, based upon not one known fact. Until we know if you're a Kovar, how many families have the fade ability, if you can fade—there's simply no point in assuming the worst."

Interesting. Heike was apparently on board with everyone's evaluation of Worth as a super-evil, way-bad dude. Lizzie liked that. It had a nicer ring than mastermind, which seemed to give him too much credit. It was a helpful discovery, insofar as it might help Lizzie to believe Heike wasn't a cooperating and fully participating member of Worth's gang.

She covered John's hand with her own, squeezed once in thanks, then moved to sit up. "I'm good."

Lachlan seemed unconcerned, but mildly curious. "Worth used teleportation to escape?" He gave Harrington a quick side-glance. "I wasn't aware."

Harrington remained silent.

Lizzie slipped Harrington an annoyed look. "I'm confused. Wasn't that in the report? Worth disappeared, and Frank—our healer—picked him up again in a neighboring house. It should have been in the report." Lizzie knew the IPPC had recorded all of the information. Why didn't the head of security—temporary though he might be—have all of that information?

"There were certain aspects of the case that we decided

required further investigation. That was one of them." That was Harrington—no apologies.

"Is there a way to prevent someone from teleporting into an area?" John asked. He rubbed his jaw thoughtfully. "I'm thinking about our perimeter security."

Harrington said, "The distance Worth seems to have traveled is very short. It's possible it was a function of his weakened state, but more likely it's a limitation of the talent."

Tavish and Lachlan murmured words of assent.

"What little I've seen has been short distances. No more than twenty feet, certainly. Probably less." Tavish seemed certain.

After a short consultation, the men seemed to be in agreement that there was minimal security risk from teleportation unless Worth could boost the distance significantly from any historically known teleportation attempt. There were multiple perimeter wards and physical security barriers in place at points in excess of twenty feet from the walls of the house.

Lizzie waved at the group of men. "We need to come up with questions for Matylda, before she returns. Clearly, she thinks she can help with Sarah. I couldn't be more thrilled, if that's true, and I'm pretty sure she's going to keep coming back until we get the message." She looked around the group. "I'm not sure about you guys, but I'd eventually like to get some sleep. And we'll be here all night at the rate we're going."

Heike nodded in John's direction. "He had a good question. You can't teleport to a place you can't see and haven't been before. Or if you can, you don't how to do it safely."

Tavish said, "How can Lizzie teleport to an unseen location?" Heike nodded and wrote it down.

Lizzie raised her hand. "Um—I can't teleport, remember? We need to tell her that. And what about an alternative entrance?" She perked up. "Wait a minute. If it's an escape route, there's another side. A passage or tunnel has at least two access points. Maybe we can find the other end."

And avoid a gruesome end to a, thus far, much too short existence. But she kept that thought to herself.

Heike spoke as she wrote. "Alternative exit—got it. Lizzie cannot fade, or doesn't know how."

And, naturally, a stack of books fell over with a loud crash.

CHAPTER TWENTY-THREE

"Are you kidding me?" Lizzie practically yelled. She didn't think she was the only one to jump at the loud noise.

There was a tapping noise coming from the table with the board. All six of the room's occupants moved to surround the table. John and Tavish quickly cleared everyone away from the side of the table near the heavily targeted shelf.

The source of the tapping was the tip of a pen, hitting the "no" word repeatedly.

Heike interpreted for anyone who missed Matylda's meaning. "She's not kidding."

And the resident ghost had a sense of humor. Either that or she was really annoyed with them. Or with Lizzie.

Heike shoved the short list at Lizzie. But Lizzie shook her head and quietly murmured, "Thanks." Two questions she could do on her own.

"You want me to fade to the other side of the wall?" Her tone was clipped, almost angry. She had to remind herself that Matylda wasn't the problem. Their limited communication was.

Yes

"I can't fade."

No. The pen thwacked the word on the board.

"You're telling me I can?"

Yes, yes, yes. The pen tapped lightly three times in quick succession.

"How?"

F-O-L-L-O-W

"Sure. I just follow a ghost, who I can't see—eek!" Lizzie was being pushed, no, pulled. But not with hands. Then she felt a soft tug deep inside, like her magic wanted to grab onto something, someone. Matylda?

Lizzie panicked. Was this what Worth had done? He'd grabbed Sarah's magic and pulled it from her body. She could hear a growling noise, as if from a very long way away—John. If she was this frightened, he was surely seeing red.

But then she felt the most amazing sensation. It was as if she was twining fingers with Matylda, even though Matylda had no hands. Like their magic touched and intertwined. It was intimate like a close hug, but not invasive. And she could feel, she wasn't sure what, but something from Matylda. Comfort? Reassurance? It was warm and pleasant.

When Matylda tugged at her magic, it was a polite question: follow me?

Remember the rules, Lizzie reminded herself. She had to find her magic, pull it to the surface so that it was ready to be used. Matylda had done that for her. Something Lizzie had never experienced before. That was what had so frightened her. She thought that Matylda was taking her magic, but she was simply calling it and mingling it with her own.

Next she imagined very clearly in her mind the connection between Matylda and herself. Or maybe she was seeing it? Then she formed a clear picture of what she wanted to happen. She didn't know where she was going, so she cleared her mind of a destination and thought only of Matylda. Of the feel of Matylda's magic. Of the connection remaining strong and intertwined.

Finally, she willed that into being.

And that's how magic worked.

She lost the sensation of intertwining magic, and slowly became aware that she was back. She hadn't been aware that she'd been gone, but now, now the reality of her surroundings intruded. She'd been drifting. She wondered how long. She couldn't hear John. She was sure she'd heard him before—

She realized suddenly that she was cold. Her fleece jacket was insufficient to ward off the suddenly lowered temperature. She tried to open her eyes and blinked. They *were* open. A tiny kernel of fear began to unfurl in her chest. It was dark, incredibly dark. Where the hell was she? She thought frantically back. What exactly had she done?

Oh my god. I'm in the wall. What the hell had she been thinking? And where was Matylda? And where *the hell* was the light? She hadn't moved. She'd been disoriented at first, then paralyzed by fear. If she took a step, what would she find?

She could feel herself getting light-headed. Her fear turning to full-blown panic. Her breath was coming in short gasps. She could not pass out. Not here. There was no one to save her, wherever she was.

No one but her, dammit. She tried to slow her racing thoughts. Her breathing was next. She tried desperately not to think about whether there was any ventilation. The space felt small and close to her. The air stale, with a sickly sweet taste. Light. She needed light. How could she make light? Wards shone brightly when they were viewed through her magical lens.

She tried to detect any existing wards. No luck. She dug

in her pocket for a handkerchief. Her mother made them for her, so she could hardly insult her mom and the environment by using tissues—could she? She found the tiny bit of embroidered linen stuffed in her jeans pocket. She took it out and unfolded it, thought for a second, then cast one of the few wards she was familiar with. A sensing ward may not be that helpful when attached to a small bit of cloth, but like any ward, it lit up and provided a small light source. Having just learned and practiced sensing wards, she created one attached to the hanky—carefully.

Lizzie's breath caught so suddenly that she choked, gasping for air. Matylda. Or what was left of her. Lizzie wasn't sure how she knew, but she was certain. An overwhelming sadness engulfed her. Matylda had died in this room, all alone.

The very faint, sickly sweet smell that had nagged at her and caught in the back of her throat took on a more sinister cast—human decomp. She shook herself. *She* wasn't dying in this room. She turned her attention to her surroundings. She'd find a way out. And if not, by damned, they'd beat that wall down until she was out. She knew her wolf. He wouldn't leave her in here.

She could just make out four walls. The ward was bright but didn't illuminate very far. She squinted and calculated. The room couldn't be more than six feet by six feet. She scanned quickly past Matylda's remains, propped partially in a chair. Behind the chair was a very small table. Lizzie forced herself to take a step closer. The ward light was bright but didn't illuminate like a lantern, outward in an even wash of light. And speak of the devil. Not a lantern, but a candle. She lit it using the flint left on the table. It took several tries, but she finally had a tiny flame.

And wouldn't you know, behind the table, illuminated

now by the candles glow, was a niche in the wall with several books. Lizzie wondered now about the dry air in the small chamber. Did that occur naturally? Or had the mysterious Kovar family done something to the chamber to make it more hospitable for the few books stored here? She cast a quick glance at Matylda. And maybe that was why she appeared to be mostly intact. Her skin was stretched and tight. She looked small and shrunken, with small bits of cloth clinging to her body and scattered around her on the ground. Lizzie's eyes welled with tears. *Oh, Matylda. What happened to you?*

Lizzie wiped at the faint wet marks on her cheeks. Now wasn't the time to be crying. Especially not over Matylda, gone a hundred or more years now. Speaking of—where the hell was she? She'd brought Lizzie here and then disappeared. Maybe Matylda had been exhausted by the effort? That didn't seem right. Lizzie thought back to her first fade. And "fade" was the right word. Teleport, her ass. She'd simply drifted or faded away. Then she was back again—but somewhere else. She still wasn't sure that she actually had the talent. Matylda had played a huge role. Lizzie certainly wasn't keen to try it on her own. What if she faded away and didn't come back? Her whole body shivered at the thought, starting with a creep in her scalp and then slithering down her back.

But she was pretty confident that it was *her* magic that got her here. Matylda did the driving, but Lizzie was the engine. So Matylda shouldn't have exhausted herself. And suddenly, she was there. Lizzie could feel her presence.

"You scared me like you wouldn't believe, Matylda. I hope that wasn't your intent." Lizzie didn't expect an answer. So when a small object nudged at her hand and fell to the ground, she was surprised. She kneeled down and retrieved it. A sapphire ring with diamond accents, Lizzie guessed. A gift? Meant as an apology? No. *Aha.* Just like the pebble and the poker chip—a small, easily moveable object.

"All right, Matylda. But if you throw this anywhere near me, you'll do some damage. So be careful."

She thought for a moment, then—carefully moving past Matylda's remains—she grabbed the books from the niche above the desk. She counted them. Seven books, of varying sizes and colors. Moving as far from the desk and Matylda as she could, she created two stacks of books. The stack on the left was low, with the three thinnest books. The stack on the right held the remaining books and was taller. She placed the candle in between the two stacks. Then she thought a moment and grabbed one of the books off the low stack, making it even lower. Flipping quickly through the book, she settled on a page and placed it typeface up, open on the ground.

"All right, Matylda. What do you think about this? The left, low stack is 'no.' The right, high stack is 'yes.' And we can try the open pages for spelling out answers." Before Lizzie had finished explaining, the ring was resting on the 'yes' stack.

"Excellent." Lizzie thought for a moment, then decided on some basic details first. "Are you here in this room when you're not in the Library?"

Yes.

"Does it tire you to speak with me or to interact with people by moving objects?"

No. No. No.

Lizzie interrupted the tapping of the ring on the low stack by placing her cupped hand over it. "I got it. I'm sorry, Matylda. We thought you were leaving the Library because you were tired."

The ring bumped up against her hand. Lizzie lifted her hand away.

No.

"Why are there no stories about you? Why didn't you speak with anyone before?"

The ring moved back and forth between the two stacks, then went to the open book.

Lizzie realized it would be easier if she used yes and no questions. But in her enthusiasm for answers, she'd forgotten.

"Sorry. Did you try to speak with anyone before?"

Yes.

Interesting. There weren't any stories that she could find about the house being haunted. "Did they understand?"

No. The ring moved to the book and stopped with the plain band curved around an 'm' that was starting a sentence. G-I-K followed.

"Magic?"

No.

"Not magic?

Yes.

Lizzie was confused. If the word wasn't magic, then—one possible meaning became clear.

"The people you tried to speak with were not magic-users?"

Yes. Yes.

"Oh, my. I can just imagine that."

Yes. Yes.

Was that a little bit of humor showing through? Lizzie realized her candle was noticeably lower. She felt as though no time at all had passed, but this method of communication was very slow. John had to be worried. No, he'd be too pissed to be worried—and probably at her. She sighed. While technically this wasn't her fault, she was starting to see a pattern.

"I think we need to hurry. They'll be tearing the wall down soon, if we're not careful." She was concerned the men would act in haste, fearful she wasn't safe. But the panic she'd felt earlier was almost completely gone, lost amidst the sadness she felt for Matylda and the challenge the unraveling of a tricky problem presented.

Lizzie considered her next question. She needed to focus more on the core questions of Sarah—and how to leave. "The books are what can help Sarah?"

Yes. Yes. Yes. The ring tapped three times in quick succession.

"Can I bring the books out with me?"

Yes. Then the ring moved away slowly.

Huh. I can but...? Lizzie thought.

"These are especially important books?"

Yes. But again, the ring moved away.

Why would these particular books be here? Hidden so very well? Hidden from Worth and men like him, surely. But that was true of the whole Library. So maybe there was something else. Lizzie reached for the volume resting topmost on the right stack. As her hand touched it, she saw a thin volume in the other stack move—the book second from the top— and push out away from the stack. Lizzie slipped Matylda's choice out of the stack.

She opened the book, trying to get a feel for it. She asked the book if it had a name, and, receiving no response, then asked about the content of the book. She received an unexpected response. Instead of a series of words, she experienced a wash of images in rapid succession. Finally, one word, overlaid with all of the emotion of a young, terrified adolescent girl—the caster who had recorded the images, Lizzie believed—Vampyr.

Lizzie placed the book back on the stack, but her hand didn't leave the book and the images continued to replay over and over in her mind. She sank slowly to the floor, her knees finding the ground, and her butt coming to rest on her heels. The images the young caster had recorded were infinitely more terrifying than the corpse that rested less than three feet from Lizzie. Blood washed across the bodies of a family. Father, mother, an elderly woman, and a small girl of perhaps five or six years. The rough clothes they wore were from several centuries past and were ripped and fouled with blood. Not with the bright red blood of a movie set, but a crusted brown. Red-tinged where thicker, sticky pools had collected. Duller and darker, where the blood was thin and streaked.

The images in her mind were made more horrific by the layers of emotion wrapped around each picture. The love the young caster had felt for her slain family. The gripping terror evoked by the torn flesh of her father's throat—a man she'd always believed powerful and capable of protecting her. The haunting guilt associated with the smallest form. Her baby sister, intended to accompany the caster on her market trip but left home at the last moment.

A sharp, stinging pain in Lizzie's hand brought her back to the present. Glancing down, she saw a small scratch, angry red but only barely weeping blood, had appeared on her left hand. The beautiful sapphire ring was inches away. She let out a long slow breath and looked at the remaining stub of candle. How long had she been lost in those images?

"Thank you, Matylda. These books are dangerous in some way." It wasn't a question, but Matylda responded, nonetheless.

Yes.

"I'll make sure everyone is warned. These are the books Worth was looking for?"

Lizzie waited. The ring didn't move.

"Are you still here?"

Yes.

"Do you *know* if these are books Worth was searching for?"

No.

"I'd like to leave now, Matylda. Do I leave the same way I came?"

No.

Well, shit. And Lizzie couldn't think of a yes and no way to get instructions. *Crap.* Could Matylda get her back? "Do you know how I can leave?"

Yes.

Lizzie couldn't help but breathe a sigh of relief. Okay, so there was just a communication problem. And not much candle left. Lizzie quickly checked the small desk for another. *Damn. Of course not.*

The ring caught the candlelight briefly as it moved to the open book on the floor.

L-I-B-R-R-I

"Library?"

Yes.

S-E-E

Please let that mean what I think it does.

"Are you telling me to visualize the Library?"

Yes.

"Then will my being there again?"

Yes.

"But you won't—" What exactly had Matylda done before? Commingled their magic? "—do whatever you did before? Because I think it was you who moved us here, right?"

No.

Lizzie frowned in confusion.

L-I-S-S-I

"*Me?*"

Yes.

If she tried and couldn't fade at all—no problem. A long wait for a wrecking crew, but otherwise no problem. But if she tried, faded, and couldn't come back—that was a horrific thought.

Lizzie's breaths started to come more quickly. She could do this. She could. "I can't do this."

The ring nudged at the ring finger of her right hand. Lizzie smiled. She slipped it over her knuckle and firmly onto her finger. She couldn't be sure what it meant, but she would take that as a showing of solidarity. Matylda was with her in this.

She pulled her fleece jacket over her head and wrapped up the seven books, creating a sling-type carrier. Then Lizzie twisted the ring so that she could feel the stones on the inside of her tightly clenched fist. Closing her eyes, she recreated an image of the Library. The three tables, angled to create a rough approximation of a triangle. Books strewn on the floor, mostly in stacks but not all. Wooden chairs scattered around the tables haphazardly. The remaining walls covered with neatly shelved books, floor to ceiling. John. The grumbling, low growl of dismay she'd heard as she'd left.

She was ready. She had a firm sense of place etched in her mind. She let out a slow, calm breath and released the magic she'd been pulling to the surface as she pictured her destination. Her last thought before she pushed—or, as Pilar had once explained it, applied her will—was of John, waiting for her to return.

She didn't experience the sensation of drifting that she'd had the last time. She was with Matylda, the candle sputtering, about to go out. Then—she was with John near the base of the basement stairs. Previously, she'd drifted away and then when she was back it was like waking from a dream. Slowly becoming aware of her surroundings. But this time, it was as if she'd blinked, and when she opened her eyes, John was there. And with his arms around her, holding her so tight she almost couldn't breathe.

As soon as John had loosened his hold a bit, she said, "What the hell?" She blinked, looking around her at a room that was clearly not the Library. She'd overshot by a few hundred feet, if she had to guess. *Uh, oh.* More than twenty feet. Much more than twenty feet. They needed to reevaluate those security plans.

"How did I end up here?" Farther than Lachlan or Tavish thought it possible to fade?

CHAPTER TWENTY-FOUR

"I think that's my line," John said. "As well as, where the hell have you been?" He pitched his voice low, almost whispering the words, trying to keep the rage that was so close to the surface from coloring his speech. "And are you all right?"

With the last question, he set her slightly away from him and gave her a thorough inspection. She *looked* unharmed. He made an effort to slow his pulse and calm his wolf.

Before Lizzie could respond to his question, Tavish, Lachlan, and Harrington poured through the door connecting the Library with the main basement room. Their faces displayed varying degrees of concern, Harrington clearly the most agitated. As he should be. Lizzie was his employee. He was her mentor. And he likely knew a good portion of the rage pouring off John just a few minutes earlier was directed at him.

John picked up Lizzie's jacket from the floor. She'd dropped it as soon as she'd appeared—literally out of thin air—in front of him. Partially untying the bundle, he glanced inside. "This is what you were looking for?"

Lizzie looked uncertain. "Maybe." She shook her head,

like she was confused or shaking off something unpleasant. "Matylda certainly thinks so."

"What did you find?" Harrington asked as he arrived on the heels of Lachlan and Tavish.

"Seven books stored in a small cell. Matylda thinks they're particularly dangerous, so I have strict instructions to make sure they're kept safe."

Tavish asked, "From Matylda?"

"Yes. She communicates well enough if you give her an opportunity." She turned to Harrington. "At least one is related to Sarah's situation but I'm not sure how." Lizzie's brow furrowed in concentration, creating tiny wrinkles in her forehead that John wanted to smooth away.

"What do you know about Vampyr?" Lizzie asked.

Lizzie and he had joked a few times about what was out in the world. If there were Lycan and spell casters, then maybe there were other things that go bump in the night. Clearly, that was true. John eyed Lachlan and Tavish. He'd learned about a number of magic-user types with talents he'd never suspected, all within a matter of weeks. True, Lycan were notoriously self-interested and exclusionary, but it was still surprising his Pack had been so ignorant of the outside magical world. John was more progressive and interested in outsiders than many of his brethren, and he planned to yank the whole lot of them with him as he became more aware of other talents and other communities—assuming he survived whatever challenges were brewing. The IPPC, or organizations like it, were the future. But *vampires*? That had only ever been a joke between them.

As informed as Harrington could sometimes be about matters in the magic-using community, this smelled of ancient history to him. He glanced at the aged texts, then directed his statement to Lachlan. "Tell me Vampires are a myth."

"What's a myth? Are there inaccurate stories circulating both within and outside the magical community of blood-drinking creatures? I think you know there will always be such stories." Lachlan hesitated briefly before delivering the bad news. "Sadly, there is some basis in fact."

"I'm not sure what Vampyr have to do with this. The attack I saw was nothing like what happened to Sarah. There was blood, quite a lot of blood." Lizzie shuddered suddenly, as if the words she'd spoken had just registered. She'd been cold since she'd arrived in the basement—easy enough to see from the goose bumps. But as he held her, it felt like her body temperature had just dropped three degrees.

After shoving against him as if she could steal his warmth, she returned to her main point. "But Matylda was quite insistent that the Vampyr book was important."

"I'm not so sure," Heike added. She'd been on the stairs, a tray in her hands, waiting to rejoin the group. At the sound of her voice, Lizzie jumped. John pulled her tighter against his side and rubbed her arm.

He looked at her closely, trying to decide if he should encourage her to head up to bed or if that would be a tactical error.

Before he could decide, she leaned in and said quietly, her voice barely a whisper, "I'm fine."

Heike finished her descent down the stairs, pausing by Lizzie and muttering, "Sorry," under her breath.

As she set the tray down, she said again, "I'm not so sure that the attacks were so different." She glanced quickly at Lizzie. "Assuming what you read—"

Lizzie interrupted her. "Saw. The spell captured images, except for the word Vampyr."

Heike looked intrigued, but she didn't pursue it. "What you read was similar to popular culture stereotypes? The consumption of blood by a fanged creature?"

"It was more of a sense of the events. I only saw the aftermath. The little girl who recorded the images wasn't there for the attack, and only recorded what she saw when she discovered the bodies." Lizzie turned away from John to gather up her fleece, quickly pulling it over her head.

Harrington asked, "Can you describe the scene?"

Head emerging from her fleece, Lizzie nodded. "Large gashes in the corpses. And wounds with ragged edges, as if the flesh had been torn away. I thought there was a lot of blood, but I realize now it was smeared across the bodies. There should have been pools of blood. There were a few very small patches that hadn't dried entirely, but none were large." Lizzie was losing some of her color as she spoke. John wasn't sure he had the patience for much more of this. He wanted her in bed, wrapped in his arms, asleep, with the images of death and blood no longer troubling her. "I didn't process it consciously at the time. I must have realized on some level what that meant, because when the word Vampyr was introduced, I wasn't surprised."

Heike said, "It's bothered me ever since I was briefed on the kidnapping. With the exception of the blood, isn't what Worth did *exactly* the same as a vampire? He siphoned off Sarah's magic, ingesting it like food—just like any parasite that feeds off a host organism." John thought that Heike looked ill at ease speaking to the small group clustered around her, but she pushed on. "Perhaps that's the connection Matylda wants us to see?"

Lachlan said, "And for additional motivation, there were men who believed that consuming the blood of their recently slain enemies would imbue them with the enemies' gifts."

"Drink the blood of a dying Lycan, acquire the ability to become a wolf? That's ludicrous." John's arm never moved from around Lizzie as he spoke, and he kept his voice even and calm.

But he was disturbed by the dragon's revelation. He could still feel the agony of separation as Worth had begun to drag his wolf—the embodiment of his magic—clawing and frantic, from his body. Even though Lizzie had interrupted Worth, there had still been a moment of despair when he feared he wouldn't be able to change. That he'd lost that part of himself. Perhaps, then, not such a ludicrous statement.

Lachlan watched John for several seconds before he replied. "Perhaps."

"Lizzie's exhausted. We'll debrief more fully tomorrow, after everyone has had a chance to rest. And then we can discuss next steps." After he made the announcement, it occurred to him belatedly that he hadn't called this meeting. Harrington could fire his ass if he had a problem with it.

John was contemplating the logistics of being an ex-Library employee while living in the house during Lizzie's internship, when Harrington said, "That sounds like an excellent plan."

Harrington had been making what John considered to be questionable management decisions—withholding from Lizzie the fact of Heike's employment, hiring the Dragon Clan and failing to disclose their particular talents, withholding several key points of the kidnapping from Lachlan. Harrington had too many agendas that didn't coincide with John's. It was a pleasant change to see Harrington's agenda briefly align with his own.

Looking down at Lizzie, he could see her lids drooping in exhaustion, and she was blinking frequently, as if she couldn't hold her eyes open. He debated momentarily, then shook his head, deciding against picking her up and hauling her off to their bedroom. Instead, he said, "Ready?"

She nodded, then turned and said, "Night," to the group.

He tugged gently on her hand as he walked up the stairs. She followed behind, feet dragging.

"Why am I so exhausted, all of a sudden?" she asked.

"Because you've been going nonstop, didn't get much sleep last night, and apparently had an unpleasant experience with Matylda." He paused. Deciding again that less was more, he said, "Let me know if you want to talk about it."

She nodded. They'd reached the top of the stairs. She turned to him and asked, "How much of a weenie does it make me that I want you to carry me the rest of the way?"

He didn't answer, just swung her up into his arms and hugged her tight to his chest. Even in the lamplight, he could see that the pinkish undertones of her complexion were still washed away. The unnatural paleness combined with the purplish smudges under her eyes to make her look particularly vulnerable. He shifted her slightly in his arms, but she didn't wake. She'd fallen asleep almost as soon as he'd settled her in his arms.

As John settled Lizzie in bed, he removed her shoes and clothes, but she still didn't wake. John knew she'd been running full speed all day, but she was unnaturally quiet and still. He climbed into bed next to her, and pulled her into his arms. He was somewhat reassured when she rolled onto her side and snuggled closer. But even then, she seemed diminished and drained.

Holding her slight frame close, in that moment he couldn't help but think how very small she was. He smiled slightly. She would disagree. But she was small and so human, with human frailties. He couldn't ever remember wishing Lizzie other than she was, but now he wished she had the physical strength and healing ability of a Lycan.

Matylda had come back as soon as Lizzie had disappeared. Wise ghost. A room full of some of the more powerful magic-users in the community—no telling what they would have done had she not conveyed Lizzie's safe arrival and imminent return. Visions of an impromptu demolition in the Library aside, John had been truly frightened. He couldn't forget the horror of seeing Lizzie literally fade from sight.

He bent down and nuzzled her neck, breathing in the warm, womanly smell of her. Letting out a slow breath, he remembered how frustrated he'd felt. He couldn't follow her. He couldn't protect her. He didn't even know what the dangers were. Why was it he only ever felt any sense of inadequacy or inability when it came to Lizzie? Protecting and caring for her was a full-time job. In the short time he'd known her, she'd been a walking magnet for magical mayhem. He sighed. She needed someone to have her back.

He fell asleep amidst his worry for Lizzie and the nagging thought that the distance between the hidden chamber and the basement stairs where Lizzie had reappeared was well beyond the twenty feet the dragons believed maxed out teleportation skill. Clearly Lizzie was unique, but what did it mean that she'd so far exceeded the anticipated scope of teleportation?

CHAPTER TWENTY-FIVE

Lizzie woke feeling stiff and disoriented. And sore. Her whole body ached, like she was recovering from a fever. For a brief moment, she thought she'd been sick. Then she remembered that yesterday had been a long day; she was just tired.

Just as she was starting to consider the idea of getting out of bed, John came back in the room with—Frank? The healer? He'd helped to rescue Lizzie when Worth held her, but what was he doing here now? Why did she need a healer? Maybe she had been sick?

"You're awake." John eyes lit up when he saw her. He sounded relieved. And surprised. Thrilled, even.

Lizzie looked more closely at him. His face looked drawn and tired. He hadn't shaved, and he had on the same clothes he'd worn last night. What the hell had been happening?

"What's going on?" she croaked. *Yuck.* Her mouth was all dry and cottony, her throat parched. She cleared her throat and licked her lips. "What time is it?"

Before he answered, John poured her a glass of water from a carafe on the nightstand. Handing it to her he replied,

"Two—in the afternoon." He spoke curtly. He seemed a little angry, but Lizzie knew he wasn't angry with her.

She rubbed her eyes, but she stopped immediately when she felt the dry, gritty residue. *Ugh.* It was a good thing she wasn't worried about John's feelings for her. Otherwise, she'd be feeling pretty damn self-conscious right now. Scratch that. She was feeling pretty damn self-conscious. She felt disgusting. The last time she'd been anywhere near this funky, she'd partied all night and woken up with the flu. Hung over and sick, she'd felt about as bad as this. Well, except for the puking. There was no hint of *that*, thankfully.

"I really need to freshen up before I see anyone this morning." Lizzie glanced at Frank and back again at John. Then she said, "Um, hi, Frank. Doing okay?"

Frank just nodded.

John walked over to the bed and sat down on the edge. "I couldn't wake you up this morning."

"I'm sorry—what?" Lizzie didn't understand "I overslept. I was pretty tired after everything yesterday."

"No. I tried to wake you up, and I couldn't." He looked out the window. "I shook you. Slapped you. Nothing."

Oh, shit. That John had felt like he had to smack her was a really, really bad sign. He was pretty staunchly opposed to hitting women that weren't actually attacking him.

She ran her hand across his broad back. "I'm so sorry. I'm okay. Really, I'm fine." But as she said it, she could feel the pull in her muscles just from the simple act of lifting her arm to rub his back. She closed her eyes. She let the feel of smooth cotton and rigid muscles continue to play under her fingers for another few seconds before letting her arm fall back to the bed.

Turning to Frank, she said, "You're here to check me out, I assume?"

Frank nodded. "If you don't mind?"

"Of course not. Go ahead." Lizzie knew that healers were very particular about how and when they used their skills. There were strict ethical guidelines that most adhered to. So Frank wouldn't begin to scan her until she agreed. Kenna had explained it to her after her rescue. Frank had played a critical part in their success, but he'd had to scan the house from a distance. Only the presence of hostages, people in need who couldn't provide consent, had made it possible for Frank to help. It had seemed an interesting ethical dilemma when viewed in the abstract. But when Lizzie considered that her life had been on the line, she'd decided the ethical question became less academically fascinating.

After a cursory exam, Frank asked, "Have you been doing magical laps?" At her confused look, he said, "Burning the midnight oil? Your magic is diminished—like you've overworked yourself. Or maybe you performed some big magic yesterday?"

"Yes," John answered for her.

She did?

"You've overexerted yourself, magically speaking." At her blank look, Frank said, "You'll be fine with a little rest. Take it easy—no magic for a day, maybe two."

"When do I know it's okay to use magic again? I'm supposed to be here, working. And how do I prevent this from happening again?" Especially since she didn't know how it had happened to begin with, she thought.

"It's not exact, but I can give you some guidelines." When she nodded eagerly, he continued. "If it hurts, don't do it. And if it's hard to bring your magic up, stop."

"Seriously? That's your advice? But I don't even know how I did this to myself. How can I prevent myself from accidentally doing it again if I don't even know how it happened?"

Frank was looking a little helpless and harassed. And well

he should, if he couldn't even answer her simple questions.

"I've got this, Frank. Is there anything you can do for her?" John avoided her eyes, but he reached down and twined his fingers with hers.

On more certain ground, Frank said, "I can help with the muscle aches and the general fatigue. I assume that's an issue?" When she nodded, he continued. "But I can't recharge your magic."

She needed to give the poor man a break. For whatever reason, John knew what was going on and he wasn't sharing it with Frank. Her muddled, sleep-fuzzy brain understood that much. "That would be great. And thank you. For your help and for coming out to the house. I really appreciate it."

"John was insistent, and Harrington wasn't far behind. But I'm always happy to help." He reached his right hand out, palm up, inviting her to place her hand in his.

She gave John's hand a quick squeeze and gently disentangled her fingers. Placing her hand in Frank's, she asked, "Do you see this frequently?"

"No. Most magic-users know where the line is and don't cross it. I know you have an unusual history with your magic being locked away. You might discuss this with Harrington, and he can help you see the warning signs more quickly." While he spoke, Lizzie could feel the ache in her muscles fade, the bone-deep feeling of exhaustion was slipping away, as well. In moments like these, Lizzie was really glad magic was a reality.

"What happens if you keep pushing?" Lizzie had a horrible thought. "Not what happened to Sarah?"

"No. No. That I've never seen before." Frank stopped his ministrations, clearly distracted. "I'm honestly not sure what would happen. I suppose you could push until there was nothing left. It would probably take you a very long time to recover. But I just can't see how it could cause you permanent damage. Based on some of Harry's observations, I'd guess Worth took more than the usable magic we generate. You tried to empty the well, but Worth took away the rain and the underground river that feed the well."

Frank snorted and shook his head. "This is not my area of expertise. Much more Harry's line. I'm a hands-on, intuitive healer. Harry's better at the theory. I understand you guys hit it off. He'd be a great person to ask these questions." Frank suddenly looked as if he regretted his words, shooting a quick sideways glance at John.

John had been patiently sitting on the edge of the bed, waiting for Frank to finish. He hadn't backed up, but he didn't seem particularly concerned by Frank's nearness. Or by the reference to Harry. Lizzie wasn't really sure why Frank had looked concerned. John had never been jealous or possessive. Maybe that was a Lycan stereotype he didn't live up to? And he certainly wasn't unreasonable, in regard to her or anything else. It was sometimes frustrating when she could see people around her viewing John—and sometimes her—through a cultural filter she had almost no information about. She mentally shrugged. She needed to get over it or get informed; those were the only options.

"That should do it. At least get you back on your feet and relatively pain-free. But take it easy for a few days." Frank's words rung in her ears as he walked out the door.

Take it easy? Seriously? There was a ghost mucking around in the Library. A secret cell to be investigated more thoroughly. The mystery of Sarah's coma to crack. And some magic books to delve into. Books that might hold the key to solving Sarah's medical mystery. Lizzie thought of them, sitting in the Library unread. She sighed. Heike would have to do it. *Damn.* She really wanted to have a look at them. But Frank was right—one step at a time. Then it hit her. She'd been unconscious for almost twenty-four hours.

She shoved the sheets out of the way and rolled onto her knees. She wrapped her arms around John, her front pressed to his back. And squeezed just as tightly as she could. She wasn't sure exactly why, but all of a sudden she had a horrible urge to cry. She pushed away the tears and clung that much tighter to his broad back.

After a few seconds, she could feel the tight muscles in his back loosen. She waited a little longer, just to be sure her voice wasn't choked with those chased-away tears. Then she said, "I'm fine. Are you ok?"

She was shocked when he said without any inflection, "Not really."

She clung that much tighter. When she heard and felt him let loose a deep breath, she let go. She reached down low with both hands and tugged the hem of his shirt up his chest. It took him a second to register what she was doing; then he lifted his arms and yanked it off.

He laughed, only a little of the strain she'd felt vibrating through his body remaining. "I'm not sure this is what Frank had in mind when he said rest."

"Pshaw. I'm up for anything." She paused a second, then she said, "Actually I was hoping for a full-body cuddle, but I'm pretty sure I could be persuaded to get naked and crazy."

"I can't believe I'm saying this—but naked and crazy will have to wait." She could hear the mock disgust in his voice. "God. Don't ever let it get out that those words left my lips."

"Hmm. Okay. How about a compromise?" she asked. He turned around, an easy smile on his face. She suspected it had taken him that long to get to the point where he *could* smile. And he wouldn't want her to see him worried. Or angry. Or unhappy.

"I'm listening."

She wrinkled her nose, taking a discreet sniff of the T-shirt she'd slept in. "Group shower?"

He laughed. "Done."

After a playful half hour in the shower, John had finally urged her to finish rinsing her hair or she'd end up waterlogged. And when it looked like that wasn't sufficient incentive, he stepped out and wrapped himself head to toe in a bathrobe—since she apparently had no self-control around his bare ass, he claimed—and bodily hauled her out.

A few neck nibbles and failed disrobing attempts later, he carried her down the hall and dropped her ungrateful butt back in bed. Some thoughtful soul had stripped the bed and changed the sheets. She sighed mournfully, but he refused to join her. At least one of the two of them had some sense, she thought, as she drifted off. She really was too tired to be engaged in anything more active and exciting than sleep.

When she woke, the sun was a little lower in the sky, and John had arranged for a meal to be brought up. He was eating—probably on his second or third helping, if she had to guess—when she rolled over and groaned.

He looked a little guilty at being caught mid-meal.

She chuckled. "I know you were starving. I'd never begrudge you a meal. And shame on you for thinking I would. Did you even eat breakfast or lunch?"

He shook his head and kept munching on a chicken leg. That was her guy.

As she stretched and rolled to her side, he started to fill a plate for her. "I figured we could eat and discuss your—" He glanced at her. "—oversleeping incident."

"My massive fade overreach?" Lizzie inquired nonchalantly. She had flipped over on her stomach, feet near the pillows and head at the foot of the bed, chin propped up on her hands.

"Figured that out?" John asked in between bites.

"Uh-huh. Hard to believe, but my brain wasn't entirely in the right place earlier. I feel much more clearheaded now, thank you." She kicked her feet up in the air a bit. She was also feeling less sore. Actually—she swung her legs again—the last bit of soreness seemed to have faded as she'd slept. Hmm.

"So—I'm actually feeling pretty great." Eyes wide, she blinked once, slowly. That was her very best I'm-so-innocent look.

He stopped mid-chew. After about two seconds, he narrowed his eyes, finished chewing, and swallowed. "You're a menace. A menace who's supposed to be resting," he reminded her. "And whatever you're thinking, I'm sure it involves cardio."

True. They'd not made it to slow, sensual lovemaking yet. Whatever their intentions, they tended to end more in the direction of boisterous, fuck-me-now sex. She sighed wistfully. *Maybe later?*

Apparently, John had better self-control than she did. He was telling her something about a meeting.

"I'm sorry. What was that?" she asked, all innocence.

He grinned. He'd totally caught her fantasizing about sweaty, rowdy, athletic sex. He definitely wouldn't let her forget that.

"I was just saying that we have a meeting scheduled in fifteen minutes. With Harrington, the dragons, Heike, Pilar, and Max."

"Wait—wow. When did that all happen?" Lizzie couldn't believe it. Max. And Pilar. Her heart melted a little that Pilar had come all this way. Lizzie was sure it was to help out with the seven dangerous books. She was so completely and utterly reliable. And motherly. *Oh, no.* "Has anyone told Pilar about my magical mishap?"

"Yes, but she knows you're fine. And as to when—it's been about twenty hours since you passed out. A lot can happen in a day," he said.

As John answered Lizzie's questions, he was careful to skirt certain details. How he'd been worried as she'd slept through the entire night, barely moving. How Max had called in the midst of him trying—and failing—to wake her. How he'd become more frantic as she'd stubbornly refused to wake up. How Pilar had harassed Harrington when Lizzie hadn't answered her phone, then immediately grabbed a flight to Prague when she pried an update from Harrington. How he'd dodged calls from Kenna and voicemails demanding to know what the hell he'd done with her friend.

"The whole gang is here—except for Kenna. How did that happen?" Lizzie groaned. "Never mind. Max is coming, so she probably skipped out to avoid him. She is being so completely weird about Max. I still haven't gotten anything useful out of her, but my best guess is that she screwed around with him and then dumped him before there could be any real relationship."

"That explains a lot." John grimaced slightly. What was Max thinking? "Max asked if we really needed her here. I thought she'd demand to come per her usual pushy, managing self. But when I told her who was here and that we had it well under control, she agreed to wait a few more hours before hopping a plane." He shook his head at Max's lack of sense. Lizzie's best friend, of all people. "And now I know why."

For a very brief second, Lizzie looked like she might argue the pushy and managing comment. But objectively, she couldn't deny that's exactly the kind of person that Kenna was. And frequently she was being pushy and managing to further Lizzie's best interests—so it wasn't exactly like he was pointing out a character flaw. There was no arguing that Kenna could be a force of nature.

John watched Lizzie roll out of bed and on to her feet, stretching her clasped hands above her head and shaking off the last bit of sleep. She seemed completely fine. He let out a breath that he felt like he'd been holding for hours. And he could feel his shoulders fall down an inch, as some of the remaining tension fell away. He hadn't realized how keyed up he'd been. She'd woken up hours ago. Frank had said she was fine. But seeing her now, doing something so small, so normal, as shaking off a long nap—it comforted him and made him feel that she truly was okay.

She was bouncing up and down on her toes, checking to see that everything was in working order. He smiled. And that was one of the things he loved about her, the way she could always make him smile, even with simple, small acts. And he did, he realized. He did love her.

Damn, but he didn't want her at that meeting. He sighed. It wasn't always about what he wanted. Sometimes it was about what she needed. And she needed to be a part of this. A part of finding Sarah's cure—if there was one. A part of the hunt for Worth. *Fuck.* He could rationally understand the need, but the thought of Lizzie anywhere near Worth tied up his insides and made him want to throw someone through a wall.

She was already dressed, almost ready to leave, and just doing the little things that women do. Lip gloss, face cream. He needed to leave. Before he did something rash, something he'd regret. Like lock her in the room. Or tie her to the bed. Or tell her that he forbade her to participate in anything, *anything at all*, that had to do with Worth.

"I'll see you downstairs? We're meeting in the main room of the basement," he said, his hand already on the door. By the time she responded in the affirmative, he was already out the door.

CHAPTER TWENTY-SIX

Lizzie had just finished reassuring Kenna for the sixth time that, yes, she was totally fine. And no, there were no lasting effects. And yes, she'd be more careful. And no, Kenna didn't need to hop on a plane immediately.

"Mom's been out of town at a conference, and I've got your boys. I thought I'd save them a kennel visit. But I've dropped them off and am ready to head out," Kenna said.

That explained why Kenna wasn't making the meeting Lizzie was about to step into. She'd seriously underestimated her friendship in thinking a little thing like a sexual relationship and an awkward break-up would keep Kenna from flying out to check on her.

"Really, everything is fine. No need for you to drop everything. And your boss wouldn't be thrilled with losing you for several days so soon after our last adventure," Lizzie said.

"If you're sure—" Kenna sounded doubtful.

"I am." Lizzie shifted the phone on her ear. "Although, it does look like Max has made it. I guess he has nothing better to do with his time."

"Hmmph. He really doesn't have anything better to do. The guy can't take a hint." Kenna sounded more than just a little annoyed.

"Ah. That's too bad." Though Max was hardly the normal type for Kenna, Lizzie had held out some hope that maybe he'd be around a little longer than the usual fling. But it was clear from Kenna's reaction that now wasn't the time to discuss it.

It had taken Lizzie another five minutes of cajoling to convince Kenna she was fine. She'd been wound pretty tightly by her failed attempts to make it to Prague quickly and adding Max to the conversation hadn't helped. Hanging up the phone, she reminded herself that it was a wonderful thing to have a friend who cared so much about her. But that had been an exhausting conversation.

She stopped at the top of the basement stairs, composing herself before she headed down to meet the planning crew. When she arrived, silence settled over the group for about four seconds, and then conversations picked up again.

Pilar rushed forward and wrapped her in a motherly, expensively scented embrace. After two quick kisses, one on each cheek, she pulled Lizzie further into the room. After greeting Max and Ewan, she did a quick head count. John, Harrington, Tavish, Lachlan, Ewan, Heike, Max, and Pilar. *Oh, my.*

After everyone had found a seat, Harrington started the meeting. He addressed Lizzie first. "You're feeling better?"

"Fine. No magic for a day or two, but otherwise great. Frank stopped by and patched me up. Thank you." She looked around the table. No healer, but Lycan, dragon, caster, and non-magical human sat side by side. She was glad to have John on her right and Pilar to her left. Her strength and her confidence were bolstered by their presence.

"We have a few items to discuss. First, Heike and Pilar

have started translating the seven books found in Matylda's cell. Pilar, what can you tell us about the books?" As Harrington spoke, Lizzie wondered if this was an IPPC meeting and an IPPC operation.

None of the group gathered at the table were regular IPPC employees, though several—if not all—were contracted to work for IPPC on a temporary or per project basis. It didn't really matter, she supposed. She'd gone beyond analyzing and deciding if her and her friends' actions were considered legal by mainstream society or under whose authority she might be acting. *Wow.* She'd never realized what an about turn she'd made. That was a wildly different view of society from her previous strict adherence to the law and societal norms. A change she'd embraced after just a few short weeks of exposure to magic and magic-users. Did that make her fickle? *Nah.*

Things change and she had to roll with it or be incredibly stressed out by it. Apparently, her subconscious had decided she'd be rolling, because she hadn't actively debated the issue —thought about it at all, really—until now. Well, except to be aware that her actions might be illegal and she didn't want to get *caught.*

Failure to report a crime was the least of her offenses, given everything that had happened to her recently. She was pretty sure she was also an accomplice to a variety of dodgy activities. Things really had changed in her life.

She reined in her stray thoughts and focused on Pilar's description of the books she and Heike had been working with.

"—categories. The Vampyr books, death magic books, and necromancy. There are three books that we categorized as death magic books and two each of the other types. The death magic books were concerning."

"And creative," Heike added. "Torture and death were

used to super-charge a variety of spells. To reinforce personal protection wards, to eavesdrop over long distances, even—" She glanced worriedly at the dragons, seated together at one end of the table. "Even to kill dragons."

At Lachlan's intent stare, she said, "I'll explain later. Your people should be aware, if you're not already familiar."

Lachlan simply nodded. The dragons were at turns taciturn, mischievous, and then forthcoming. Dependent on what, Lizzie wasn't certain. She did know she wanted them on *her* side.

Pilar picked up the thread again. "Death magic is little understood, and I'm certain that these books will provide valuable insight. Not only into death magic, but also into the underpinnings of casting. Why certain casts work and others don't. As disturbing as the material can be, it is useful. But I don't think it relevant to Sarah's case."

Now that Lizzie looked closer, she saw that Pilar looked careworn and slightly frazzled. In her earlier enthusiasm, she'd missed the slightly less than perfect chignon and the faint shadows under her eyes. And how she had failed to notice Pilar's attire, Lizzie did not know. Pilar was wearing a pair of jeans. Stylish jeans, but jeans. Lizzie hadn't spent that much time with Pilar, but she'd only ever seen her in dresses and slacks. Not a single Facebook picture showed a hint of jeans. They'd have to talk later.

"Understood," Harrington replied. Lizzie guessed that meant the books wouldn't be destroyed. "The necromancy and Vampyr books?" he prompted.

Pilar sat straighter in her chair and clasped her hands in front of her, as if steeling herself for an unpleasant task. And in that moment, Lizzie realized, maybe Pilar felt the same way that she did. Not guilty about Sarah, more an assumption of responsibility. An acknowledgment that *someone* had to make her a priority. That Sarah was important and that she wouldn't be a forgotten casualty of their rescue.

And there was another important point that Lizzie had overlooked. *She* hadn't been rescued. *They* had. Both of them. This was Pilar's story as much as her own. Lizzie frowned. More so, actually. Pilar had been held longer than Lizzie. Her beloved daughter captured and detained by truly terrifying people. And amidst it all, Pilar had made time for Lizzie, had tried to teach her. Hell. It was Pilar who had figured out that her magic was blocked. She was an amazing woman.

"There were some concerning pieces of information in the necromancy books. They'll certainly require additional study—much like the death magic books. The Vampyr books, however, stand apart. Matylda was convinced they would be the most useful in aiding Sarah, and I have to agree. I see strong parallels between the Vampyr's and Worth's attacks." She looked to Heike for support of her conclusion.

Heike said, "The first book showed the aftermath of a Vampyr attack. We missed some of the relevant pieces of information initially, likely due to the graphic nature of the images recorded. The family were magic-users. You can actually see what remained of the wards protecting the home, if you look closely enough. The attackers were either very sophisticated casters or had a top-notch caster aiding them. The family's protection had been deconstructed. Conceptually, it's a simple work-around for a ward but quite difficult in its execution. And the family would certainly have known the attack was happening."

Lizzie shook her head slowly, trying to process the implications. "So the family members were magic-users? And they were warned? But…." Her words trailed away.

"I don't think you've ever understood how powerful your magic is, Lizzie." Pilar spoke directly to her in low tones.

Funny, really. Almost everyone in the room had super-hearing, so trying to speak privately was a joke. A little louder, at a normal, conversational volume, she said, "Even forewarned, the family had no opportunity to escape."

Pilar's comment was not helping. Her distress must have been clearly written across her face, based on Heike's next words.

Heike spoke tentatively now, as if she wasn't sure what to say but felt obligated to speak. "There's little doubt—it was all very fast. Once they were inside the house, the family wouldn't have had much time. From the wounds—well, it would have been over quickly."

"That's some comfort, I suppose," Lizzie said. She felt foolish for such a response, for being so upset by something that had taken place hundreds of years earlier. But she couldn't change how she felt. At least she still found the images disturbing. How much more death and blood would she have to see before it *stopped* upsetting her?

Pilar returned to the books. "The second book records a caster's first experiences as a Vampyr. The high he experienced the first time he ingested blood soaked with a dying man's magic. The difficulties he had ingesting human blood, regurgitating the blood almost as quickly as he consumed it. Also, his frustration as his victims' magic unwound itself from the blood in their bodies, sometimes before he could harvest the blood. He struggled with tying the magic firmly to the blood, to make it more readily accessible."

Lizzie looked appalled. "Are you telling me that those people's blood acted as a medium to carry the magic the Vampyr actually wanted?" Lizzie's voice started to shake. "That the Vampyr hadn't perfected their technique, hence all the blood?"

"We think so," Heike said. "I know the images were terrible—"

Pilar placed a hand on Heike's arm, quieting her. "It makes sense that Worth solved the problems that are discussed in the book. Either through experimentation or research. Because there are too many similarities between our Vampyr caster's experiences and what happened to Sarah."

John had been silently watching the proceedings. Now he turned to the dragons and said, "Lachlan mentioned a group of men who drank the blood of their slain enemies. That they believed drinking the blood would allow them to steal their enemies' magic. What about that group? Any connection to Vampyr? To this caster whose book we've got now?"

Lachlan replied, "The men I described were considered cannibals and their acts determined to be against the natural order of magic and man. They assumed the name Vampyr. Though they were more like a movement or an organization, unlike the myths that portray them as a type of magic-user. Any magic-user type could be found among the Vampyr. Casters, Lycan." A look of acute distaste crossed Lachlan's features. "Even healers, if such an abomination is imaginable."

Harrington's typically neutral expression was showing distinct signs of cracking into interest. "What became of them? IPPC has no record of Vampyr."

Lachlan's expression firmed, his green eyes hinting at the fire deep inside. "We hunted them into extinction several hundreds of years ago." In moments like this, Lizzie could easily believe Lachlan hid a mouthful of vicious teeth and rock-hard scales.

Lizzie was starting to wonder more and more about those glowy green dragon eyes. She shivered a bit, then snuck her hand under the table searching for John's fingers. Once she found his hand, she twined her fingers in his. He glanced down at her, worry clear on his face. She just shook her head once and turned back to Lachlan. She had no problem at all with her boyfriend turning into a fluffy tailed, monster-sized wolf, but fiery, glowing eyes were a little freaky. Her mind was a mystery.

"I'd thought their methods had been lost with them. Until now." That was the sound of a pissed off dragon, Lizzie thought. She glanced at Lachlan's eyes. Yep, fiery green. She was starting to wonder if no one else saw that. She'd have to remember to ask John later.

"And Sarah? How does this aid in discovering some kind of cure?" Harrington asked.

Pilar checked her watch. "I'd hoped Harry would arrive by now. We've been updating him on what we've found, and he's had a few thoughts."

"And what were Harry's thoughts?" Harrington did not sound enthusiastic. Downright disapproving, in fact.

Lizzie wondered what had caused such strife between the two. Surely the breadth of Harrington's disappointment and disapproval couldn't be solely due to Harry's refusal of an IPPC position.

Harry breezed in, right on cue. "Replace what was taken. Replenish her core magic." He stopped, looking for an open seat. Finding none, he grabbed a chair and dragged it to the table. "Apologies for my tardiness. My flight was delayed."

Once seated, he kept speaking, as if he'd not been late and there was no awkwardness between him and his uncle. Maybe there wasn't on Harry's side. He was an odd duck. A cute, frenetic, brilliant guy. But absolutely an odd one. "The challenge is in determining how to affect the replacement. If we can determine how the magic was removed, then the chance of reversing the process is much improved."

Max had been silent up to this point, but he was troubled enough by something that he raised his hand up a few inches to catch everyone's attention. "Maybe I'm the only one seeing a flaw in that—but where exactly does this core magic come from that you'll be putting back into Sarah? I mean, Worth made off with whatever he took from her, right? It's not like he's going to swing by and make a donation. So even assuming you figure out the *how* of this process, where do you get the juice?"

Harry smiled. "Excellent question. Braxton solved that problem for us quite nicely."

John looked up in surprise when his name was mentioned. "Me?"

"The night Sarah was injured, Worth attacked three people: Sarah, John, and Moore. The result of each attack was different. Based on the reports and a physical examination of Sarah and Moore, the conclusion that I've drawn is that the quantity of magic Worth siphoned was the determining factor. With only three subjects, it's impossible to be sure, but it does make sense."

John had assumed a thoughtful expression. "I'm not sure about Sarah and Moore. I do remember being—" John stopped, as if choosing his next words carefully. "I was very concerned. I thought I'd lost the ability to shift."

"And I remember the feel of the magic moving through the connection. It felt Lycan," Lizzie said.

"And it's these impressions that lead you to believe that only a small amount of magic was taken from John, explaining his full and rapid recovery?" Harrington attempted to clarify.

"Correct. More was taken from Sarah, resulting in a coma. And even more from Moore, resulting in death." Harry looked pleased with the conclusion, but Lizzie still wasn't exactly sure what that meant.

"I won't approve such a risky procedure," Harrington said.

Now Lizzie was really confused. What was Harrington

talking about? And why the stare down between him and Harry?

Heike shared her confusion, probably less aware of the conflict between the two men. "I don't understand. What's the problem?"

Max answered before either of the two men, currently staring each other down, could reply. "Donors. Volunteers. Each person only giving a little, so that none suffer ill effects."

Harry looked away from Harrington casually, as if nothing had happened. He smiled at Max. "Exactly. Preferably spell caster donors, in case there's a compatibility issue."

Max cocked his head thoughtfully. "That sounds a lot like a blood transfusion."

Harry assumed a professorial tone and was settling in for a lengthy explanation. "We don't actually know how much of a role magic plays in the normal functions of the body. But we do know that it becomes intertwined with the body on a very basic level, and that's expressed in different ways depending on the particular talents of the person. Lycan, for example, heal themselves with their magic. Is it possible that magic, like blood, flows throughout the body carrying some vital components that feed our magic needs? Why not?" Lizzie looked around. If she had to guess from the reception Harry's speech was getting, magic-users didn't get much insight into how their magic worked.

"I can tell you that magic is not static, it ebbs and flows. And it certainly moves throughout the body. Even the least talented healer can tell you as much. A much more challenging and interesting question relates to volume and quality. Unlike blood in a human body, the magic each person possesses can vary in its strength and quantity. One person's normal levels of magic could be significantly higher than another person's, because they generate more magic more frequently. And since our magic is not contained within a closed system—one significant difference from blood—some magic-users leak unused magic. It's one of the easiest ways that healers can identify a magic-users talent type." Harry blinked. Then he gave a sheepish grin. "Sorry. I get a bit carried away."

Surprisingly, it was Harrington who spoke for the group. "Not at all. Useful information." Then he frowned and said, "I still find the idea of experimenting on Sarah and several hapless volunteers unacceptable."

Ewan, who'd been silent for the duration of the meeting, added, "I agree." He looked at Heike briefly. Lizzie was startled by the intensity of the look between the two of them. Clearly intended to be private, it was scorching. "It's hardly safe."

"The question remains, how do we remove magic from one person and give it to another?" Max asked.

"Worth." John looked annoyed that he opened his mouth.

"Agreed." Lachlan spoke, but several other heads at the table nodded curtly in agreement. "Given Worth's fascination with finding the Lost Library, I find it not unlikely that he discovered other spelled texts."

"And?" Harrington prompted him.

"And if we can't get the information out of Worth, perhaps we get the information from Worth's source," Max answered, looking at Lachlan for confirmation. As Lachlan offered a small smile, Max continued. "He's liquidated several assets, and he's gone into hiding." Max turned to Harrington. "Your people are surely still working on locating assets?"

Harrington responded in the affirmative. "They are and they have. I've got half a dozen possible locations. All were buried even deeper in a series of complex transactions, the sole intent of which was to obscure the buyer. But we need weeks, maybe months to determine which locations, if any, he's actively using. If we're not careful, we'll spook him and he's in the wind again."

Ewan cleared his throat. Not an attention getting sound. More an embarrassed, damn-I-have-to-speak-now sound. "Uh, I may be able to help. That's actually why I'm here at the meeting today. Lachlan asked that I come and offer my—" He halted mid-sentence, reluctant and pissed. He looked at Lachlan, who gave a nasty snarl. Lizzie did a double take. What the hell was that? "I'm to offer my tracking skills."

Harrington looked intrigued. Never a good sign, in Lizzie's opinion. Lizzie stopped and had to laugh a little at herself. She wasn't biased, or anything. She was still pissed about Harrington springing Heike on her. But at least she was big enough to admit that she was seeing Harrington through a very skewed lens these days. The asshole.

"Scent tracking?" John asked.

"Magical tracking, I suppose you could say," Lachlan replied for Ewan, who was still looking ticked. "Ewan says the stink of Worth's magic is still all over this place. So no problem finding trace magic to work off of."

"So not all dragons track?" John looked confused.

"We can smell prey from miles away, little wolf. It's magical tracking that is unique." *Uh oh.* "Little wolf" was never a good sign. Lizzie squeezed John's hand. Hard. Well, as hard as she could. But he'd locked in on Lachlan.

Lycan were preternaturally strong and violently efficient in a fight. She'd seen John in action. It wasn't at all like what she'd expected. Quiet, no fuss. Just vicious clawing, crushing, and shaking. She'd come to terms with that aspect of John's life much more quickly than she could ever have hoped. Circumstances had helped, since he'd routinely been saving her life whenever someone's butt was being kicked. But imagining her wolf up against a dragon—not good, was her conclusion. She knew she was being an unsupportive little wolfy-wife, but it didn't change the conclusion. Not good.

Her grip must have finally registered, because he looked down at her and winked. The bastard. Here she was, worried he'd get his ass kicked, and he was playing silly games with a flying lizard. No, not just a flying lizard, but one that could roast him from well beyond twenty paces. Not cool. And on top of it, she had lost a little feeling in her hand from gripping so hard. Again, not cool.

Ewan must have gotten over his mad, because he finally spoke to the assembled group. "We didn't know you'd narrowed down the possibilities so much." Was that a mild twinge of annoyance she heard in his voice? She did believe that it was. "But now that you have a few locations, I can do a reconnaissance flight, scout each of the locations, and tell you how saturated Worth's magic is in each location. The idea being that the most saturated location with the most recent spores will be the most likely hiding place for both Worth and his most precious assets."

"Fucking bloodhound...hunt for humans...fucking bastard...owes me." Lizzie looked up at Ewan. That was Ewan; she was sure. But he wasn't speaking. She recognized the voice, and who else would be griping about being sent off to track Worth for the puny humans? But she'd heard it as a static-filled echo. She turned to John. "Did you hear that?"

"What?"

No reason to stir the pot. "Nothing," she said. Just one more creepy thing about those weird dragon guys. Someone was getting grilled at some point...but she wasn't sure how exactly that would play out.

While she'd been contemplating freaky dragons and her sanity, the dragons and Harrington had come up with a plan to hit all the locations. Night was coming, so they'd start this evening. Ewan preferred to fly under the cover of darkness. It was only then that Lizzie realized that he'd literally meant *fly* earlier. As in—dragon with wings, flying. Cool as that may be, she'd take her wolf over that any day.

"One last item." Lizzie thought she'd strangle Harrington. This was turning into the never-ending meeting. "Thoughts on how you ended up well over twenty feet from your original location when you faded, Lizzie?"

"A few. The first of which is that you guys—" She motioned to the dragons. "—have a crap memory and twenty feet was never the outward fade limit. And—I may have made a tiny error when I cast the fade earlier." She blushed.

"Understandable. You'd never faded before," John said. Either he missed the blush or he ignored it.

Not so, Harrington. "I don't think that was the problem, was it, Lizzie?"

"Um, no. But I'll be much more careful in the future. And specific. I'll be more specific." Who knew her magic would perceive John as a place? How was that even possible? Trying to keep John out of her brain, especially if she was stressed and under pressure—that might be hard. Because that's exactly what had happened. She'd been worried and thinking about John made her feel better. So she'd had John on her mind when she'd faded. The only problem was that he'd been a little far away. She wanted to stamp her foot and protest that it wasn't fair. She'd *also* been thinking about the Library. But practically speaking, her connection to John was so very much greater than any she had to the Library.

Realizing Harrington had never responded, a hopeful note crept into her voice and she said, "Maybe we can discuss this in a mentoring session." She looked around at the curious faces surrounding the table. "In private."

"Enough for now. Lachlan and Ewan, let me know if you

need any assistance with your reconnaissance. Max, perhaps you can assist with long-range transport? Finding a pilot last minute might be difficult. I know Frank's not available to leave right now." At Max's nod, Harrington turned his attention to Pilar and Heike. "If you can go through the Vampyr books one more time? I know it's repetitive and tiring, but any piece of information that you can glean might be helpful. You've both been a great help so far."

"Harry? Would you mind to have a look at Lizzie before you leave?" Polite. To the point. Harrington didn't betray any other feelings about Harry's presence.

"Naturally. I am planning to stay a bit, though. Sarah is stable and will be fine with a colleague checking on her for the next day or two." He paused. "I've made arrangements for accommodation not far from here."

Lizzie could see a slight stain of pink beginning at Harrington's collar and running up to his ears. They really did rub each other the wrong way. She couldn't perceive anything objectionable in Harry's words. In fact, he seemed quite helpful. As she turned to John, she heard Harrington reply, "You'll stay here."

Lizzie was ready to stretch her legs. The meeting had been much too long. As she stood up, her vision narrowed slightly, her peripheral vision turning black. Before she could blink, John had a firm grip on her elbow and was lowering her back down to into her seat. "Head down?" John murmured in her ear.

She took a breath. "No. I'm fine. I must have stood up too quickly." And she was fine. But tired, she realized. Frank had said to take it easy. And she understood she wasn't to run a marathon—but a marathon meeting? She'd been sitting on her tush. She sighed. *Stupid magic malfunction.*

John interrupted what looked like a heated conversation

between Harry and Harrington. "Can you have a look, Harry?"

"Of course. What happened?" Harry turned sharp eyes to her. While John explained her magical mishap, Lizzie figured she was recovered and they could continue this someplace more private. Except this time when she stood up, there was no tunnel vision to warn her.

CHAPTER TWENTY-SEVEN

Lizzy woke up warm and comfortable, wrapped in John's arms.

"Umm." She grinned, wiggling just enough to make sure he was awake and interested.

"I don't think so." His voice was sleep roughened. And incredibly sexy. As was the stubbly feel of his chin on her cheek.

She slowly rubbed her cheek up, then down against his chin. Just enough pressure to feel the hard line of his jaw and the soft scrape of day-old whiskers. She could feel him inhale slowly, and then she felt little nibbles and kisses along the sensitive tendon of her neck. And then a bite. Not painful, but firm. She was sure it was intended as a mild reprimand—his way of saying "don't tease me"—but he failed. All she could think about was the clenching feeling deep inside her, when the bed dipped.

John rolled quickly out of bed. "Witch." Shaking the last traces of sleep away, he turned and knelt next to the edge of the mattress. "After passing out again, you need to take it easy."

"Then put a shirt on," she grumped. Bare chest, bare feet, jeans riding low on his hips. He needed more than a shirt to squelch her desire to yank him back in bed.

She blinked. Wait a minute. He seemed awfully casual for a Lycan whose mate had just passed out. Last time she woke up after passing out, he was a mess. She chewed on her lip. She hadn't really thought about that. He really had taken it hard. She frowned. She hadn't *meant* to overreach with her magic. Or get kidnapped. Twice. She sighed. Realistically, she wouldn't want to date herself. She was—she scrunched up her nose—high maintenance.

"You don't seem too concerned about it." She ventured a peek under her lashes.

He smiled, a slow, sexy smile. "Do you want me to be?"

"Just saying. Last time you were less—" She waved her hands in his direction. "—however you are now."

"Relaxed? Calm? Not worried sick?" Fully dressed, he sat on the edge of the bed to tie his shoes. Looking down as he fiddled with the laces, he said, "Harry gave you the green light. He said you'd overdone it a bit, that you likely hadn't eaten enough, were a little dehydrated, and otherwise seemed fine." Finished with his laces, he caught her eye as he said, "Although, you are to rest if you feel at all tired today. He expected you to be completely fit tomorrow."

"Hmm. Okay." Weird, but cool. She liked this relaxed, charming John. Here was the man she'd met and originally fallen in love with. And yes—she was completely head over heels. There was no getting around the fact.

"And I may have woken you up a few times last night. Just to make sure he was right," he said sheepishly.

Aha! Lizzie knew something was up. And now that she thought about it, maybe she remembered him gently shaking her in the middle of the night. She shrugged. Whatever made him sleep better. Lizzie wasn't sure what exactly she would do if the tables were turned. She frowned. She really wasn't the type of person she'd want to date. She'd be worried sick all the time. That wasn't a very reassuring feeling.

"What time is it? And is there any news on Ewan's targets?"

"Nine o'clock, and I have no idea. I haven't been downstairs yet." He looked at her scantily dressed self, still wrapped up in the duvet. "Since you're not in a rush to get up, I'm going to head down for breakfast."

"I'll join you in a few minutes," she replied. The poor man was probably starving.

She'd only managed a quick bathroom break and to throw some jeans and a top on when there was a knock at her door. "Yes."

Heike poked her head in. "Can we talk?"

"Come on in." Lizzie still wasn't entirely sold that Heike was someone she could trust, but Lizzie was typically a good judge of character. She liked to believe that particular piece of herself had survived her transition into spell caster, that one piece of her had remained intact through the constantly changing landscape of her life the last few weeks.

But now she wasn't sure. She'd experienced a strong sense of unease when she'd first met Lachlan and Tavish. Now, however, she believed them trustworthy and honorable men. So that first impression had been some kind of glitch. A magical glitch, maybe. Or maybe her second impression was wrong. She wasn't sure. And that was enough to make Lizzie just a little sad. She didn't want to lose her faith in her own judgment.

And Heike. She'd mistrusted Heike from their first introduction. She considered her, at worst, a member of Worth's gang. At best, complicit by virtue of inaction. And now—Lizzie sighed. Now she wasn't sure. She was young. Much younger than Lizzie had initially realized. And shy. She'd as much as admitted to Lizzie that she wasn't good speaking with people she didn't know. What Lizzie had seen as disinterest or self-interest might have simply been uncertainty. When a shy person is placed in an uncomfortable social situation, or a very stressful situation with strangers, Lizzie supposed the result could look something like her initial experiences with Heike. Lizzie was also starting to get a nagging feeling that she was missing some vital piece of information or had failed to observe something important.

She narrowed her eyes in consideration. She just bet that Harrington had all the pieces. That would explain why he'd been so completely obnoxious about placing her trust in him and relying on his judgment when it came to Heike. He had the pieces, and he wasn't sharing.

Lizzie had been waiting for Heike. She was the one who knocked on Lizzie's door, not vice versa. But it was clear that Heike was hesitant to speak now that she was here.

"You wanted to talk about something in particular?" Lizzie prompted her.

Heike nodded slowly as she sank down onto the love seat placed at the end of the bed. She clasped and unclasped her hands in her lap nervously.

"I know you don't trust me," Heike started.

Great. One of those conversations. There was no right answer to that comment, so Lizzie remained silent and waited for her to continue. What came next was not at all what she expected.

"Ewan found Worth. Not Worth's hideout—he actually found Worth. And I'm not sure anyone will tell you." Heike's words were rushed.

Lizzie felt her throat close and tried to decide if she was about to have some kind of panic attack now that she knew —had some proof—that Worth was alive. She hadn't realized until that very moment that she'd wanted so much to believe he was dead that she'd half convinced herself he hadn't survived. Which was ridiculous. Of course, the evil genius who sucks people's magic to heal himself is still alive.

"Shit," Heike said, looking at her with wide eyes. "You don't look so good."

And Lizzie laughed. Doubled over, from the belly, make your side hurt, laughter.

"Shit," Heike repeated with even more emphasis.

Which, of course, only made Lizzie laugh all the harder.

"I'm going to get John. This was a huge mistake." Heike had stood up and was halfway to the door, before Lizzie caught her by the arm.

"Stop. Please." Lizzie wiped away the tear tracks where her eyes had watered from laughing so hard.

"You really don't look good." Heike pulled the arm that Lizzie held. "And you're hysterical. I need to get John."

Lizzie didn't let go initially. After a second, she dropped Heike's arm and said, "If you feel you need to. But I promise I'm not hysterical. It wasn't even Worth that made me laugh. Well, mostly not Worth. And there's a reason you told me." Heike always seemed such a cold, distant type; Lizzie figured calm reason would work.

And she wasn't wrong.

"If you're not upset about Worth, then—um, what were you laughing at?"

"I am upset about Worth. But I was laughing at—uh, sorry—you." Lizzie snorted. "I was thinking how maybe I hadn't been fair with you. And you pick that moment to come in like you want to have a heart-to-heart. But contrary to all indications that you want to talk about our stuff, you're here for an entirely different reason. You're here to share something that's clearly supposed to be a secret. Thanks for that, by the way." Lizzie shot her a sheepish smile.

Lizzie stopped when she saw how confused Heike was.

"We have stuff?" Heike frowned at her. "What are you talking about?"

Well, shit. "Sorry. Apparently, *I* have stuff. With you. Gah. Forget it. The point is, you pop out with 'shit.' Which, by the way, is a lot like watching a twelve-year-old swear—fascinating in its incongruity but just wrong." Lizzie thought she was doing a bang-up job explaining herself. Until she saw Heike's dismayed look. "It was funny. And I was already a little stressed by the news about Worth."

Heike watched Lizzie, suspicion all over her face.

"You're totally ratting me out to John and telling him I flipped out," Lizzie said.

"Yes, it's headed in that direction." Heike hadn't looked comfortable since she stepped in the room, but she seemed even less comfortable with the direction the conversation had taken.

"Please. Do I sound like I'm hysterical now?" Lizzie attempted to portray a reasonable, sane demeanor.

She wasn't sure exactly how to convey sanity—but it must have worked, because Heike tentatively shook her head.

"Why wouldn't Harrington share that information with me? I'm the one person we *know* can stop him." Assuming Lizzie could figure out how to repeat what happened before, but she'd keep that questionable tidbit to herself.

"When you had your magic." Heike's dark blonde eyebrows quirked up, and she tilted her head. "You know. Before your accident."

"But this is temporary, right? That's what everyone keeps saying." Panic edged into her voice and Lizzie took a short, sharp breath. She'd just gotten used to *having* magic. The thought of losing it was distressing.

"Oh—yes. I think so. No, I just meant, right now. You're not much help now, right? You're not recovered yet, are you?

I mean your magic is still gone?" Heike looked hopeful for a contrary response.

"I'm not sure, but I don't think it's back yet. I didn't really want to short circuit anything, so I haven't tried to do any kind of magic yet," Lizzie replied absentmindedly. Her brain was already racing to the next conclusion. If they knew where Worth was, that meant they had a plan. And she really hoped that they'd simply not gotten around to telling her. She had just woken up.

"I think Harrington is going to keep you out of the loop. I owe Harrington, for this job and for giving me a second chance. But I'm worried that Ewan will be a part of the raid, and I have to consider his safety, too." Heike was clearly conflicted, and it was causing her a great deal of stress. Quietly, Heike added, "Ewan is more important to me than a job. Even this job."

Her tone firmer and more certain, Heike said, "And I think they need you."

Hmm. If they were planning an immediate search of the property, then they might leave her out of it. *Damn.* And if Heike was concerned for Ewan—well, Lizzie couldn't help but think John would be in on anything having to do with Worth. A raid of his property? An attack on him directly? What were they planning?

Lizzie squared her shoulders. "I'm heading down to breakfast. Have you eaten?"

Heike nodded mutely in response.

Lizzie said grimly, "Good. I'm not sure you need to be a part of the conversation I'm planning." As Heike turned one way down the hall and Lizzie another, she realized she'd forgotten something important. "Heike?"

Heike froze and then turned around slowly.

"Truly, thank you," Lizzie said. And she meant it.

CHAPTER TWENTY-EIGHT

If Lizzie could have guessed how the breakfast conversation would end, she might have chosen a less direct confrontation with Harrington. Or maybe avoided the conversation all together. Maybe then she wouldn't have found herself a prisoner in her own room a few short hours later.

When she arrived in the breakfast room, Harrington was just finishing his coffee.

"I'm surprised to catch you here this late," Lizzie ventured.

"We just finished up a meeting." He eyed her cautiously. "That you clearly know about." Shaking his head, he said, "I told John it would be easier to leave before you were up. You're in no condition to join us. Without your magic, you'd be more of a liability than an aid and you might get someone hurt."

Lizzie didn't correct him regarding her source. "It only makes sense to take the one person who might be able to fight Worth effectively," Lizzie reasoned.

"Your magic is back?"

Lizzie sniffed. "Not yet, but at any moment. I could easily be ready to go by the time we arrive."

"No." His voice, face, even his posture were implacable.

Lizzie narrowed her eyes at him. Why was he being so unreasonable? Surely Harrington wasn't worried about her? *Nah.* He must be really concerned she'd place the crew at risk. "You're wrong."

He looked up, catching her eye. "Maybe." Carefully folding his linen napkin and placing it to the side of his plate, before leaving the room, he said, "I'll ensure you can't follow us. For your safety and everyone else's. And John has already agreed that this mission falls under the IPPC umbrella. He won't help you."

Lizzie grabbed some toast and bacon, making an impromptu sandwich, and filled a mug of coffee to go. Then she headed out to find John and see exactly what the hell they'd been discussing in her absence. It didn't take her long to find him.

The conversation went something like this:

She said, "What are you thinking?"

He said, "Not my jurisdiction; I'm not in charge."

She said, "Bullshit."

He said, "I'm not arguing."

When she couldn't do magic on the spot, he rested his case. And for some reason she just couldn't work up a good mad. Not at John, at least. She kept thinking, what if he was somehow diminished in a serious way and then *he* wanted to go off and pick a fight with Worth. She'd do her damnedest to make sure he didn't.

Which left her locked in her room with Tavish on the door as her jailer. And still seriously pissed at Harrington.

"Hey. You guys gonna feed me?" Lizzie yelled through her door.

Tavish popped his head in and said, "Sure. Sandwich okay?"

"You're an ass."

Tavish ignored Lizzie's derogatory comment. It was a lot milder than some of the profanity she'd spewed during the previous two hours, so Lizzie wasn't surprised by his lack of response.

"Sandwich?" he repeated.

She sighed. She was in a quandary. She could use her magic to break out. Maybe. She hadn't checked to see if it was back since she'd spoken with John. And if she was honest with herself, she didn't feel quite right. Better than yesterday, but off. And since her magic was a strange and foreign thing she hadn't quite worked the kinks out of, she couldn't say for sure what that meant. She did know that she was saving any magical effort for a good, workable plan. If she was going to short circuit herself because she used her magic too soon, better it be for a successful effort.

And realistically, even if she did manage a breakout, she'd have a dragon on her tail. She wasn't sure exactly what that meant, except for flying (Ewan had done his recon by air), fire (none of them denied it), and knowledge (they all lived a really long time). But that was enough incentive for her to avoid a chase scenario.

Maybe she'd have to be patient. And wait. *Hell, no.*

"That's fine. I've been kind of light-headed. You'd think I'd be used to it after all of the fainting I've been doing." He probably didn't know she ate a late breakfast and had been feeling great this morning, right?

"Um-hm. I'll get you something." And he shut the door firmly with a little snick.

Maybe if she kept dropping hints, they'd give Harry a call to check her out. She knew he wasn't on the mission—his authority issues with IPPC or his uncle had cropped up again? —and he was friendlier with Lizzie than the IPPC. He seemed a good ally in an escape attempt. She huffed. She couldn't believe that she was plotting an escape from her own employer.

It turned out Heike needn't have worried. Her concern had been misplaced, since Ewan wasn't a part of the raiding party. None of the dragons were. Lizzie hadn't caught all the details, but it seemed that a raid on Worth's residence was well outside the scope of any favor Lachlan owed to Harrington. So Lizzie wasn't counting on additional help from Heike.

John, Max, Pilar, and, surprisingly, Harrington made up the team. Harrington was their warding expert—reputedly at least as good as Sarah. Before IPPC had taken control of the Library, Worth had it heavily warded and secured with traps. And Sarah had gotten them into the Library without injury. So, if Lizzie was doing the math correctly and Harrington trumped Sarah on talent, then he should be up for the challenge.

The question was—could the four of them get back out once they'd broken in? When she'd pitched a fit earlier, they'd responded by explaining they planned to avoid Worth. But that seemed beyond naïve, asinine even. Of course Worth would know they were there. And he would defend himself and his property, of that Lizzie had no doubt.

Maybe they had a better plan than she imagined? They hadn't exactly shared all the details. And what the hell were they looking for? Maybe there was a book, but what if there wasn't? What if the knowledge they needed was in Worth's head? What if he'd made the improvements to the process himself?

Lachlan said it was unlikely in today's climate that as many deaths as would result from perfecting the process would go unnoticed. Unlikely, her ass. What if he chose some area with high crime? Or poor infrastructure? The world seemed full of places—dark and faraway places—where Worth could hide as many bodies as he liked.

Harrington had mentioned that his people were starting to see patterns. They believed that the Lost Library wasn't the only magically significant project that Worth was pursuing. If that was true, then Worth's operation was massive. Which made Lizzie even more convinced that he could hide away the effects—the casualties—of experimentation on other magic-users.

Lizzie had worked herself into a frenzy of worry by the time her lunch arrived. Like she could eat. She had absolutely no idea how she would get past the good intentions of Harrington, embodied in her dragon guard, and it was making her sick to think of her lover and her friends facing Worth without her.

"I have your sandwich." Heike poked her head in.

As soon as Lizzie looked up, Heike came all the way in the room carrying a tray.

Lizzie was still trying to decide what to say when Heike set the tray down and said, "I know how much you like orange juice, so I had them put some on the tray for you."

Huh? She did, in fact, like orange juice. But she drank tea or coffee in the morning when they both breakfasted. No way Heike knew orange juice was a favorite. She thought fast. Gamble that the OJ meant something and be quiet? Or ask Heike for help and indirectly inform her keen-eared jailer that she was contemplating escape? She stuck with her gut and remained silent.

After Heike had gone and Tavish was safely on the other side of the door—good lord, surely they didn't have x-ray vision? She needed more info on these dragons—Lizzie checked the OJ. Sure enough, there was a note. "Breaking you out. Be ready. H."

That sneaky bastard. Harry really was quite out of sorts with his uncle if he was willing to disobey Harrington so directly. Before the smile could stretch completely across her face, she caught movement out of the corner of her eye—her window opening. Harry was waiting at the open window. He motioned for her to hurry. "Come on, then, if you're ready to go."

Lizzie looked at the door, frowning.

"Afraid of heights? I hadn't really considered that." Harry looked thoughtful.

Lizzie looked at Harry like he'd lost his mind. "No. I'm just waiting for someone to hear us and open the door."

"Ah. No worries. Heike took care of that. She waited until the last possible minute and then placed a ward against sound. But I'm not really sure how long it will take them to detect the ward itself or notice the absence of rude complaint emanating from your room. So get a move on." Harry's head disappeared as he made his way down a rope ladder, not even giving Lizzie a chance to argue the rude complaint comment.

As Lizzie eyeballed the skimpy rope ladder, she reconsidered her denial regarding heights. Then she shook her head. She was *not* afraid of heights. She was, however, pissed that she had to go to such extremes to do what was clearly the right thing. The ladder twisted and swayed under her. Making her way down this flimsy ladder, three floors from the ground, definitely counted as extreme. Two overprotective men deciding on her behalf that she wasn't fit—well, one deciding and the other not arguing—when she was the only chance they had in a direct confrontation with Worth equaled stupid men in her mind.

She paused, letting the movement of the ladder settle a little. John had played scarce after their mini-discussion. She was only mildly annoyed that he hadn't argued her case with

Harrington. She totally got it, but— he hadn't actually tried to prohibit her from joining them. He hadn't even made a token effort.

Maybe they were more of a team than she realized. She *was* his mate. Mostly. *Gah.* They really needed to sort that out. Maybe if they actually got to the point of defining their relationship and being in agreement on what she actually was, they'd be speaking the same language. She was starting to suspect that though John may not be expecting her, he wouldn't be surprised if she landed on his and Harrington's doorstep.

More than halfway down, the muscles in her arms burning and her toe hunting the next rung on the ladder in vain, she decided she'd have to maim Harrington to make up for this. John may or may not get a pass, depending on her mood. But Harrington was totally on her shit list. Her hands were starting to ache from the death grip she had on the ladder. Yep, she'd figure out a way for Harrington to pay.

"Could you move any slower?" Harry asked from about ten feet below her. "This is actually an escape, a prison break so to speak, so some speed is preferred."

She glared down at him but quickly decided that was a bad idea. "I hate to be unappreciative"— she said as she stared firmly at the wall in front of her—"but this is just a touch outside my regular skill set."

"No complaints," he admonished her. "I almost had you belay down and then decided that might be asking a bit much and assuming some skills you didn't have. You see before you the compromise." He sounded quite proud of himself.

As her feet touched the ground, she regained her sense of fair play, thankfully. Because, otherwise, she would have told her rescuer where he could stuff his ladder. Likely ruining poor Harry's excellent mood and definitely shattering his pride in a job well done. She reminded herself—he had done a good job. She was out of her room and free of a dragon shadow. For now.

Harry handed her phone to her. "Thought you might be missing it."

And her feelings of charity toward Harry tripled. Saving her was one thing, but saving her phone as well was another level of wonderful entirely. "You, Harry, are a gentleman and a hero. What's next? Or am I on my own?"

"I managed to find a buddy who can fly us." He hustled her away, moving in the direction of the one of the cross streets.

"Thank goodness. I just realized that I have no idea where we're going. Worth's actual location didn't come up, just that he'd been found."

He grinned. "Heike told me what a snit you were in. And that they planned to leave you behind because of your medical condition. Since I'm the resident healer and they didn't consult me, I thought I could at least have a look at you before they left. Harrington declined, saying they were opting for a conservative approach, they wouldn't be confronting Worth, and so you wouldn't be needed." He turned toward her and peered intently at her face. "You know he feels guilty, right? About you being injured. Or maybe responsible is a better word. You're his mentee, and you made one of the most basic errors a magic-user can make when you outstripped your readily available magical reserves."

"It's a little more complicated than that. And there was no way Harrington could have helped. I made a mistake when I used my completely unknown, untried, and apparently rare fade talent. How is that Harrington's fault?" Lizzie was starting to puff a little with each step. They'd made it to a side street, and Harry was pointing out a rental car about halfway down the street. They were walking at a pretty good clip, and Lizzie hadn't even noticed. Probably riding the last of that adrenaline rush from her ladder adventure. She flexed her sore fingers—stupid swaying ladders.

"What exactly did happen?" he asked.

Harry wasn't puffing. In fact, he looked like he was out for a stroll with his grandma, his long legs covering ground without appearing to. That was vastly annoying, although why she'd focus on something so small in the grand scheme of things she had no idea.

"I'm supposed to have a clear picture in my mind of where I'm going. Typically, one would be going somewhere familiar, a place one had already visited. No problem, because I was heading to the Library. I constructed a detailed mental image of the Library. John was in the room when I left, so I unthinkingly included him in the image. My guess? By having John in my target location image, there was a conflict as to my intent. My connection to John was stronger, so there I went. I just didn't think of John as a place. Now I know—no people in location images."

As she hopped in the passenger seat, she added, "Why *did* it work if there was any confusion as to intent? I thought that was an essential part of any cast—clear intent?"

Harry shrugged as he looked over his shoulder and started to pull into traffic. "I'm no caster, but maybe your intent was clear? Maybe John is essentially a place." He looked at her briefly as he zipped along between cars. "If that's true, be careful. A moving destination target could cause you worlds of problems if I understand this fade talent correctly."

As Harry slid in between two speeding cars, Lizzie thought she might be better served to keep her mouth shut during the ride. Harry drove like he did everything else, with a barely contained energy and clear purpose, overridden by a bizarrely at odds casual, devil-may-care demeanor. In a car, it was mildly terrifying.

Within a short time—made shorter by some breathtaking speed—they were at a private airstrip. *Where did all this money come from?* That was Lizzie's first thought. Then she quickly revised that, thinking instead, how did Harry know such a wide array of people? Looking at the tiny plane, with its not-so-shiny exterior, and its tiny hunched pilot, Lizzie had a moment of doubt. She looked at the plane again and revised her opinion. Her reservations were quite large.

"How far exactly are we going?" Her skepticism must have shown through in her voice, because Harry laughed in response. She'd made strides recently. Flying didn't freak her out nearly so much as it used to when she was traveling for work. But this was no commercial plane or posh private jetliner.

When he didn't follow that laughter up with an answer, Lizzie punched him in the arm. "Seriously. That was a real question."

"First the ladder, now the plane. You are turning out to be an incredibly unintrepid adventurer." Harry grabbed a small duffel from the trunk of the car.

"That's not even a word," Lizzie replied distractedly. Then she realized—"You're going with me?"

She must have sounded shocked, surprised—something noteworthy—because for the first time since her jailbreak, Harry was completely still. After a brief moment passed, he slowly turned to her.

"Of course. I wouldn't send you off with James—" He jerked his head in the direction of the wrinkled, stooped pilot. "—alone. And I should be there."

Lizzie had no idea whether he'd declined an invitation to join the group or been prohibited from going. But she wasn't about to ask.

James must have decided they'd been standing around long enough, because he opened the plane door and waved them over. Lizzie eyed him with some trepidation. The man truly did not inspire confidence. Neither did his tiny patched plane.

Clearly seeing her anxiety, Harry smiled. "To answer your earlier question, we're headed to Freiburg, Germany. It's a few hours. And James, well, let's just say James has a way with the wind. You've got nothing to worry about."

"We're talking magic, right?" Lizzie tried to clarify. But Harry had already picked up his bag and headed to the plane. She scurried after him. "Wait," she yelled after him. "What if I have to pee?" They'd be in the air a few hours after all. And she'd actually drunk that orange juice with the message underneath it.

"Go now," James offered this sage bit of advice while pointing to a small building. Then he spat on the ground.

Several minutes later as they were about to take off, Lizzie was busy trying not to think about possibly needing a potty break at some point. Trying to keep her mind on other things—*not* on having to pee while trapped in a tiny plane, *not* on how most accidents occurred during takeoff and landing, and *not* on how old and frail James seemed to be—Lizzie asked Harry, "Why don't you go by Alistair? It's a lovely name."

"I've nothing against the name, rather the person it belonged to before me and after whom I'm named." He considered his words for a moment. "I'm not a fan."

She was pretty certain Harrington's name was Thomas. Maybe it was the mysterious Alistair who was the root of their disagreements. She liked them both—even if Harrington was on her shit list right now—and really wanted them to get along. She mentally chastised herself. Everyone had family drama. She really shouldn't get invested in the lives of people she didn't know that well. She sighed. *Right.*

"What's the plan?" When Harry looked at her and shook his head, she said, "When we arrive, I mean. Where are we going? What are we doing?"

"We call Harrington and John and tell them we're on the way." He shrugged. "Give them an estimated arrival time."

"You break me out of IPPC holding, and that's your plan? It's seems a little overly simple." Or maybe stupid. Then she immediately felt remorseful. Harry had gone to a lot of trouble: breaking her out, getting a plane, and risking Harrington's anger. And Harry was no fool.

"Once we're there, there's not much for them to do. They don't have the manpower to keep both of us under lock and key. And, quite simply, they need our help. Leaving you behind was ridiculously sentimental of Harrington. Something I'm sure he'll realize once we arrive." He cocked his head and studied her for a minute. "And John—well, John didn't say much about the situation to begin with. You likely know more about his reception than I."

"No idea," she replied. Which wasn't exactly true. She had her suspicions that she might be expected.

Why hadn't she pushed John harder? Maybe because they had enough to worry about right now between the two of them. Or maybe because she didn't really want to go. An image of Worth—in his bespoke suit, his gray hair recently trimmed, his face handsome and tanned—flooded her mind. She remembered him politely handing her a surveillance photo of her parents, as if he was doing her a favor by providing the picture. A fine sheen of sweat broke out on her upper lip. Damn that man and his ability to terrify her.

She kept getting accused of having no sense of self-preservation. When, in fact, it was thriving. She frowned and muttered, "I'm not a coward." *Was she?*

He looked at her oddly. "Never said you were. Unintrepid doesn't actually mean cowardly."

Lizzie just shook her head and said, "Never mind. And unintrepid is not a word, Harry."

Then she settled in to mentally prepare herself for the possibility of a face-to-face meeting with Worth.

CHAPTER TWENTY-NINE

Lizzie sat in the kitchen of the small house on the outskirts of Freiburg that Harrington had found for the team. Contact with Harrington had gone better than she'd expected. Harry called his uncle as soon as they touched down. While Lizzie had no idea what Harrington had said on the phone, the conversation had been short. Harry hadn't said much more than, "We're here." And when Harry hung up, he had directions to the team's hideout.

Although maybe hideout wasn't exactly the right word. Lizzie looked around at the cozy kitchen, full of cat-themed kitchen paraphernalia. A soap dish and a hand towel, she could understand. But the theme carried through to the wallpaper, curtains, kettle, and refrigerator magnets. It was a little overwhelming initially. Lizzie craned her neck to scope out the cat-themed light fixture.

John walked in at a good clip, almost screeching to a halt when he saw her. "Max said I'd find you in the kitchen."

He held out his arms to her. She hopped off the kitchen chair and stepped into an almost smotheringly tight hug. She could feel the gentle pull of air as he inhaled her scent. When she could breathe again, she said, "Miss me?"

"Not enough for you to come here." He held her a moment longer, and then he set her away from him just far enough so that he could easily look into her eyes. "But I can't say I didn't expect it."

"You have more faith in my abilities than I do. They left Tavish at my door." She scrunched up her nose. "He can be really big and scary when he's not on your side."

"Harrington actually locked you in? With a guard?" A small chuckle escaped from him. "I'm not sure whether to be pissed, or pat him on the back for making a solid effort. You did notice my restraint on the topic when you were arguing your case?"

She poked him in the chest. "You left me on my own to make an argument for the only reasonable course of action. It makes sense to have me here."

"You're not wrong, but why would I ever argue to bring you into danger? Especially when you make such a fine case without my help." Bastard. He was so rational. And absolutely correct—she had made an excellent case. Unsuccessful, but excellent. He continued, "From Harrington's standpoint, it makes sense to have you here if you can protect yourself. About that—can you protect yourself? Is your magic back up?"

Lizzie knew there was a right and a wrong answer to that question. If she was still recovering her magic, then why had she come? She'd had a quick chat with Harry on the drive over—who knew the stooped, wrinkled pilot, James, would be such a wicked fast devil in a car?—and he'd told her she looked to be recovering well, but her magic battery wasn't fully recharged. And was told "no clue" when she asked when she'd be up and running. Apparently, that varied from individual to individual. At this point, she wasn't sure she'd ever fade again. Even though she'd only just recently acquired her magic, doing without it was turning out to be a massive inconvenience. And hazardous.

"I'm guessing from your silence, that's a no." John's voice was grim.

Oops. She hadn't intended to avoid the question. She'd just been considering her response. "That's why I have you?" she said hopefully, a small question in her voice.

"Nice try. Play on the poor Lycan's protective instincts. You know what you're describing is just a smidge hypocritical, right?"

Lizzie sighed. "Yes," she said dispiritedly. "Do you have to be so consistent and so honest? It can be really annoying. Lovable, but annoying. And what's with 'smidge'? What kind of word is that? You and Harry—oh, speaking of Harry. Harrington was surprisingly restrained when I showed up on the doorstep. In a good way. But—what's going on with him and Harry?"

"A very large argument that I'm trying *not* to overhear." John face reflected his distaste for unintentional eavesdropping. They must have raised their voices, if John couldn't avoid the conversation.

"Ah. Forget I asked." Lizzie stared at the cat kettle. Where did one even buy such a thing? "So, um, how angry are you on a scale of one to ten?"

His answer surprised her. "Not."

At her assessing look, he said, "You forget. It wasn't that long ago that I handed you over to Worth's men in exchange for your best friend. Against my better judgment and every desire I had to keep you safe."

"But I wasn't your mate then."

"And you think that's why I didn't stop you?" He sat down in a kitchen chair, pulled her hand until she was right in front of him and pulled just a little bit more. She tumbled into his lap. "Really?"

She hooked her arm around his neck and looked into his eyes. "Okay. Then why didn't you?"

"Because it was your choice, and you needed to go." Before he'd finished the sentence, she pulled him closer for a soft, appreciative kiss. That was the plan, anyway. Minutes later, her heart was racing, her bra was too tight, and she was really annoyed that they were in the kitchen.

"Although I did consider tying you up," he said. "Briefly."

"Huh?" *Oh.* She thumped him on the shoulder. "You couldn't just let that go, could you?"

He grinned mischievously. "You said I was honest."

"So you're really okay with me being here?"

"Not even a little. I'm just not angry about it." He tipped her head so her cheek rested against his shoulder. "You gonna pass out now?"

"What?" Her voice rose slightly in aggravation.

"Get your pulse up a little, wear you out slightly, and that's your go-to response since you over-extended your magic." His voice was light and teasing, but she could hear the underlying concern.

"Harry says I'm completely fine. Different people recharge, recover, whatever you call it, at different rates." She grimaced. "I'm sick of feeling like a used-up battery. But he's not worried at all. And you know Harry's a badass in his field, right?"

"So I hear. Harrington was pissed when he refused to come with us. He claimed the kid's ethics were fucked up—my words, not his—and started blaming his mother."

"Hmm. Mom must be the healer. Although I'm surprised Harrington was so forthcoming."

"It was a brief moment in time." John pinched the bridge of his nose. "Now Mom's a hippie healer."

"Sorry. I don't follow."

John stopped massaging his temple and said, "Their argument. I can't quite tune them out." He sighed. "This is not one of the perks of improved senses. I have no desire to be involved in, or have any knowledge of, their private family disagreements."

John looked frustrated. Lizzie got it. The house was small, and he really *couldn't* tune them out if they were yelling at one another. She could even hear some of the noise of their voices occasionally, though no distinct words.

"Maybe I should go knock on the door?" Lizzie wondered aloud.

"Bad idea. Besides, I think Pilar might beat you to it."

Sure enough, the voices stopped.

Pilar walked into the kitchen a few seconds later. "Meeting in five here in the kitchen." She turned to Lizzie, who was rapidly climbing off John's lap, and said, "I'm glad to see you up and around. And the color is back in your face."

No wonder, since she was blushing an unattractive crimson color. At least from the heat in her ears, that's what she guessed. Lizzie smiled. "I'm feeling quite a bit better."

Harry breezed in next, no trace left on his expression of the argument raging between him and his uncle only minutes earlier. After briefly greeting John and Pilar, he took a seat on one of the kitchen chairs, legs casually sprawled out in front of him. With his tousled, carroty hair, Marvel T-shirts, and almost perpetually upbeat demeanor, he was a likable character. And he set people at ease. It saddened Lizzie that those feelings didn't extend to his own family.

When Harrington appeared, everyone turned as one in his direction. "Lizzie, I understand you're not yet back to your full capabilities."

"That's correct." She decided now wasn't the time to elaborate. She was just glad Harrington wasn't trying to lock her up.

"John, you're ready to relieve Max in a half hour?"

"I am." John affirmed.

"Pilar, you're heading in to town for some supplies?"

"Yes. I thought I'd bring Harry with me, since Max might need to rest, and John will be on watch." Pilar looked between the two men, waiting for one of them to agree with her plan.

"Good idea." Turning to Lizzie, Harrington explained, "We're keeping an eye on Worth's house, waiting for an opportunity to enter and search the premises when he's gone."

Lizzie's brow furrowed. She had been on the inside, had been one of the kidnap victims, when John had led a team to rescue her and Pilar from the Prague house and Worth's control. While she'd not been privy to the team's efforts at the time, she had read the reports afterwards. She was certain that when Sarah, the team's warding expert, had moved them through the several layers of security wards Worth had created, at least one had alerted Worth to their presence.

"Won't he still know that you're here? Even if he leaves? Or is there a critical distance, a point where he can't sense interference with his wards any longer?" Lizzie had visions of Worth returning in the midst of their search. She couldn't articulate how bad that would be.

Her skin started to crawl, her breath came a little shorter, and she felt a hot flush of panic wash through her. When would that man cease to have a hold on her? She took a breath, and she reminded herself—it may feel like her kidnapping was a lifetime ago, but it wasn't. In practical terms, it had just happened. Her reactions were reasonable, just not very convenient.

For a moment—a very brief moment—she was frightened enough that she considered removing herself from the team. Assuming she was even on the team. *What the hell.* She mentally berated herself. She needed to be in the right place mentally, or Harrington would never include her. He'd ship her butt back to Prague in a heartbeat if he thought he could. She was here because she could help. And Sarah deserved it. And she needed to conquer her fears where Worth was concerned. And she wanted to be there for John. And, dammit, it was just the right thing to do.

Okay. She was good. Well, she could breathe. Good was probably a few months away. Or perhaps it was just seeing Worth locked up that she needed. Maybe that would make her feel safe again.

Harrington responded to her question. "The purpose of this mission isn't directly related to catching Worth. I'm willing to risk exposing our knowledge of this and his other remaining residences to accomplish our goal. That said, my hope is to enter undetected."

Lizzie raised her hand. If she didn't know better, she'd have thought that was an eye roll from Harrington.

"Yes?" he asked politely. Must have been her imagination.

"What exactly is our purpose? I missed that meeting." Maybe it wasn't her wisest move to mention her exclusion, given the fact that she wasn't sure why Harrington hadn't shipped her right back as soon as she arrived in Freiberg.

"To search for any evidence of Worth's Vampyr technique —how he manipulates someone else's magic and how he can utilize or absorb it. In the short term, the information could aid in finding a cure for Sarah. Longer term, we need the information to curb what could be the next rise of Vampyr." Harrington's voice had turned quieter as he spoke. And he looked grim.

She hadn't considered the broader implications. But of

course Harrington had; that was his job. And if she had to guess, so had John. She was new to evil masterminds, world domination, political power plays, and magical factions. If she had her druthers, she'd stay that way. Well, not new—but completely uninvolved.

She sighed quietly. As unconvinced as she might be that the bigger picture held any relevance to her life, she did know that the people sitting at the kitchen table in this room today were becoming more important to her with each passing day. Not just John, all of them. Which made this whole mess relevant to her life.

"On the positive side, I seriously doubt Worth would ever willingly share his Vampyr knowledge. So a resurgence of the old movement isn't very likely, right?" Lizzie figured a little optimism wouldn't be a horrible thing. Because right now, their mission seemed like a risky endeavor with massive consequences and very little chance of success. In summary, no bueno.

Pilar leaned forward, elbows resting on the table. "Unfortunately, it doesn't work that way. This is a secret too great to be kept. If Worth isn't the engineer behind the improved process, then who was? How did Worth discover it? Has anyone else discovered the source of Worth's knowledge? And assuming a best case scenario—that no one else has the information, that Worth alone is in possession of the key to Vampyric feeding—how long can he keep the information secure? With this much power, infinite questions arise."

Lizzie rested her head on her arms and closed her eyes. This situation sucked. She felt John's warm fingers rub the exposed base of her neck. Were these the types of situations that John dealt with as the Alpha of the Texas Pack? Was this what she had to look forward to if she finally accepted the position he'd so casually bestowed upon her? Could she feel more overwhelmed? *Argh.*

She was an adult. Adults had responsibilities. So hers involved saving the world (sort of) and her friends (definitely), and maybe meant she had to risk her life (probably) to keep other people safe (damn straight!). But that was okay, because she had badass magical powers—she hoped—and an incredible side-kick-hero boyfriend.

And she *really* needed to make some changes in her life, because eventually she wouldn't be able to pep talk herself out of some terrible situation.

Harrington said, "If you're feeling like the situation is too dangerous—"

Lizzie lifted her head up, looked him square in the eye, and said, "I didn't break out of IPPC holding so you could send me back. Realizing we're in a difficult situation is hardly an admission of defeat." She needed to stop worrying about Harrington shipping her off. She wouldn't let him—and she'd found her sass. She might lose it occasionally, but Harrington didn't need to know that. "What's the plan? And how are you going to prevent Worth from detecting us as we breech his wards?"

CHAPTER THIRTY

A country compound, surrounded by a combination of stone walls and wrought iron fencing, security guards —some Lycan, based upon scents John was picking up—and wards zinging around the entire place like invisible laser beams waiting to melt intruders. No problem.

The plan had been relatively simple. Keep a man on Worth's house round the clock. When he left—they could only hope he would—have Harry do his magical headcount. Turned out, that was what at least part of the argument between the two men had been about. Healers had strict ethical guidelines that they followed. And Harry, though unconventional and creative, was turning out to be very ethical. Scanning a person without their knowledge was considered a violation of healer ethics. Harrington reasoned that the good of the entire magical community was at risk, and surely *that* weighed more heavily than some hired goons' privacy rights. Harry wasn't so sure. He had a problem with the lack of immediacy of the threat.

But without Harry's aid, John, Max, Harrington, Lizzie, and Pilar would go in almost blind. Their knowledge of the occupants would be limited to the men who had come and gone while the house was under surveillance. And there would be no specific location known for those guards within the compound.

Frank, the healer who had participated in Lizzie's rescue, had agreed to help in the instance of Lizzie's kidnapping only because there were two known hostages—Pilar and Lizzie—inside the house. He'd weighed the various factors, and the safety of the hostages had weighed heavier than the rights of the scumbag kidnappers. John's words, not Frank's. That was a very different situation than the one Harry was facing today.

Lizzie wasn't sure what Harrington had finally said to convince Harry, but he had finally acquiesced. And it was a good thing, because it hadn't been long after that Max had contacted them to say Worth had left the house. Dusk was falling when Harrington got Max's call.

The next part of the plan was even simpler. Harrington was the king of wards, or so he claimed. Perhaps not in those words, but stress was making Lizzie mentally glib. Harrington claimed with ninety percent certainty that he could dismantle Worth's wards without alerting him, so long as Worth was more than a mile or two away. And Worth was actually the caster who created the wards. Where he got the math on that, Lizzie didn't even want to know. What she did know was that if he pulled this off, there was no way she'd ever let him wiggle out of mentoring her. She wanted some kick-butt warding skills. With her current life choices and the direction things were headed, they'd come in handy.

"Wow, pretty," Lizzie uttered, before she could stop herself. Her eyes popped at the sprinkling of tiny pink and purple lights that showered down around them. Lizzie would have to ask Harrington why she could see the diffusing ward but the guards couldn't. She was sure that was the case. Harrington would never be so careless. *Oh.* Lizzie wanted to do a jig. If she could see it, maybe her magic was coming back.

Pilar shushed her. She was holding the ward together that muted their presence, both audio and visual. Pilar wasn't the most sophisticated of warding casters, so she'd asked the group to remain quiet and move deliberately without sudden spurts of speed to help her ward "stick." *Oops.*

As Lizzie continued to watch the colorful dissolution of one of the perimeter wards, she hoped Harrington's reasoning had been sound. He'd claimed Worth's ego was too great to have another caster set the wards—at least any of the important ones. Some of the perimeter wards might be another caster's, assuming Worth employed one. But—since Harrington never had a chance to speak with Sarah about the wards Worth cast on the Prague house—he wasn't sure what to expect. That was one of the gambles in the plan.

Harrington waved them through a small side gate. Max had picked the lock, and the ward Harrington had just diffused had been attached to the gate and fence. Warding, like most caster magic, did require an anchor. Language casters frequently chose books as the anchor for their recording spells, for a variety of reasons. But with wards, the caster chose whatever would help the spell along a little. The ward Harrington diffused was likely a perimeter-sensing spell of some kind.

None of the other wards Harrington pulled them through fizzled out with a magical fireworks display. A little anticlimactic, she thought, and then she almost bit her tongue. What the hell was she thinking? She was in Worth's backyard. That was more than enough excitement for anyone.

John pushed gently on her lower back. She followed Pilar through the back door. Harry had found only three men. Worth had taken two with him when he'd left. So there were six total staying at the house and three in the house now. That seemed a little light on staff to Lizzie. If she was an evil mastermind, she'd have twenty guys on staff acting as bodyguards. Worth must have a more than average number of enemies. It seemed like a smart move. But for reasons of ego or discretion, this was the second time they'd found him with a small security contingency.

She couldn't believe she was in Worth's house. She tried to shake off the icy shiver that ran up her spine at that thought and turned down the hall to a room on the right. They'd entered into a side hall from outside, but now she, John, and Harrington were covering the rooms to the right, Max and Pilar the rooms to the left. Lizzie didn't have her magical spidey sense for spelled books—no magic, no spidey sense—but she and John could certainly look for any books, and Harrington would catch any wards. Pilar could at least see any wards that were there—if she looked very carefully—and certainly could spot spelled books. Although Max had no magical skills, Lizzie learned in the aftermath of her rescue from the Prague house that Max was handy with a gun. Very handy.

They'd discussed briefly how Worth might be hiding his research or his source. John and Harrington agreed that he would likely use a combination of magical warding and traditional security measures. Worth could trap it, hide it, or place sensors on it using warding. And traditional security was a likely initial deterrent, keeping less determined thieves or the nonmagical from stealing it. Whatever *it* was. Lizzie was getting annoyed. Looking for something (she wasn't sure what) that was hidden (she wasn't sure where) was a huge pain in the rear.

Her team had cleared a parlor and a living room and were working on a large full bath—you never knew where someone might hide a valuable spelled book—when

Harrington got a text. Or Lizzie assumed it was, because he checked his phone then waved her and John out of the bathroom. Lizzie replaced the lid on the toilet tank with a small wrinkle of her nose. *Thank you for small favors.*

Harrington flashed the screen at John, who nodded and changed. He was John, then he wasn't; it still freaked her out a little. Not the massive wolf standing in front of her; him she was fine with. It was the change itself that was disconcerting. She hadn't blinked but felt as if she had—and presto, wolf. It was disconcerting. She snapped to attention. Her wolf was just about to leave. He usually took a moment to orient to his new form. And from the deep stretching bow he was rising from, she could tell he was about done.

She leaned over, grabbed a handful of dense hair on either side of his massive jaws near his cheeks and pulled his head to face her. Just inches away, her voice barely a whisper, she said, "You will be careful. You will *not* get seriously hurt." When his wolf eyes stared intently back at her, unblinking, she said, "Right?"

One single, sharp dip of his head. Then he wrenched his head to the side, pulling the fur easily from her fingers. He was gone, the low-lying tip of his tail the last thing she saw before he disappeared around the corner. She looked down at the small bit of fluff left in her hand. She hadn't realized she'd been holding on so tightly, she thought absently. She wanted to growl her frustration. If her magic was back—

Before she had a chance to finish that thought, Harrington nudged her. He held the screen on his phone towards her and waited for her to figure out what it meant.

Lycan. There was only one way they'd know a Lycan was approaching—he had to be in wolf form. Max and Pilar had seen him. Had the guard seen them?

Lizzie's mind raced. If the guard was in Lycan form, he was prepared for a fight. Had he scented them? Or had they tripped a ward? Maybe he did his rounds in wolf form, she thought hopefully. Worth's Lycan henchmen had guarded her during the first kidnap attempt Worth made, and they had chosen to patrol in wolf form. So it wasn't completely out in left field that the guard was patrolling as a wolf and unaware of them—but she didn't have a good feeling.

A whole of ten seconds must have passed before a loud crash sounded, propelling her into the hallway. She walked to the corner, pulling Harrington behind her. She was surprised when he didn't resist. She peeked around the corner, not sure what to expect. If it was bad, she was helping—magic or no magic. What she saw as she turned the corner made her heart pound in fear.

CHAPTER THIRTY-ONE

Lizzie gulped in a quick, short breath. She'd been startled into holding her breath, and now it was coming in short, fast pants. Her first coherent thought wasn't very complimentary to Max. Her next thought was a little more rational. She'd kick Max's ass next time she saw him. Two Lycan guards. He couldn't just take an extra second and type that little "2," could he? *Idiot.*

She looked frantically at Harrington for some guidance as to how they could help John. That's when she realized Harrington *was* trying to help. He was inspecting the room for wards, she suspected to make sure John didn't accidentally trigger a trap. They hadn't cleared this room yet. He must have been casting as she'd dragged him along behind her. That suddenly made a lot more sense.

She searched the room. Max was in a corner, gun drawn. But there was no way he could risk a shot. His gun wasn't silenced, so a shot would alert the remaining guard—assuming he didn't already know. And—Lizzie cringed, looking at the tumble of wrestling furred bodies—he couldn't get a clear shot. He was just as likely to injure John as one of the other wolves.

Pilar. Where was Pilar? The room they were in was the large entryway with a sweeping, curved staircase. Pilar had positioned herself on the staircase, several steps up. Perhaps she'd been caught unaware and retreated there. Even in her panic, Lizzie could see that Pilar was riveted, but not to the thrashing bodies wrestling below her. Her attention was pinned to the wall opposite Lizzie's hallway. Fearing yet another guard, Lizzie turned and found...nothing. Her gaze flew back to Pilar and to the wall opposite again. Only on the second look did she register the tapestry hanging on the wall. She turned once again to Pilar, and this time, Pilar saw her. She pointed repeatedly at the tapestry.

Shit. That's what they'd come for. Not a book, at all. A tapestry. She tried to calm herself, so she could consider her options. Clearly, she had to retrieve the damn tapestry. Max would hold his position so long as there was an opportunity to pick off one of the guards. Pilar was trapped on the stairs by the unpredictable movements of the fighting Lycan. And Harrington was otherwise occupied, if she had to guess, deconstructing a ward on, near, or around the tapestry.

She narrowed her eyes, trying desperately to pick out which body was John's and which the guards'. She'd never seen a close quarters fight between Lycan. There was no retreat and reengage, just sliding and twisting, angry teeth and vicious claws. And their movements were lightning fast. It made it almost impossible to track individual movements. She could finally see that bright blood splashed down John's side, but she thought—she hoped—it might be from one of the other wolves. A rangy, tawny wolf had a mangled ear that was bleeding profusely, so perhaps it was his blood.

Suddenly, the fight shifted. She hadn't realized that John had been fighting defensively, until he wasn't. The seething mass of tawny, silver, and reddish fur seemed to heave. Before Lizzie could properly process what had happened, the body of a red wolf—much smaller than John—was lying in a pile next to the tapestry wall. Her ears were ringing from the sound of the two shots Max had fired almost immediately, hitting first the torso then the head of the prone wolf. She couldn't imagine he had survived his impact with the wall. Whether a broken neck or a bullet killed him, the result was the same. Even from across the large entryway, Lizzie could clearly see the open, staring eyes and the motionless body heaped into a pile of unnatural angles, loose skin, and bloodied fur.

Her stomach roiled and her mouth started to water in a way that predicted the very real possibility she'd lose the contents of her stomach. She inhaled cautiously. Then exhaled very slowly, fearful a fast breath might push her nausea into vomiting. She'd seen a Lycan killed before—but she hadn't been this close to the corpse. She took another slow breath.

As she struggled to stay calm, she couldn't help but see John. His silver and black body intertwined with tawny pale patches of fur. With just the two wolves, she could see more detail as the fight continued: the paler wolf's dangling and useless foreleg, the blood—definitely not John's—splashed across his rib cage, the increasingly sluggish movements as both wolves tired. Wrapped up in the push and pull, the clawing and grabbing, Lizzie could feel her nausea recede. *John would be fine. John would be fine.* Almost a chant in her head. The reminder kept her moving when she saw her chance to cross the floor. Both of the wolves, bodies still wrapped around one another, had moved closer to the stairs. Closer to Pilar. And that meant further from the tapestry.

Before she had a chance to reconsider her actions, she darted across the floor stopping only inches from the wall. It was then that she realized she hadn't a clue if the tapestry was still warded or if Harrington had managed to disable whatever Worth had placed to protect it. She spun around, frantically searching for Harrington.

When he saw her panicked look, he yelled, "Clear."

As Lizzie pulled the tapestry from the wall and began rolling it, she had the irreverent thought that it was about time she heard Harrington raise his voice like a normal person and it just figured that it took life or death circumstances. She also thought—where the hell was that last guard? They'd made enough noise to wake the dead.

Having managed to reduce the tapestry to a more mobile size, she stopped suddenly. While the wolves had been mostly silent as they'd fought, there had been the background noise of movement, the slide of fur on the floor, and an occasional whimper or groan of pain. That was gone, replaced by the singular, softly huffing sound of labored breathing. Looking up, she saw John standing on all fours, his head and body sunk low in exhaustion, his sides heaving, and blood sprayed across his muzzle and chest. But standing, definitely standing. She felt some of the tension seep from her. A growing pool of blood caught her eye, drawing her attention to the ground. The tawny wolf's neck had been ripped open and the blood was draining at John's feet.

Reality and a sense of place reasserted itself. They needed to leave—now. There was a third man unaccounted for, and Max had fired his weapon. They needed to retreat quickly. Harrington and Max both came to that conclusion a hair earlier. Max had reached Pilar and was walking her down the stairs. Pilar looked pale, and she took Max's arm when he offered it. But when she moved, her steps were sure and purposeful.

Harrington had crossed the room and stood before her, hand outstretched. "Check on John."

She must have been in a mild state of shock to have to be told to check on her wounded mate. She handed the tapestry to him, and moved toward John. Realizing he was still on four legs, panting heavily, she turned back to Harrington and said, "He needs to change, right?"

At Harrington's nod, she turned back and continued on to John. She frowned, the furrow deepening as she got closer. He should have changed by now.

She had an uneasy feeling as she approached the last few feet. She had the distinct feeling she was facing not John, but a wild animal. Her heart said to touch, but her eyes and common sense said to stand very still. As she watched, John swayed and his glazed eyes swung in her direction. She reached a hand out to his shoulder to steady him, unthinkingly. John's response was shockingly swift. His posture became rigid and he lifted a snarling lip at her.

Harrington called to her, "Hurry him up. We're leaving."

Lizzie was frozen in place. Not by John's snarl. It had lasted a second, and with a tiny dip of his head and a slow blink, he'd stopped. But her indecision and uncertainty couldn't be banished as quickly. Body still, she tried to relax —as much as she could while her brain zoomed along at rapid speeds. He was clearly injured, or he wouldn't be acting like he was. If he didn't change, he'd never make it out of the house. Not as injured as he was.

She glanced quickly at Harrington, Max, and Pilar. They had the tapestry. If it contained the information she believed it did, they needed to leave with it immediately. "Go."

At their incredulous looks, she repeated herself. "Go. While you still can. I'll be right behind you."

Pilar said, "No."

"Worth is on his way. He has to be. Please," she begged. "Leave."

Finally, she said, "I could see the sparks. When Harrington dissolved the ward."

Harrington nodded in understanding, grabbed Pilar, and spoke quietly in Max's ear. Max shook his head. Then Harrington left, pulling Pilar behind him.

"You better not be full of shit," Max said grimly.

She was about ready to cry. She didn't need to be bullied right now. "Fuck you. Help me move him. I can't get near him, let alone get him to change. Something's wrong."

Her terse words must have made some impression, because he jogged toward her immediately.

"What do you suggest?" Max asked.

Tears leaked down her face. She brushed impatiently at her cheeks, looked at John, then at Max. "Muzzle and carry him." She said it with much more certainty than she felt.

"Fuck." Max ran a hand through his hair. "You muzzle; I'll carry him." He yanked off his rigger's belt and handed it to her.

Okay, she had one shot at this. No way could she ever muzzle a healthy wolf, but the half-wild, swaying, exhausted animal in front of her couldn't keep his eyes open. She could do this.

She looked at the belt, tried really hard to remember that Pet First Aid class she took—five years ago? Three? At least she'd actually attended the whole thing, unlike that self-defense class.

She was procrastinating, because she really didn't want to get bit. Worse yet, for John to ever find out he'd bitten her. She took a breath, waited for him to sway, and just as he was blinking, she wrapped the belt around his mouth, then behind his head. As soon as she had crisscrossed the straps, Max had reached out to hold them in place. If he hadn't— well, John was pissed and he was a wolf with preternatural speed, injured or no. She worked as quickly as she could to make the final wrap around his muzzle one more time. Was that right? She wasn't sure, but it looked secure. She hoped it was. Otherwise, Max would likely suffer some serious puncture wounds wrestling an unhappy wolf. She cringed at the thought.

"All right. How do we do this?" she asked, eyeing a very disoriented but increasingly agitated John. He was temporarily distracted by the muzzle, alternately pawing at it and shaking his head.

"*I* do it," he said, looking at the drawn-back lips of the wolf with little enthusiasm. "A modified fireman's carry, I think."

He kneeled down and heaved the wolf over his shoulder. In that moment, it was crystal clear to Lizzie that the wolf was still mostly John. A confused and pissed off John, but still John. Max would have been torn up, muzzle or no, if not. As it was, he had a deep furrow of claw marks on his stomach before Lizzie could grab the wolf's hind feet and hold them still. She could see the blood already oozing through the T-shirt Max wore.

It took them another try before they finally figured out he would have to rest behind Max's neck, front legs dangling to the right side of Max's chest and hind legs to the left. Even then—he was just big. Max would have to work to get him as far as the gates of the property. As soon as the wolf was firmly settled, Max's hands steadying all four limbs, he took off at a good clip. Lizzie was directly on his heels.

CHAPTER THIRTY-TWO

Lizzie had no difficulty keeping up with Max—the man was carrying more than two hundred pounds of wolf—but she was trying to keep an eye out for guards, as well. She was just starting to consider giving her magic a tiny test, when she spotted two guards. She thought there had been only one guard left...which meant Worth was somewhere near. "Guards."

She and Max had just cleared the side door leading out onto the grounds when she spotted the men, so they either had to return to the house or make a run for it through the grounds. There wasn't much cover outside, but it was by far the better choice over being trapped in the house. And she was relatively certain Harrington had cleared any harmful wards, especially if they followed the same path back to the gate. Max must have agreed, because he kept to the same route as he headed to the gate.

Shit. The men were catching up. But not at Lycan speed, she realized. As one drew a gun, she considered that they might be non-magical humans.

"Gun," she warned Max.

She got a grunt in reply. He'd already increased his speed when she'd warned him of the guards. There wasn't much else he could do with no cover.

"Don't shoot." The clipped command came from none other than Worth. "I want the woman alive."

Lizzie's foot caught on a tuft of grass when she heard Worth's voice. Dammit. As she caught her balance, she hoped that his men wouldn't aim at Max and John for fear of hitting her. She slowed down slightly. If she could keep herself in between Max, John and the guards, then—*uumph*. Her nose was suddenly mashed into the dirt, one of Worth's men pinning her to the ground. *Hmm*. Perhaps she hadn't planned that so well. If she didn't distract the guards, they might still manage to catch or possibly shoot Max or John. That panicked her enough to make her struggles with her tackler and his buddy last an extra ten or twelve seconds.

Face pressed to the ground, arms twisted behind her, she frantically hoped that Max would keep going. She thought—hoped—that Max would get John somewhere safe. Once John had changed and was recovered, they were more than welcome to come retrieve her ass.

The thought of being stranded here and under Worth's control made her want to bawl. She also realized a rescue might not be such a simple thing. John's failure to change up to this point was inexplicable and deeply troubling. His injuries might be more severe than Lizzie understood. He might not be *able* to help her.

They marched her toward the house, a guard on either arm. She scanned the surroundings. The fence surrounding the property was so close, maybe 100 feet away. What would happen if she attempted a fade and her target was too far? She'd overextend aiming past the fence, no doubt. She'd deplete any magic she had left, which would be fine if she was safe from Worth. But on the other side of the fence wouldn't give her much of a head start. And what if she attempted to fade and couldn't? Would she still be magically tapped out? Those were chances she couldn't take right now.

When they reached Worth, he nodded at the guards, which was apparently a signal to let her go. She stumbled on the uneven ground when the harsh hold they held on her upper arms was suddenly released. As she tried to regain her balance, she thought frantically of her options.

"Long time, no see," she said. She tried to sound calm and confident, but it came out breathless and higher pitched than her normal tone of voice. She couldn't help it. Making eye contact with Worth was harder than she'd imagined.

Worth backhanded her sharply across the cheek. *Son of a bitch, that hurt.* She blinked tears from her eyes and realized she'd fallen to her knees. Small pebbles from the rough path gouged at her knees. Before she had a chance to even think about standing, black spots still dancing around the outer edges of her vision, he kicked her in the ribs. *Fuck.* This wasn't the man she remembered. She swallowed the gorge that was rising up. She *did not* need to puke on his shoes. No telling how much that would piss off this angry, volatile man. He was very different from the coldly calculating strategist she remembered.

Lying on her right side and curled in a ball, it was all she could do not to moan. But he didn't touch her again. After about a minute, she recovered enough to look beneath her lashes at him. Gone was the cool head, polite manners, and urban attire that had been Worth. This man wore khakis, a crisp T-shirt, the beginnings of a beard, and a gun in a shoulder holster. Lizzie closed her eyes fully again. Her mind reeled. He looked human, non-magical human. Casters and Lycan didn't usually carry guns.

"I know you can hear me, pretty little Lizzie." His voice was the same—yet different. There was scorn and unconcealed disgust. He'd been so controlled before. "I have need of you and your tidy little supply of magic," he spat. "Or you'd be dead."

She felt a hard yank on her scalp. She wanted to cry out, but no sound emerged from her lips. Someone was dragging her down the path. Her muzzy, pain-filled brain tried to put the pieces together. If he was carrying a gun, he might have a very good reason to hate her. A personal reason to become emotional over her appearance at his front door. Maybe he'd lost his magic for a time. Given the wards surrounding the compound, he had it back. But if he'd lost it—even for a short while—she couldn't imagine the level of virulent anger such impotence would generate in Worth.

The painful pulling at her scalp was joined by a steady wrenching feeling in her shoulder. She must have passed out for a moment, because suddenly she was inside the house and being pulled across a floor. She could feel the wood floor and then the rug underneath her—but it was all distant and fuzzy, like she'd just woken from a dream but wasn't yet able to think clearly or move. She could feel even these sensations start to slip away as her thoughts became hazier. A sharp pain pierced through the darkness. Her body slamming into a wall? A doorway? She made a half-hearted attempt to grab at the doorjamb she was being yanked past, but her fingers wouldn't move to clench the frame.

She was so tired. Even her mounting terror couldn't keep her awake. She didn't want to die like this. She didn't want to die *at all*, she thought right before she lost consciousness.

She woke briefly as a guard pulled at her feet. The movement made her shoulder scream with a tearing pain, and tears were running down her face. She could just barely make out Worth speaking in the background. He was giving instructions for evacuation to one of his men. As she struggled to hear anything that might hint at their destination, the guard finished binding her feet and moved to her hands. He pulled her hands together, wrenching her damaged shoulder. She bit down on her cheek frantically as waves of pain tore through her. She didn't want Worth to hear her scream, she thought, a fraction of a second before her mouth filled with her own blood, and she lost consciousness.

CHAPTER THIRTY-THREE

John woke to blackness. God, he was tired. And sore. What the fuck had happened to him? He felt like he'd run straight into a wall, running at full speed. *Shit.* Now he remembered. He practically had run into a wall. Or, at least, he'd been thrown into one headfirst. And as soon as he thought about his head, he felt a piercing pain shoot through his skull. Murmuring voices were getting louder in the background.

"…concussion. No bleeding in the brain and I've stopped the swelling…"

His brain was swelling? *What the fuck!* He tried to stand up, and that was when he first realized that a) he was still wolf. And b) someone had restrained him. Oh, and c) he was in a moving vehicle that was hauling ass down the road.

It might be time for an attempt at communication. A rumble started low in his chest and vibrated through his entire body. The sound grew louder as he struggled against his restraints and failed to break free.

"…any drugs…sedate…"

He still couldn't see, but he recognized the voice.

Harrington was speaking in that clipped, controlled tone he used so often. John tried to open his eyes. He knew being sedated right now was a bad idea—terrible, in fact—but he couldn't remember why. He panted in agitation trying to remember. Then suddenly he knew—Lizzie. And with that thought, he snapped and snarled. His movements were blind, since his eyes still refused to open. But he didn't care who he grabbed. Apparently, everyone in the vehicle was colluding against him. He heard his name….

"Braxton." More firmly. "Braxton." The second time, a hand shook his shoulder roughly. Pain, but more of an ache than the shooting pains in his head. He growled. The third time he heard his name, he recognized Harry. Harry was a healer. He quieted.

"No. No drugs. And he's at least partially aware of what we're saying right now. Isn't that right, Braxton?" Harry's voice was calm and even. Much more soothing than the hand on his shoulder.

"If you can hear me, wag your tail," Harry said.

John thought for a moment, took a discreet sniff, did a little math, then grabbed the hand resting close to his muzzle. He didn't bite down, just held it. *Wolves don't wag, you bastard.* He realized they must have removed a muzzle, because he did vaguely remember the sensation across his nose and neck, and having difficulty panting. They'd tightened the thing too much.

Harry let out a low chuckle. "Told you. He can hear just fine. Can I have my hand back?"

John spit it out, like it tasted foul.

"Cute," Harry said wryly.

John lifted his lip, showing a little canine.

"Can I touch you? Now that the swelling is reduced and you're thinking more clearly, I'd like to get you well enough to change. All right?" Harry seemed pretty damn chipper.

John knew something wasn't right and that there was a reason Harry shouldn't be so damn cheerful. He was having difficulty hanging onto any one thought, and his head was still pounding terrifically. Then his thoughts slipped again to Lizzie. *Dammit. Where was she?* She should have been with him. She'd never leave him in this state unless she had to. Since Harry hadn't begun to heal him yet and the thought of Lizzie had him slowly working himself into a panic, he thumped his tail emphatically against the seat they'd laid him on.

"I got it. Just give me a second. We're going to remove your restraints." Harry had toned down the chipper and was now calmly efficient.

John held himself perfectly still. Whatever moved this mess along. His restraints—melted, for lack of a better word. Those bastards had warded him somehow. He had more important things to worry about, but he wouldn't forget that. He needed to know what they'd done and if anyone could repeat it. He tried to pull his eyes open, and this time he succeeded. But the small amount of light in the car moved straight from his eye to the back of his brain like a needle.

As he was closing his eyes, Harry said, "Sorry. Should have warned you. You've had a pretty good thwack on the head. You'll be light sensitive until we get you fixed up. Hang on."

After some shifting, Harry said, "I'm going to touch your head. Okay?"

Since his head hurt when he moved it too much, he thumped his tail again. Max would never let him live this down. And he knew Max was present. He could smell him. And blood. Max was covered in his own blood. What exactly had gone down after he'd lost awareness of his surroundings?

His attention pulled back to Harry as his head was gently

but firmly grasped. He'd never been healed like this. He'd gotten a general boost from a healer before. Frank had helped him out after Worth had tried to suck him dry. But serious injuries were more quickly healed by a change. How bad had his head injury been? He could feel whatever Harry was doing take hold. The shooting pain in his head lessened, becoming a dull ache.

"Think you can change?" Harry asked.

John considered seriously before he tried. He'd been pretty seriously damaged if a change hadn't been possible. *Was* he recovered enough to change? He tugged at his magic, expecting some resistance, but it flowed to the surface of his skin just as it always had. He gave the tiny mental push that brought about his change.

"Where's Lizzie?" The first words out of his mouth immediately dampened what appeared to have been a moment of relief when he changed.

"He doesn't remember." Max stated the obvious.

"Clearly." What little patience he had was disappearing. "Where is she?"

Pilar spoke up, eyes forward. "Caught as you were escaping. There was no way to stop it. Max had to carry you out, and Harrington and I had the tapestry—the source that we came for. And even if we hadn't, neither of us is a match for Worth." Leave it to the only woman in the vehicle to have enough balls to answer him.

They'd arrived at a house. "A different house?" John asked as he pulled on a pair of sweat pants Harry threw at him.

"A safety precaution," Max replied shortly. "We need to get Harrington, Pilar, and the tapestry back to a more secure location, back to Prague." He looked at John. "Then you and I are going to get you as close to Worth's as possible. If Lizzie's magic comes back, there's a chance she'll try to fade to *you*. And we all know how that turns out if you're too far away."

"Pilar told me Lizzie could see the residual magic dissipate after Harrington dismantled a ward on your way in. That's excellent news. Her magical battery is getting close to being recharged." Harry grimaced. "I know. A terrible analogy."

"But good news," John said thoughtfully. "What's the time frame? I know, I know—it's not an exact science. But give me your best guess."

Harry gave him a look. "One hour? Six? Chances are good you can get back to her before her magic returns. What I can't figure out, is how you'll stay under Worth's radar if you return."

"And how long we have before Worth has packed up and left. His hidey hole is blown. He'll evacuate right away," Max said. When John shot him a nasty look, he replied "Hey, we needed to get you in your right mind and a car ride worked to get us away from Worth. I'm sorry, but that was the option that seemed best at the time, even if it left him open to bolt. And it was always our backup plan to come here if we didn't make a clean getaway."

Turning to Harrington, John said. "You need to leave."

Harrington nodded.

Harry interrupted them. "Bad news. You'll need to drive out. At least to the next nearest airport." He looked a little sheepish. "When it was clear Lizzie was not coming out, I made some arrangements to ensure Worth couldn't abscond with her by plane. But it means you can't leave by plane either."

Harrington looked suspicious and angry. "What have you done?"

Harry ignored him.

"Fair enough," said Max, almost simultaneous to John's "Thank you."

"No problem. It's a temporary fix, but Worth should

already know that flying is out of the question for the next two to three hours. My friend can only make very small, localized adjustments," Harry said.

"Can you have the dragons meet us and escort us out?" Pilar asked. When three male heads turned her way, she clarified. "They wouldn't help with a raid but would do the flyover. I just wondered if escorting us home was within their"—she fluttered her hands—"their guidelines or rules."

Rather than respond, Harrington picked up his phone and made a call as he walked out of the room.

"Are we ready to head out again?" he asked Max. He was impatient to get back to Worth's. He'd never forgive himself if something happened to Lizzie while they plotted and planned. His instincts were pushing him to hustle.

"My friend can give us a speedy lift home, so I'll stay in Freiburg to coordinate our flight back." Harry ducked his head. "I'm not much use in a fight, but I'll be here for medical care and transport."

Harrington walked in on that statement, and he narrowed his eyes at Harry. John could smell the anger leaking from his pores. These two definitely had some unresolved issues.

"Fine," Harrington said curtly.

"If they do attempt to relocate by car, wouldn't that be ideal? Or even if they drive to the airstrip?" Pilar asked. Seeing the confusion around her, she explained. "It's doubtful Worth knows Lizzie can fade. As long as he doesn't try to siphon her magic—if it's back—then she can fade to a car that's not far away, correct?"

John's heart stuttered when Pilar mentioned Worth stealing Lizzie's magic. It was an obvious outcome that none of them had articulated. What was to prevent Worth from simply killing her immediately? From sucking her completely dry as he had his henchman Moore in Prague?

A hand touched his shoulder, and the muscles twitched

in response. He was incredibly distracted if Pilar could sneak up on him. "She's quite valuable alive, John. She has special knowledge, and she's a precious bargaining chip. Also, Worth doesn't act on emotion, not that I've seen. He's thoughtful, calculated really. He'll recognize her value alive."

John nodded. He wasn't in a frame of mind to tell her, but he appreciated her efforts. Turning to Harrington, he asked, "What did Lachlan have to say?"

"He's sending two men to Munich. We'll drive to the airport, and they'll meet us there. It's the best we could manage, taking into account the urgency of our departure and our grounded plane." Harrington glanced quickly at Harry and away.

Either Harrington and his nephew had different priorities, or Harrington didn't appreciate losing control. Either way, all John cared about was that Lizzie's departure had been slowed.

Losing his patience, John said, "We're leaving. Need anything else from us?"

"Wait." Harrington stepped in front of them before they reached the front door. "I can tell you with some certainty that Worth hasn't left. I laid a detection ward around the fence. Worth would find it before he passed through, and I suspect he'll disable it soon. But it still stands and no one has passed through it."

Noteworthy. Why wouldn't Worth immediately remove it?

Harrington must have seen his doubt, because he said, "He may not have found it yet. He's quite possibly busy with other concerns. Or it could simply be too much trouble and he has other priorities."

Each group began gathering their things and splitting apart. Max, John, and Harry in Harry's rental. Pilar and

Harrington took the more conspicuous van since they wouldn't be remaining in town with Worth.

John wasn't mollified by Harrington's assurances. He still drove like mad to Worth's property. En route, Harry leaned forward from the back seat and quizzed him about his head injury.

"Fine." He glanced at Harry out of the corner of his eye and right back to the road. "Lycan, remember? Shifting heals most wounds. You should know that."

"Don't be an ass. Most wounds, not all. And it was your pathetic furry self who *couldn't* shift without my help." When John didn't immediately respond, Harry prompted him again. "So—?"

"Like I said—fine." John sped up a few miles per hour.

Harry started to tick off a list. "Headache?"

John sighed in resignation. "No."

"Scalp tenderness? Light sensitivity?"

"No and no. Enough; I'm fine."

Harry leaned into the door, bracing himself as John took a turn at high speed. "Okay." He exchanged a glance with Max. "We'll call that good."

CHAPTER THIRTY-FOUR

Lizzie woke up in the trunk of a car. *Seriously?* Could these people stop shoving her in the trunk like she was luggage? Well, those other kidnappings had actually worked out all right. And she had to admit that waking up at all was a major win. If she was alive, there was hope for escape.

There was some reason Worth wanted her alive, and, again, she could only be thankful for that. But from there, it all went downhill.

Losing time was incredibly unsettling. And it didn't help that she'd been shoved in the trunk, all while unconscious. Someone had touched her, and she hadn't been aware of their hands on her body. It made her skin crawl. She needed to focus on the here and now. She took a deep breath—and inhaled the artificial fabric stink of an enclosed car trunk. The darkness of the trunk closed in on her. *No. No.* Panic would not help. Taking another—shallower—breath, she started to take stock of her condition. She found that her right cheek and jaw ached, and her lip was swollen. Wiggling, she found her ankles and wrists bound, which drew her attention to her left shoulder—which was a bad thing. Her movement had aggravated her shoulder injury, and the searing pain in her left shoulder made her eyes tear up. No more wiggling. None. She panted in distress, hoping it would stop.

Several minutes passed before she was able to think about anything but the pain. She was sure there were other scrapes, bruises, and sore areas, but she couldn't bring herself to even contemplate moving to try to discover the extent of her injuries. Five minutes, maybe ten, or an hour—she'd lost her sense of time—she was thinking about how she could investigate the trunk with as little movement as possible.

She rationalized that her abduction was completely unplanned. And they'd tied her for a reason. They may not have been able to kidnap-proof the trunk, like they had in the previous Lizzie-abduction-mobiles. She smiled. At least her sense of humor was trying really hard. If she could just get her hands to do the same. But as much as she steeled herself—as much as she told herself the pain would be over quickly—she couldn't make her body move. Her instinctive aversion to excruciating pain was too great, and she was paralyzed.

She contemplated alternatives that kept her shoulder as still as possible. Just when she had come up with a plan, the car hit a particularly large pothole or speed bump, and she dissolved into tears and gasps of pain. She thought she might have passed out, because she realized her shoulder was significantly better than her last recollection. How much time had passed? She couldn't let herself blackout again. Whatever she did, she had to remain awake.

It took a moment, but her plan came back to her as she became more aware of her surroundings. She felt for the taillight cover with the toe of her shoe. There was a slim chance, but she hoped that she could kick out the cover and somewhere along their route the missing taillight would be noticed. She thought it was still dark outside, and that would certainly help make the missing light noticeable. She'd prefer to remove one of the covers by her head so that she could see, but there was no way her shoulder would tolerate that much abuse. She'd pass out for sure.

It was a slow process, and it took her several tries before she could gauge how hard she could kick without jostling her arm so much she risked passing out. She finally got into a rhythm, and after several good solid kicks she was starting to worry she wouldn't be able to do it. Then her boot—and was she ever thankful she'd chosen boots—made solid contact and the plastic cracked. She continued to kick, hoping all the while that her activities would go unnoticed by Worth and his men.

After a few more solid kicks, she'd managed to crack most of the plastic. She was pushing it out with her toe when she was startled by the sound of an intermittently blaring horn. The noise surprised her, and she rolled and bumped her injured shoulder. Her head immediately began to swim. She was on the verge of passing out when it occurred to her there might just be a reason someone was honking. *Dammit.* She fought back the blackness that was closing in on the edge of her vision. She clenched her teeth, panting in short, sharp bursts. She desperately needed to stay awake for a few moments longer.

CHAPTER THIRTY-FIVE

M ax was driving. He had insisted after they'd arrived at their surveillance point near Worth's compound. Max claimed he'd barely survived John's driving and would prefer to be killed—if it came to that—by Worth and not one of his best friends. It hadn't been long before they'd spotted a car leaving with four occupants. It had to be Worth.

Max had tailed him, but it was John who laid on the horn when they'd seen the pieces of Worth's taillight fall away.

"What the fuck?" Max had asked in confusion. But being the smart man he was, he also leaned to the left out of John's way.

"It's her. Which means she's awake. Which means she can fade if she knows we're here. If she knows I'm here," John said.

"And she has her magic back," Max added.

"Yes. Given the alternatives, I'm willing to gamble." John was convinced this would work. But if it didn't— "Be ready to do some creative driving. And get closer."

"Closer?" Max asked with some concern. "We're already…got it." At the blaring horn, Worth's vehicle had increased in speed, pulling away from their car. "You have a backup plan besides chase the bastards and hope we don't kill her and us in the process?"

But before he could get an answer from John, a bizarre thing happened. A transparent, almost ghost-like Lizzie appeared in John's lap. Max's sudden jerk on the wheel caused the car to skid momentarily, and it consumed his attention to keep all four wheels on the road. By the time Max had regained control of the car, Lizzie—solid and quite real—was sprawled in John's lap. And she was screaming.

Max pulled over to the side of the road immediately. All four occupants piled out of the car and onto the grassy area next to the road. It didn't take long for Harry to diagnose a dislocated shoulder. He turned to Lizzie and asked, "Bad news or good?"

She was sprawled on the ground with John holding her as still as possible. She'd already thrown up once before Harry had been able to do anything, so she was trying desperately to stay still. "Shit." Lizzie panted in pain. "Bad."

"We've got to move the head of the humerus back into the shoulder socket." Harry was atypically grim.

Pale and sweating, Lizzie just looked at him as her chest heaved.

"It's going to hurt," he added.

John was done with the delays. "Fix this already." Lines of tension radiated around the corners of his mouth and eyes.

Lizzie grunted in agreement.

Harry took Max aside, presumably to give him instructions. When they returned, Harry spoke directly to John. "Keep her still."

Sweat poured off her face, and every small breeze made her teeth chatter and her body shake with cold. John gripped her hand and pushed wisps of hair away from her face.

As Max and Harry moved into position, Lizzie gasped, "The good news?"

Max and Harry shared a glance and then simultaneously pushed and pulled. In the blink of an eye, Lizzie was out. John gathered Lizzie's now unconscious form close to his chest. Taking up position next to her on the grass, he raised his eyebrows a bit when Harry spoke.

Harry belatedly answered Lizzie's question, "You won't be awake for long. T*hat* is the good news."

Harry performed his healer magic hunched over Lizzie's shoulder. He worked longer than John would have expected. As time passed and Lizzie didn't wake, he asked, "Shouldn't she be awake by now?"

Harry looked up from where he kneeled over Lizzie. "I gave her a nudge to keep her unconscious." Clearly noting John's worried and tense expression, Harry clarified, "It won't hurt her to be under for a little while. And I thought she'd appreciate missing most of this. Once I've healed her enough to be mobile and relatively pain-free, I'll pull her into consciousness."

John wasn't sure how much time had passed, but it seemed like a hell of a long time. Harry finally stood up and stretched out his neck, shoulders, and back.

The color had returned to Lizzie's face quite some time ago. So she really had just looked like she was sleeping, cradled in his arms. When she did finally wake, he shouldn't have been surprised that after a slow blink or three, her first words weren't about her shoulder.

"Where's Worth?" she asked.

Max responded. "Long gone. When you faded to the car, he kept going."

John knew Max was pissed to lose Worth again. He knew it, because he was, too. But there hadn't been much they could do as Worth's taillights had disappeared up the road.

They were preoccupied by Lizzie's sudden appearance, the near wreck, and treating Lizzie's injury.

She nodded slowly in response. Standing up, John helped her fit an improvised sling Harry had cobbled together from a fleece jacket.

Harry was looking rough, and John wondered what exactly he'd done for Lizzie. Healers were good at injuries. But even so, they usually just gave a helping hand to an injury, a magical push to speed the process. What Harry had done—taken stretched and torn tendons and coaxed them back to their normal placement and condition—John hadn't known that healers *could* do that. No wonder Harry looked wiped out.

Max called Harrington to update him on Worth's direction of travel—not Munich, possibly Frankfurt—and to let him know that Lizzie was retrieved. Injured—but safe and healing. While Max was updating Harrington, Lizzie called Kenna and left her a message. She couldn't reach her friend, which was weird, because John said she'd been harassing Harrington for updates.

After hanging up, Max claimed the driver's seat. Harry took the front passenger seat, so Lizzie and John could sit together in the back. As they drove to the private airstrip where they'd flown in with James earlier, she heard all about what Kenna had been up to. That she'd left John messages—he wouldn't say how many. And she threatened him with castration if he didn't call her back today. Classic Kenna. At least Harrington had been saved that indignity. Lizzie had to try hard not to laugh at the picture of Kenna leaving a castration voicemail on John's phone. It was utterly ridiculous.

Harry piped up from the front of the car, "I told you no strenuous sports, right?" Turning to John, he said, "No strenuous sports."

When it looked like John might actually growl at Harry,

Lizzie intervened and promised, "Scout's honor." It was only later that she revealed to John, "Of course, I'm not and never was a Scout. Do I look like I know how to start a fire, pitch a tent, or fish for supper with a ball of twine and a safety pin?"

John's reply, "Um, that's not exactly what the Scouts are about," earned him a frown and then was ignored.

James, Harry's pilot, had agreed to meet them at the airstrip. Halfway there, Lizzie wrinkled her nose and looked at John. "I've just remembered that you're not so fond of flying."

"It's only a few hours. I'm sure it'll be fine," he said dismissively. And if it wasn't, he'd puke in the toilet.

"Uhh—it's a small plane." She peeked at him from under her lashes. Something he found absolutely adorable, especially since she always did it when she was a little bit worried or embarrassed. "Really small."

Her words registered. "How small?"

"If you all weren't so huge, we might fit one more." She bit her lip. *Great.* Now she was worried about him flying.

"I'm sure it'll be fine," he reassured her, not sure at all himself.

Lizzie tried to distract him with various questions as they took off—in a tiny tin bucket with an octogenarian as pilot.

"Don't you ever wonder what happens with all these rental cars that we leave about everywhere?" she asked, out of the blue.

He chuckled. "We have people," he replied mysteriously.

"Um-hm." She eyed him suspiciously. "It's like the European version of Enterprise—*we'll pick you up*—isn't it?"

He was about to answer, when the plane dipped and rattled. And that was the last conversation they had for the remainder of the plane's ascent and well into the flight.

CHAPTER THIRTY-SIX

John's face had a greenish cast. Lizzie looked out the window and away from him, cringing in silent sympathy. She knew being in such a small plane would be a problem for him, but he was making every effort to act as if nothing was amiss. And in that moment she had a revelation. She wasn't incredibly brave or particularly adventuresome. But she could be brave; she could be adventuresome. She was the kind of person who was willing to face Worth—a man she was terrified of—on the chance that a cure could be found for Sarah amongst his possessions.

Here was the kicker: while Sarah was a dear woman, she was no John. And John's pack was certainly no Worth. So why was it so simple for her to take risks for Sarah, but not for John? Why was she so worried about the Texas Pack, when she was dealing with the likes of Worth?

Becoming John's mate in truth meant accepting a position within the Pack. It meant being a politician's wife and dealing with pack politics. It meant accepting additional responsibilities that she wouldn't have, under other circumstances, sought out. That didn't seem like such a leap right now. Okay, she'd been in the trunk of a car—her shoulder dislocated, her scalp on fire, her ribs aching, her cheek throbbing, and a gnawing fear that Worth would kill her soon eating at her belly. So sure, her perspective was a bit skewed right now.

But maybe that's what she'd needed in order to realize that becoming John's mate wasn't the huge hurdle she'd believed it to be. Yes, he'd basically moved their relationship to a new level without her informed consent. Yes, that was pushy, controlling even. Yes, he needed to learn to share power, control, and decision-making. But seriously, the man had not blinked when she'd traded herself to kidnappers to save her best friend. Well—he'd not been happy, but he hadn't tried to prevent her.

And that was no fluke. He didn't want her anywhere near Worth. She got it—she didn't want to be near the egomaniacal jerk any more than John. But he'd said not a word of recrimination when she'd shown up in Freiburg.

So in summary, she'd be John's mate. Accept whatever responsibilities that entailed. Accept whatever that meant for their relationship. He kept proving, over and over, that he was willing to compromise—she just hadn't been looking hard enough to see it.

She was a complete nut job if she didn't accept whatever responsibilities a position as his mate might bring. It was so simple. He was worth it. At the very minimum, he was worth her trying to fit in with the Pack.

And all of this was churning through her brain, while she sat next to John on the flight home. She couldn't discuss it, because—well, John wasn't exactly at his best on a small plane. She gave him a little room, left him in peace, and hoped he wouldn't be too miserable. She was much better with flying than she used to be, but she wasn't thrilled either to be in such a small aircraft—magical pilot or not.

As they approached Prague, she began to fret over Sarah. Her concerns about her relationship with John were temporarily allayed. So unfortunately, her mind moved on to the next big worry. She wanted to poke herself and say give it a rest. But that's how she rolled.

Would the tapestry reveal enough to help them develop a cure—a way to transfer magic back to Sarah? Would Harry's method of skimming magical energy from a number of sources be possible without harming the donors?

She looked at John. Finally, he'd fallen into a fitful sleep. She'd told him that the best cure for motion sickness was to fall asleep and it seemed to help him. She had no empirical evidence to support her claim, but she'd been a poor traveler —stomach and nerves—for years, until her magic had been released. She'd always found that it helped her. His complexion was still off, and his sleep was hardly sound, but he looked more comfortable now than he had the entire flight. She realized as she looked at him sleeping next to her, he grew dearer to her every day.

He surprised her by waking up about fifteen minutes later, looking almost fit again, the greenish cast gone from his skin. He rolled his shoulders, working the kinks out. Which reminded her—how had he been so seriously injured?

"You're okay? You seem okay—"

He gave her an odd look.

That concern was a little out of the blue, she realized. "What exactly happened at Worth's? When you weren't yourself." She didn't want to bring up a difficult memory, and she was sure injuring Max and almost injuring her weren't easy for him to think about, but it was important. She needed to know if it would happen again.

"Ah." He closed his eyes and tipped his head back toward the headrest. After about two seconds, he tipped his head to her, looked at her intently, and said, "I'm sorry. I had a head injury. I don't think I would have actually hurt you, but I can't honestly be sure. I don't remember most of you and Max getting me out of Worth's compound."

"I agree. I don't think you would have hurt me. You snarled at me." She said it with a smile in her voice.

"God. Seriously? I'm so sorry." He sounded horrified. Then he must have registered the tone of her voice. "Okay, how does that make you want to laugh?"

"Sweetheart, you don't snarl at anyone when you're a wolf. You take their head off. If there is one thing I've learned about Lycan in watching you fight…" She had to roll her eyes at her own statement. She couldn't believe she'd seen these guys fight enough to draw conclusions. "You use your words when you're on two legs. But once you're four-legged, there's no more talking, warning, or much vocalization at all. It's actually quite creepy. If you're furry, you just bite." She smiled. "But you didn't even try to bite me."

"So even out of my head, I know you're my woman," he summarized with a leer.

"I'm sure there's a more romantic way to say that—but, yes. And I got a muzzle on you. What are the chances I could do that—even with you injured—without a little cooperation on your part?"

"Good point," he agreed with a self-satisfied smirk.

"Not to pierce your massive ego, but how exactly did you get the head injury? Harrington and I missed the beginning of the fight. And I already know that idiot, Max, forgot to mention there were two guards." She was still pissed about that. She heard a grumbled "hey" in the background. Max must have heard his name.

"Why would he? I should be able to smell the number, age, sex, and a number of other characteristics. Especially if I know to check. No, this wasn't his fault at all. Damn. I meant to talk to Harrington about this before he left." He looked seriously troubled. When he continued, she could see why. "There was no scent. An absence of scent so extreme, it was like a bubble. I should have noted it, as unusual as it was, but —I was actively hunting for Lycan scent."

Lizzie had gotten a crash course in warding twice now. Once from Pilar, who was admittedly not strong but could explain the basics, and a second time from Harrington when she'd literally fallen on her ass learning how to cast a sensing ward. It was theoretically possible, she supposed.

"Maybe warding is a possibility? A moving ward—one attached to a Lycan—might be able to scrub the air as it passes." She was hypothesizing, but that was all she could do without more research.

John looked thoughtful. "What's the anchor? It can't be the Lycan, right?"

She considered for a moment. "It would be unlikely. I'm apparently the only animate anchor Harrington, Pilar, or Frank have all come into contact with. I'm pretty sure an object would be used. Easy enough to do if they're either carrying it or it's attached to the Lycan's wolf form after the change."

Any item on the Lycan during the change wasn't likely to survive the change, from what Lizzie knew of the process.

"Let me think about it. Then we can toss it around again before I call Harrington. It was noteworthy, for sure." He reclined his seat, getting more comfortable. "After that, it was simple. They jumped me and bashed my head in by tossing me against a wall. It took me several minutes on autopilot before I was aware of what was happening."

How he could be so casual, Lizzie didn't know. It had been a frightening scene to witness. But it would have been even more so if she'd realized at the time how injured he was. "I could see that."

When he looked over at her inquisitively, she continued,

"I could see the moment you became aware. The fight was basically over after that."

"If it makes you feel any better, two nowhere-near alphas of middling size wouldn't have lasted a minute if not for the scent trick." He winked at her.

Winked. After telling her a story where—with a few different twists—maybe he dies. *Men.* But she just said, "We should figure out the scent void. What caused it, if it's unique to Worth's henchmen. Warding is so flexible in the right hands. I'm almost certain it's the work of a caster."

"Hmm. Good plan. Mind if I take a nap?" he asked. *Seriously. Only a man.*

When they arrived back at the Library, they found that they'd only arrived about an hour after Pilar and Harrington. Both had claimed a need for sleep before pursuing the tapestry lead. They'd left the tapestry with Heike. And Lizzie was surprised to discover that she had no concerns for the safety of the piece. She knew Heike would have some good information for them when they met again. Since Heike was well rested, it only made sense for her to work until the rest of the party could rest and reconvene. Lizzie wasn't sure when she'd turned the corner— maybe when Heike had busted her out of her room?—but whenever it was, she trusted Heike now.

CHAPTER THIRTY-SEVEN

"I love you," John said. He was calm. Very calm. Lizzie looked at him, trying to figure out what was going on. They'd arrived in their room only a few minutes earlier. She'd been gathering her things to head to the shower. She stopped in her tracks. She'd thought it, but she hadn't realized that she'd not said it.

Simple enough answer, and she saw no reason to dissemble. Lizzie looked up into his bright, beautiful, kind eyes. Without hesitation, she said, "I love you, too."

"You know I love you so much that it sometimes makes me want to scream and shake you and lock you in a room?" His blue eyes held hers.

Since Lizzie was a walking magical disaster, had almost died (a few times), and was only alive, in fact, because John had refused to give up on her—well, yes. She did have an idea that he felt that way. And she didn't blame him for any urges to scream, shake, or otherwise express frustration with her. It seemed that anyone who loved her did so at some risk. She was a magical mayhem attractant. She wrinkled her nose. That was singularly unattractive.

He was patiently waiting for an answer. And an honest answer was certainly the least she could do. "Yes. But I'm not sure that's something I can change."

He smiled. "That much I know." He sat down on the edge of the bed. "I had some time on the plane to think."

"Hey—I thought you were sleeping." Lizzie narrowed her eyes suspiciously. "Sneaky."

He replied wryly, "I definitely slept, too. But I also had some time to consider some advice a cranky old dragon gave me."

Lizzie busted out with a laugh. "Lachlan?" At his nod, she asked, "Do I want to know what advice Lachlan, of all people, is giving you?"

His voice serious, John said, "You do. He said I needed a partner, not a responsibility."

The laughter left Lizzie's face. She wasn't sure she liked where this was going. *Dammit.* If he broke up with her ass, just when she'd figured out she could deal with his stupid Lycan political bullshit, she wouldn't forgive him.

He grabbed her hand and pulled her into his lap. "Have I told you you're nuts?" he whispered quietly into her ear.

She was getting some seriously conflicted signals now. So she pulled a John trick and shut her mouth, betting that silence would pull more information out of him. She was right.

"You're insanely loyal. You have a foolishly strong sense of what's right. And you act with a courageous heart in pursuit of your frequently unreasonable goals." John tugged her closer.

"Not unreasonable, just ambitious goals," she corrected him.

He hugged her close to his chest and laughed. A huge, deep laugh that resonated through his body. Then he tucked his nose into her neck and said, "Ambitious, it is." He chuckled quietly. "What I'm trying to tell you, and what Lachlan was trying to tell me, is that we're better as a team." His voice took on a serious tone, the laughter gone. "You're not my responsibility. You're my partner."

Lizzie blinked in confusion. Then she said, "Equal partners, right? Fifty-fifty?" She wasn't letting this opportunity pass.

John grinned. "Don't be greedy, wench." Running his hand down her back, he said, all humor gone again, "I'm going to ask you a question, and I'm warning you—there's only one right answer." He paused significantly, then he said, "Will you be my mate—and my partner?"

"I will," Lizzie replied without hesitation. She'd already decided it was time to woman up and accept the job. Little had she known that the job would change.

"So—what brought this on? Just Lachlan?" Lizzie asked.

"It's becoming clear that trouble likes you. And much as I'd love to be your hero, much as I'd love for you to able to protect yourself, it seems that it's a group effort. Together, we have a better chance of keeping you safe." John didn't sound thrilled by the idea, but he sounded certain.

She frowned slightly. Not incredibly flattering. "Well, let's say together we can keep both of us safe."

"If that makes you happy—"

Before he could finish that sentence, Lizzie punched him in the arm. "Partners, right?"

"That's right." He smiled and stood up with her in his arms.

She squeaked in surprise. "Hey, where are we going?"

"I thought you wanted a shower?" John grinned as he headed to the showers with her in his arms.

An hour and a *very* thorough shower later—Lizzie was sparklingly clean in all her nooks and crannies—she and

John were both lying in bed, trying to catch a little rest before everyone reconvened to discuss the tapestry.

"We'll go see the Pack as soon as we get back." She knew the pack believed it was past time. And she was finally ready.

"Yes. That's about to explode," he murmured very quietly.

"What?" she yelped.

"Hmm. It'll be fine." He was licking the delicate whorls of her ear.

She frowned in concern. "So you say." She pushed him away far enough to get a good look at his face. "This—the mate thing—it means we have to move in together, doesn't it?"

It was more a statement than a question. He didn't respond right away as she thought through the ramifications of that particular nugget.

"What am I going to tell my parents?" she asked with just a tiny tinge of horror shading her voice.

CHAPTER THIRTY-EIGHT

Five hours later, the group met once again in the basement. The dragons were the only ones who looked fully rested. Everyone else in the room gripped a coffee, had a fatigued look, or both. The surprising addition to the group was Kenna. Lizzie hadn't been able to reach her earlier because she'd been in transit, headed to Prague even though Lizzie had assured her she was fine.

Other than some awkwardness between Kenna and Max, which Lizzie didn't get at all—Kenna was always casually friendly with her ex-flings, never silently awkward—Kenna fit right into the group. She was on her very best manners. She didn't even threaten to castrate John once. Maybe because when she'd arrived, Lizzie had been in one piece. Lizzie grinned at her friend's obnoxiously over-protective streak. It was cute in small doses.

Harrington got the meeting rolling with a quick recap. "The tapestry was acquired from Worth and is currently our best clue as to how Vampyr operate. Heike, what did you discover?"

With the meeting turned over to her, Heike looked uncertain. But once she started speaking, her words flowed more freely. Lizzie wasn't sure how she'd missed the signs before. Heike's youth, her uncertainty, her shyness. Lizzie just had to shake her head. Being kidnapped put a lot of strain on her, and she'd just made a mistake where Heike was concerned.

"There are a number of layered images. All of them related to a specific Vampyr faction from several hundred years ago. Several of the images seem to be an initiation ceremony, bringing new members into the group. Those were the most interesting." Heike stopped and looked at Lizzie. Blinking and holding her coffee a little firmer, Lizzie perked up. *Uh-oh.*

Heike sent a small, sympathetic smile in Lizzie's direction. "I think that the ability to fade is key to the process the Vampyr use to syphon magic."

Her heart sped up and her palms started to sweat. *No problem.* The last time had worked out okay. She'd been half out of her mind with pain and couldn't remember the details, but it had been okay. And what was the worst that could happen? She could disappear and never come back...she shook herself. *Idiot.* That wouldn't happen—she didn't think. But she could be magic-less for a few days. She sighed. Defenseless, more like.

"What do you need me to do?" Lizzie asked, hoping none of her reservations were evident in her voice.

Heike looked more than a little annoyed, but Lizzie didn't think her annoyance was directed at anyone. "I'm not sure exactly. I'm hoping that if I describe to you what I see, you can tell me more. I don't know how fading works, so I'm mostly guessing right now." Heike did not like to guess. That much Lizzie knew for sure.

Lizzie had a thought. Reinforcements were definitely in order. "I know we're a big group, but can we squeeze into the Library?"

Harrington nodded. "Good idea. Having Matylda's input could be quite valuable."

After a few minutes of shuffling, the whole crew—Harrington, Harry, John, Max, Lachlan, Ewan, Tavish, Lizzie, Pilar, Hieke, and Kenna—were all situated around the three tables in the Library. The table where Lizzie sat held her homemade Ouija board and a pebble. Lizzie wasn't really worried about Matylda beaning her any longer. She smiled. Poor Matylda, dealing with a bunch of thick, modern idiots.

Everyone was situated. And after an affirmative from Matylda that she was here and would stay as long as she could, Heike started over again.

"Initiates to the Vampyr cult went through a ritual with one member of the group—I suspect he was the leader of the group. He guides them through what looks something like their magics touching." As Heike spoke, something tugged at Lizzie's memory. But then it slipped away.

"Can you describe what it looks like?" Harrington asked.

"Imagine a visual representation of calling your magic. That's what the tapestry figures look like to me. They're covered head-to-toe in a soft glow of magic. Then the leader becomes transparent—just like Lizzie did when she faded." Heike looked down at her notes, then up at Lizzie. "I think that's what happens when you fade, right?"

When Lizzie turned to John for clarification, he nodded. "That's right."

Heike continued, addressing the entire room. "He never actually disappears, just stays transparent. Next he touches the new member briefly, and then he's solid and the magic glow is gone.

"I'll make a leap in logic," Max said. "If it's true that the magic taken by a Vampyr retains some of its talent qualities, maybe those images show the initiates getting their first bit of stolen magic from their leader. They might gain a very limited ability to fade."

Heike nodded. "I think that's what's happening. It would also explain the perversion of the process with blood and the diminished capabilities of the frustrated Vampyr from Matylda's book. The fade magic isn't native to most Vampyr, so it didn't work as well for them as the leader. That could easily lead to experimentation in an attempt to make the magic of their victims more accessible."

Lizzie felt a little light-headed. That you could take something as relatively innocuous as teleportation and make a weapon out of it—it was appalling.

She felt John's fingers wrap around her own.

"So, enough speculation as to how this plays into history. We can pursue that at a later date. How do we make it work as a cure for Sarah?" John clearly wanted to push this meeting to a close.

She squeezed his fingers appreciatively. As she looked at the table, Matylda moved the pebble.

1-S-T-F-A-D-E

First fade. She was an idiot.

Just to be sure, she asked Matylda, "When you first brought me to your chamber? How you helped me to get there, even though I didn't know where I was going?"

Yes

"Matylda, you are brilliant and an absolute angel." She looked up and every eye in the room was on her. "I think I know what we need to do. At least part of it."

Thinking through what had happened before, she wasn't sure how the transfer would work. She'd never felt as though she'd given or taken anything from Matylda.

"But how do I transfer it? The magical energy? I think I understand the merging. How do I take it and give it to someone?" Lizzie asked Matylda.

P-U-L-L

"Pull," Lizzie repeated with a small laugh. But Matylda wasn't done.

S-O-F-T-L-Y-?

Lizzie laughed, but it was slightly hysterical. Once she was sure she could form a sentence, she said, "Show me how to merge again?"

Matylda didn't answer; she just hugged her. Before, she'd felt the warmth of intertwining energies like a pleasant handhold. This time, it was a hug. It engulfed her whole body. And she realized why she had never made the connection between this and what Worth had done to Sarah and John. Because, quite simply, they weren't the same. Worth prodded and poked. He sucked and stole. What Matylda did felt more like the loving embrace of a mother hugging close a dear child.

When she felt Matylda leave, she felt a small sadness. Because she was losing a close and comforting touch. No—this was nothing like what Worth had done. The experience made her more confident that she could do this.

When she opened her eyes, everyone was looking at Harry with varying degrees of anticipation. He said, "Yes. I think that's it. At least it looks like what Heike described."

"All right," Lizzie said. "Let's do this

CHAPTER THIRTY-NINE

In the end, it had actually been a pretty simple process once Lizzie got the intermingling concept down. A short trip to London, a quick checkup to ensure that Sarah was still stable, and they'd done it.

They found five volunteers, including Pilar, Heike, Harrington, and two additional brave souls from IPPC to act as donors. Harry had been more than a little surprised when Harrington volunteered. Harrington's response had been a gruff, "Your father will kill you if you kill me."

Lizzie wasn't certain if he'd been joking or not. Sometimes with Harrington it was hard to tell. The man could be an ass, but he did take his responsibilities very seriously.

The first attempt had actually been funny. She'd started with Harrington at his insistence. She hadn't wanted to, because—well, the act had felt quite intimate with Matylda. And the thought of—god forbid—magically *hugging* Harrington, it was just weird and unsettling.

She'd been so tentative that Harrington had told her, "Get on with it already. I'd like to have my tea at some point today."

He was such an ass sometimes, but a funny ass. And it had helped to loosen her up. And when she'd tugged, she'd taken only the very smallest amount possible, immediately pushing it to Sarah. She'd never even felt it mingle with her own magic—like it had skimmed the surface of her magic to land with Sarah.

"What do you think Harry? Harrington?" They'd both looked at her like she was nuts. Apparently, she'd taken so little, neither had registered the change.

So the remainder of the process had been experimenting with increasing the amount of magic she took, always remaining conservative. They could certainly have finished the process much sooner, but everyone was happy the process had proceeded as smoothly as possible.

Lizzie had expected to meet an awake and alert Sarah when they'd finished. But Harry had called a halt long before she'd gained consciousness. Lizzie was confused that they would leave her in that state.

"Why are we stopping?" she asked worriedly.

Harry explained, "I think she's fine now. We won't know for sure until she wakes up, but she's no longer in a coma. She's currently in a restorative sleep, much like the very deep sleep you were in when you overused your magic."

"You're sure?" It seemed so anti-climactic. Sarah seemed much the same to her.

"I'm sure," Harry assured her. And Harry was the expert.

So Lizzie had a few quiet words with Sarah privately, because she felt she should, and she'd left. She and John had more than earned the few weeks' vacation that she'd pushed Harrington to give her. The dragons were staying, so security wasn't an issue. Lachlan was even discussing a long-term contract that would keep a few dragons on site running security for the Library indefinitely. Lizzie suspected that had more to do with Heike and Ewan than with any desire

Lachlan had to provide such a service. But it meant John had no commitment to Harrington that couldn't be fulfilled long-distance. And, seriously, Lizzie had earned a little time with her wolf.

Just before she left, she took Harrington aside to discuss Matylda.

"We know her body is behind the wall." Lizzie sighed. "Is there anything we can do for her? Provide her with a burial, maybe?"

"I had a little chat with Matylda," Harrington said.

Lizzie looked at him incredulously. "When did that happen?"

"As soon as you found her. Late that night, when you were recovering. We talked about a possible burial. But you're right, we can't move her." Harrington had hidden depths.

Lizzie wasn't sure how he still surprised her. She should know by now to expect the unexpected.

"Is she okay with staying there?" She was all alone. It seemed wrong to leave her body in that tiny room. Lizzie looked down at the sapphire on her finger, a gift from Matylda.

"She is, because leaving her there means she can stay with the Library. No one knows how long she'll be with us. But she does want to spend her time in the Library. And while it's not certain that her physical remains tie her there, it's the only reasonable conclusion at this time." After a small hesitation, he said, "She also wants to spend more time with you. She's certain you're related, though she didn't explain why."

"Can you tell her I'm coming back?" Lizzie frowned, twisting the sapphire ring on her right hand. "Tell her I'm sorry I didn't get a chance to say goodbye."

Harrington nodded solemnly. "I will."

CHAPTER FORTY

On the flight home, John seemed to be traveling especially well. Lizzie didn't comment, because to do so seemed to point out all the times he *didn't*. So she just enjoyed her shared time with him. Harrington had splurged on a private plane for them, well—an IPPC plane—and they were flying home from London as the only two passengers.

When she'd taken the two weeks away from her internship, she'd simply told Harrington, "I deserve it after this mess, and I have family business to take care of."

That was the understatement of the year. She could just envision how that first scene would play out.

Mom, Dad. I'm moving in with my boyfriend of a few weeks. And we're sort of common law married. Exciting, right? She'd never be that flippant, but if only she could be. Then the disappointed looks wouldn't be so bad.

She turned to John. Before she could even begin, he said, "You look terrified." He looked at her again then he modified his conclusion. "Or very worried, at least. What's up?"

She probably smelled like stress. She still wasn't sure how okay she was with the fact that her boyfriend could smell her emotions. No, not her boyfriend, her mate. She smiled. It felt good to say mate, even in her head, and mean it.

Damn. She probably smelled like nervous sweat. *Ew. How was that ever sexy?* But he swore that she smelled like heaven to him, and her emotions were just a tiny little overlay to the sweetness that was her. He really was a wonderful man. She smiled.

She shook her head. Mom and Dad. "My parents. I have no idea how to tell them I'm moving in with my boyfriend of a few weeks. A few weeks of crazily intense relationship-building, granted. But still only a few weeks." John's laugh interrupted her. "What?"

"Intense relationship-building? That's what you call your life-threatening activities over the last several weeks?" John looked a little doubtful but amused.

"We've spent more time together than I can possibly imagine any normal couple managing in such a short time. What would you call it?" Lizzie wasn't sure it mattered. Once she started down this path, disclosing her magic to her parents wasn't far behind. And then they'd have to talk about who the skeleton in the closet was.

"Dating?" he said hopefully.

"Huh?"

"You asked what I'd call whatever it is that we've done over the last several weeks. I say we call it dating." And he grinned.

Easy enough for him. His people knew about her, and they knew that she was a spell caster. *Good lord.* How was she supposed to break the whole, my-boyfriend's-a-Lycan thing to her parents?

"I'm opting for radio silence. We don't speak of it—any of it. I cannot tell my parents you're Lycan. Or that I'm a spell caster." Just saying it out loud to John made all the blood leave her head.

She chewed her lip while she waited for him to respond. He touched her lip with his thumb. She wanted to bite the pad of his thumb. What was it about him that made her want to bite, and scream, and yank his hair, and wrap her legs around him, and—she sighed. They were on a plane for goodness sakes.

And she lost her amorous glow when she heard his reply. "You're being dishonest," John pointed out gently.

She frowned at his words.

Seeing her look, he said, "You're stressed out about your parents. If I had to guess, primarily because you're considering being dishonest. Not something you're comfortable with when it comes to people you love. Granted, it's an omission, but still—it's dishonest." He paused, looking intently at her. "Tell them the truth."

"That their little girl has magic and is dating a werewolf?' She frowned even harder. "You're not helping."

"Be serious. You sit down and discuss the family tree. Someone, somewhere, is holding out on you. And your parents, for that matter. Magic can sometimes be finicky about where it lands. Hitting every generation, then skipping two. And someone failed in their duty by not informing your parents of their heritage." He cocked his head. "You could even do a little genealogy research beforehand. It's almost certain you're related to the Kovar family. Maybe approach them with the guilty ancestor's name in hand."

"That is a good point. Not that I'm looking to blame them, but someone bound my magic. And someone should have released it. I'll think about it some more." She peeked up at him covertly. "But just to check, I can tell them about you?"

"I recommend it. You never know how they might be affected by our positions. And if they take it poorly—we just have them institutionalized." His face looked bland. She was pretty sure he was kidding.

"You're kidding, right? You *cannot* send my parents to a psych ward because they flip out over werewolves. Anyone would flip out." She stopped and listened to herself. Speaking of insanity, this was an insane conversation. And it led nowhere good. "Okay. I'll work on a plan to tell them. After we meet the pack."

EPILOGUE

They'd been back in Austin for only a few hours. Just long enough to unpack enough necessities from their bags for the night and think about sitting down for a few minutes. They discussed heading out to meet the pack, but decided they both needed a day to recover. And prepare. They agreed they'd head out early in the morning the day after tomorrow.

Lizzie had just crawled into bed, deciding she might give in to jet lag and take a nap—or not, she thought of John with a grin—when she'd felt the crinkle of paper under her pillow. She didn't think anything of it, until the paper was in her hand and she'd read it three times.

If you act like a pretentious, self-important bitch, then we'll treat you like one. Watch your back, little girl.

Reading the note one more time, Lizzie couldn't help but think it might be real. It was basically a threat on her life. She huffed out a pent up breath of air. Or was it? *Shit.* They'd been in her house. She felt nauseous, her stomach churning with uncertainty. *In her home.* Strangers had been in her home.

John needed to know about this. Right now.

"John," Lizzie called as she walked through the house. It was a stupid note. It could mean anything or nothing. But something about the note Lizzie gripped in her fingers made her sick. A feeling pushed at her, like someone was out there —somewhere in the world—hating her, wishing her ill. The vitriol of the author's feelings seemed to have soaked into the paper. Because the words alone really weren't that bad. Right? She was too tired for this shit.

"John," she called a little more loudly. John had exceptional hearing. And she could feel the edge of panic in her voice. He would certainly have responded if he heard her. Where was he? He'd gotten a call from his uncle on the drive home from the airport. The conversation had been a little mysterious, and he hadn't wanted to discuss it right then. Later, he'd said. Was he speaking with his uncle on the phone again?

Lizzie walked through the living room, heart thudding. He should have responded. Something was wrong. And then movement from the backyard caught her eye. Two wolves, crouched low, standing at opposite corners of the yard. The first was the familiar mottled grey, black, and white of John. The other…Lizzie swallowed reflexively. The other was a massive black wolf. Bigger than John.

The first coherent thought Lizzie had was a flashback to the conversation they'd had on the plane about masking scent and scent voids. John would have known if a stranger had been in her home. The note, and now, the strange wolf— had the wolf's scent been masked? Could there be another wolf that John didn't know about? That's what had happened in Freiburg. It was the unexpected appearance of two wolves that had given John's enemies a temporary edge.

She wasn't sure if she had time, but she needed to know if the black wolf had brought reinforcements. She took a breath, and brought herself back to the present and away from the edge of panic. She yanked her magic to her, did some rapid calculations, improvised, braced herself against the nearest wall, and then—she exhaled. She imagined that breath slowly spreading snowflakes, small pieces of her sensing ward, across the entirety of the house. It was a massive cast, and she wasn't sure if it was diffuse enough or delivered with enough care to prevent a correspondingly large repercussion.

As she waited for the repercussion that never came, the results of the cast became clear. She'd done it. *Wow. I really did it.* There was only the one wolf inside the house. He was covered in spell caster magic, but he was alone. Leaning against the wall, her mind trying to process what exactly she'd just done, it took her a brief moment to recall John and the uninvited visitor. She didn't have time to jack around.

She lifted her hand and inspected the mild tremor. Not good, but good enough—if she hurried. Walking with calm deliberation, mentally pushing herself to slow her breathing and her pounding heart, she went to the hall closet. After a brief search, she pulled out the .357 Magnum she'd recently acquired. She'd never been much for guns, but she was discovering that in this new life she'd entered—things change. This was her life now.

THE END

BONUS CONTENT

Sign up for my newsletter to receive release announcements, bonus materials, and a sampling of my different series. Sign up at http://eepurl.com/b91H5v

PREVIEW: DEFENSIVE MAGIC

PROLOGUE

Worth shifted his cell to the left ear. While it was necessary to keep this particular player well within his sights, he wasn't overly concerned. He had more power, more experience, greater resources—but someday she might become a problem. Worth was certain she had a scheme of some kind in the works. Hardly surprising. She was a creative, ambitious little thing—which was exactly why he'd recruited her.

"You want her gone," she said in the passionless way he'd previously admired. "I'll take care of it."

Perhaps *too* dispassionate.

"I want IPPC out of my business more than I want Lizzie gone—for now." He allowed the faintest hint of disapproval to enter his voice. "Killing Lizzie will only push them even further into my affairs. And Braxton—no. I have no interest in dealing with him or his Pack right now."

"Then we act covertly," she replied blandly. "It's not as if they don't have any number of enemies. Especially Braxton. The blame is easy enough to shift."

"No. Lizzie Smith and the Texas Alpha are off-limits for

now. I have more pressing concerns than dealing with the trouble that would cause."

"Of course," she immediately agreed.

"But—keep an eye on them." He had no intention of losing sight of any of his enemies.

∼

SHE WAS glad this conversation wasn't in person. Her acting skills were exceptional, but it was so much easier by phone. With Worth hiding in the Philippines as he waited for several financial transactions to clear, she was guaranteed a few weeks free of his interference. And a life free of Worth suited her just fine. She owed this respite from Worth's attention to the Inter-Pack Policing Cooperative. Thank you IPPC for being clever enough to find, let alone seize or freeze, such a sizable chunk of Worth's assets.

She was brilliant. But she had been a little careless recently. Worth was beginning to understand the full extent of not only her brilliance, but also her ambition. That was a problem. But apparently he didn't know *that* much. Because she lived for the long game. And her goals were loftier than her current position as runner-up right-hand man, second not only to Worth but also his heir apparent. A shame Worth wouldn't figure that out in time. Well, no. It wasn't actually.

And Lizzie and John? They'd work quite nicely for what she had planned. With a bit of luck, their elimination would be a happy side effect to her plan.

PREVIEW: DEFENSIVE MAGIC

CHAPTER 1

Lizzie Smith had just crawled into bed, deciding she might give in to jet lag and head to bed without John, when she felt the crinkle of paper under her pillow. She didn't think anything of it, until the paper was in her hand and she'd read it three times.

> *The Pack doesn't need a pretentious, self-important bitch like you. Watch your back, little girl.*

What the...? Lizzie couldn't help but think of someone walking through her bedroom, touching her sheets, her pillow. The small scrap of paper was basically a threat on her life. She huffed out a pent-up breath of air. Or was it a threat? *Shit.* Did it matter? Threat or warning, someone had been in her house. She felt sick, her stomach churning with uncertainty. *In her home.* A stranger had touched her things and walked unimpeded through her home. She grabbed a pair of shorts, feeling vulnerable and exposed in her tank and underwear.

John Braxton, her mate and Alpha of the Texas Pack,

needed to know about this. Right now. The note screamed pack politics, and she knew trouble had been brewing in the Pack for the last few weeks.

"John," Lizzie called as she walked through the house. It was a stupid note. It could mean anything or nothing. But something about the note Lizzie gripped in her fingers made her sick. A feeling pushed at her, like someone was out there hating her, wishing her ill. The vitriol of the author's feelings seemed to have soaked into the paper. The words alone really weren't that bad—right? She was jet lagged and exhausted from the last few days of magical mayhem and drama, which meant she was too tired for this shit.

"John," she called a little more loudly. With his Lycan super-senses, he should have heard her. She could feel the edge of panic in her voice. He would certainly have responded if he had heard her. Where was he? He'd received a call from his uncle about an hour ago on the drive home from the airport. The conversation had been a little mysterious, and he hadn't wanted to discuss it right then. "Later," he'd said. Was he speaking with his uncle on the phone again?

Lizzie walked through the living room, her heart thudding. He should have responded. Something was wrong. And then movement from the backyard caught her eye. Two wolves, crouched low, standing at opposite corners of the yard. There was enough moonlight to see the first was the familiar mottled gray, black, and white of John. The other... She swallowed reflexively. The other was a massive black wolf. Bigger than John.

Scent void—her brain latched onto one reason that a strange wolf could appear without warning on her property. John's fight a few days ago with two of Worth's Lycan guards had involved some trick that masked or scrubbed away any trace of scent from the air. There'd been an absence of any scent in the corridor and room where the guards had ambushed John. Without the warning of their scent, he'd been surprised and the guards had gained a temporary advantage. Afterwards, he'd explained that he'd never before encountered a scent void—that's what he'd called it—an area scrubbed of all scent.

John should have detected a stranger's scent as soon as they'd arrived home, and he hadn't. No way would he have left her undefended if he knew another wolf was here. He wouldn't have missed the signs of another wolf on the property. *Something* had prevented him from scenting the other wolf. *Shit.* What if there was another Lycan that John didn't know about? Or a spell caster, one who was masking the attacker's scent?

All of these thoughts raced through her head in a few brief seconds. She collected herself and tried to think what she could do, how she could help John. First, she needed to know if the black wolf had brought reinforcements, Lycan or spell caster. She took a slow, shaky breath, trying to bring herself away from the edge of panic. She yanked her magic from deep inside, envisioned as best she could how to create a sensing ward so large it could encompass the entire house, braced herself against the nearest wall, and then she slowly exhaled. She willed that breath to softly push out tiny pieces of her sensing ward, like drifting snowflakes on a calm winter day. She gently prodded the small bits and pieces of her ward until it softly blanketed the surface of the house, including the walls and floors. It was a massive cast. As she cast, she briefly considered whether it was diffuse enough or delivered with enough care to prevent a correspondingly large repercussion. But it didn't matter—if it revealed anyone else on the property, the bumps and bruises were worth it. She grimaced, the memory of falling on her ass after she cast her first sensing ward sharp enough to bring a twinge of remembered pain. It had been a small ward, but in ignorance she'd clumsily shoved an excess of power into it as she'd cast and the recoil had bounced back on her.

As she waited for the recoil that never came—her care and finesse had paid off—the results of the cast shone brightly in her mind. One wolf, the one facing John in her backyard. The black wolf was covered in spell caster magic. Where was the spell caster? Head whipping back and forth, she checked the far corners of the yard. But her ward revealed no spell caster hiding in the shadows, only the residual magic of a caster.

Her body sagged against the wall as relief coursed through her. The sensing ward had worked, and she wasn't hurt. Leaning against the wall, her mind failed to fully process what exactly she'd just done—the size of the ward, the method of delivery, both completely outside her experience until she'd attempted it. She blinked, her mind sluggish. John. *Dammit.* John was alone with that massive wolf. And immediately her feet began to move.

She lifted her hand and inspected the mild trembling of her fingers. Walking with calm deliberation, mentally pushing herself to slow her breathing and her pounding heart, she went to the hall closet. After a brief search, she pulled out the .357 Magnum she'd recently acquired. She'd never been much for guns, but she was discovering that in this new life she'd entered, things were changing.

∼

WANT TO KEEP READING? Get your copy of Defensive Magic today!

ALSO BY KATE BARAY

LOST LIBRARY
Lost Library
Spirited Legacy
Defensive Magic
Witch's Diary
Necromancy

LOST LIBRARY SHORTS
Krampus Gone Wild: A Lost Library Christmas Short
The Covered Mirror: A Lost Library Halloween Short
Lost Library Collected Short Stories

SPIRELLI PARANORMAL INVESTIGATIONS COLLECTIONS
Spirelli Paranormal Investigations: Episodes 1-3
Spirelli Paranormal Investigations: Episodes 4-6
Entombed

BOB VS THE WORLD
Bob vs the Cat

ABOUT THE AUTHOR

Kate Baray writes paranormal and urban fantasy and lives in Austin, Texas with her pack of pointers and bloodhounds. Kate has worked as an attorney, a manager, a tractor sales person, and a dog trainer, but writing is her passion. When she's not writing, she sweeps up hairy dust bunnies and watches British mysteries.
Kate also writes sweet romances and cozy mysteries as Cate Lawley and thrillers as K.D. Baray.

For more information:
www.katebaray.com